MIRANDA

Jane Holland

Jane Holland has asserted her right under Section 77 of the Copyright, Designs and Patents Act 1988 to be identified as the author of this work. No part of this book can be reproduced in part or in whole or transferred by any means without the express written permission of the author.

This is a work of fiction. Any names of places or characters are the products of the author's imagination. Any resemblance to actual events, places or persons, living or dead, is entirely coincidental.

THIMBLERIG BOOKS

Copyright @ Jane Holland 2015, 2019
All rights reserved.

Previously published under the title, WHY SHE RAN. This new paperback edition 2020

ISBN: 9798662857575

Other novels by Jane Holland

KISSING THE PINK
LAST BIRD SINGING
GIRL NUMBER ONE
LOCK THE DOOR
FORGET HER NAME
THE HIVE
DEAD SIS
UNDER AN EVIL STAR
THE TENTH HOUSE MURDERS
THE PART OF DEATH

Also
as
JJ Holland
IN HIGH PLACES

*'Be not afeard; the isle is full of noises,
Sounds, and sweet airs, that give delight and hurt not.'*

William Shakespeare, *The Tempest*

Chapter One

Summer 1978, off the Isle of Man

Lawrence put his shoulder against the large metal door and pushed. Reluctantly it yielded, and he felt the wind blast at him as it opened slowly outwards.

'Juliet?'

His shout was ripped away into the night as the ferry plunged sickeningly. He lurched through the doorway, and saw a vast wave crash over the ship's railings and across the deck, the wooden boards left swimming with water. The reflected floodlights gleamed in its pools, illuminating the deck but no further, the sea beyond still dark and oily. Lawrence shook each foot, then waited for the water to drain away before venturing out of the doorway. His shoes were new, and salt water would soon perish the expensive leather.

His wife was standing in the shadow of a huge orange funnel, her hands cupped to light a cigarette. The wind made it an almost impossible task.

He staggered along the deck towards her, supporting himself on the slick, white-painted walls of the ferry. Juliet had told him she wanted to catch the view as they approached the island. But when he looked out over the railing, the Irish Sea was nothing but a rolling black swell alongside the ship.

He shouted, 'We're nearly there.'

Juliet leant into his jacket for shelter. She managed to light her cigarette at last, saying something incomprehensible as the wind tore across the open deck.

He shook his head. 'Sorry, I didn't catch a word you said.'

Smiling, she gestured at his watch.

'Ten to midnight,' Lawrence yelled back. 'Bang on schedule. My father's expecting us for about one o'clock.'

'What?'

Lawrence gave up the struggle, pointing back over his shoulder. His throat was hoarse. 'Come on, let's get back inside. This wind is appalling.'

Juliet showed him her half-smoked cigarette.

'Five minutes,' he insisted, spreading his fingers out to make sure she got the message, then dragged himself back along the wall towards the door.

The ferry dipped violently, and another wild deluge came flooding over the side, sending a group of kids in plastic macs and trainers squealing for cover. The ship ploughed on through the waves as though struggling to leave the storm behind.

Lawrence turned to look back, unsteady on his feet, but his wife had climbed onto one of the benches against the railings and was staring into the blackness with her hair flying back, one hand on the rail, the other still holding her cigarette. She looked like the ship's figurehead, forcing them ever onwards through the waves. There was something decidedly witchy about her these days, he thought. Perhaps there always had been but she was only now allowing it to show. As though she had grown tired of the old veneer, and this was her new, less civilised face. Whatever had caused this latest crisis between them, he could feel the tension in her, hidden just under the surface. Like a rock under the water.

He began to wish he had never agreed to visit his father. This summer storm had blown up out of nowhere, Juliet was in one of her moods, and they had not even arrived on the island yet.

Yet how could he have refused his summons? It had been years since his last visit, and his father had sounded so urgent on the phone. Through the hissing rain of spray across the deck, he watched another group of kids run past with mischievous faces, shrieking and clutching at each other before vanishing round the corner into darkness.

One minute they were there, the next they were gone, like water sprites.

And where were their bloody parents? Snug in the downstairs bar, he suspected, or asleep in one of the cabins. Lawrence knew that's where he would be if he was crossing the Irish Sea on a night like this with a parcel of brats in tow.

God, only just into his forties, and already he sounded like an old man.

Had he been like that as a child? Tearing about with his friends, making a racket, not caring what anyone thought? He recalled himself as a strange, diffident boy, quiet and with his nose in a book much of the time, but then suddenly, inexplicably rage-filled, striking out at the world without any clear idea why. Some fleeting awareness of failures to come, perhaps, along with a futile desire to escape them. He still harboured that desire, of course. But at least he was rarely angry these days, though he had his moments when Juliet was at her most imperious and impossible. His father had always mildly irritated him too, he realised, wryly conscious of a desire to take the next boat back to England rather than face going home. Probably because his duty as a son irked him now that he was older.

Besides, he had found his father hard to talk to since his mother's death. When he had come to stay with them in England, the old man had been forever staring at nothing, or disappearing to his room for hours. Sometimes he had been heard whispering to himself. Other times he had gone striding out on a long walk without telling anyone and even without a coat, whatever the weather.

'His second childhood,' Juliet had called it, shrugging off his father's behaviour as quaint and amusing. But then, she had not known Gil in his prime, so could not appreciate the ever-quickening rate of decline that had occurred these past few years.

Whatever lay ahead, they could not hope to escape it now. Less than a mile away, he could see the first lights of the island waiting for him, strung out like ghostly pearls round the dark neck of a bay.

'Lawrence?' It was his father's voice, echoing through the temporary tunnel they had erected to protect foot passengers on their way in and out of the terminal building.

Lawrence could not see him at first. Rain was still falling hard, thundering on the tin roof above their heads, making conversation impractical. There was some barely audible announcement going on over the loudspeaker system inside the main building, reduced to a kind of whisper out here in the tunnel, its sibilant crackle permeating everything. Kids with sodden anoraks, hoods up, trudged past them, followed by sullen, bleary-eyed parents. The sea slapped up against the grey stone quay, then rushed back to prepare for another assault. What had happened to summer?

Beside him, Juliet was looking wild, trying to light a cigarette while struggling with her luggage. He could hear the click-click-click of her lighter in the draughty tunnel, and her impatient breathing.

'Here, let me.' Lawrence grappled with her trolley case, though he was already laden down with two suitcases. 'Over here, Dad!'

His father was waiting to one side of the steady file of foot passengers. He looked old, Lawrence thought suddenly. Stooped shoulders, narrowed chest, his trousers hanging looser than he remembered, held up with a sturdy belt. But his eyes were as fierce as ever, his embrace fumbling and impatient.

'Sorry to hurry you,' his father said by way of welcome, 'but I'm double-parked. Hello, Juliet, good to see you again. Can I help carry something?'

Reluctantly, Lawrence parted with his wife's trolley case. 'What the hell is this weather about? Who cancelled summer?'

'Blame Manannán.'

Juliet kissed his father on the cheek. 'Hello, Gil. You're looking well,' she lied, glancing at Lawrence as she did so. Unsubtle code for *he's not looking well at all* that was not missed by his father. 'Man who?'

'Manannán mac Lir,' his father explained briefly, waving his hand towards the sea. 'Irish God of the sea. Much associated with the Isle of Man. When danger threatens, they say he spreads his cloak of mist and rain across the isle to protect it.'

'He doesn't sound much fun,' Juliet remarked flippantly, then caught Lawrence's eye and added, 'You must tell us all about him though. So we can make votive offerings to his misty Godliness. Maybe get a few sunny days during our stay.'

'Tomorrow should be better weather,' his father promised her, his tone distracted. 'Now, where did I park the Land Rover?'

They were outside in the dark terminal car park, all concrete blocks and swaying lamp posts. The storm seemed to gain in intensity, lashing them with rain, the wind howling and tearing at their coats. 'You should never have come out in this,' Lawrence told his father as they forced the cases into the back of his Land Rover. 'We could have got a taxi.'

'Nonsense.'

Eventually they were on their way, following the rear lights of other cars disappearing into the rain-mist. Then came the hour-long drive south, their car buffeted by gusting winds, his father rambling on about arrangements for the week, gloved hands gripping the wheel. And Manannán and his rain clouds doing their best to prevent Lawrence from hearing a word anyone said.

Crossing the narrow Fairy Bridge on their way south, Juliet sat forward to stare at the sign. 'They have fairies here?'

'The *Mooinjer Veggey*,' his father agreed. 'The Little People. If you believe in such things.'

Lawrence grinned, remembering an old superstition. 'You have to say hello to the fairies as you cross the bridge,' he told his wife. 'Or it's considered unlucky.'

Juliet hesitated. 'Hello, fairies!'

'Good evening, fairies,' Lawrence said dutifully, though he noticed his father said nothing.

They reached Port St Mary in the early hours of the morning. The small seaside town, more of a village really, lay asleep under the rain. There were no windows lit in the houses they passed, only the glow of streetlights along the quiet curve of the Promenade, each lamp surrounded by a thousand blades of rain.

Gil's house stood on the hill above the village, overlooking the bay, nothing out there tonight but whipped darkness, the air itself trembling.

'Here we are.' His father swung in through the green-barred entrance gate and juddered to a halt outside the arched front door. The wipers stopped their furious to-and-fro, reducing the world outside to a rain-streaked blur. 'You two go inside, the door's always open. I'll bring the luggage.'

Now it was Lawrence's turn to say, 'Nonsense.' He nodded to Juliet in the back of the Land Rover, who was tidying her hair. 'You and Dad put the kettle on while I bring in the bags. No, I insist. Leave me the keys, I'll lock the car.'

'No need,' his father said, though he headed for the front door without any argument. 'No one steals cars here,' he called back. 'This is the Isle of Man.'

Juliet looked at Lawrence through narrowed eyes, as though blaming him for the weather, then turned and followed his father into the house without a word.

So, this was to be his fault too, he thought, bending to retrieve the suitcases. She had not wanted to come, hating the idea of a long sea journey. But he had worn her down. 'You're always at work these days. Take some time off, look on it as a holiday. You love the beach, don't you?' He had hoped they could find some peace here in the island, just the two of them. But then it had started raining …

At first, in that sodden darkness, he thought the big house unchanged since the day of his mother's funeral, still a mess of white-washed wings and annexes added long after the original build and now linked by archways and steps. But then Lawrence noticed new flower beds where lawn used to be, and a swing hanging from the old sycamore tree, its wooden seat twisting in the wind. Feminine touches to a very masculine house.

He thought of Cathy, his father's housekeeper, prosaic and unsmiling, and could not imagine her on a swing. Someone else, then? Had his father fallen in love again? It was a disturbing idea, although he could not articulate why.

Lawrence wrestled with the slippery luggage in the rain. Not an easy thing to do on his own but he did not want his father getting soaked too. Then a diffuse light came on in the house, illuminating a small rectangular patch of grass to his left.

He glanced up, surprised, and a face appeared at one of the top windows, staring down at him, back-lit.

Lawrence wiped his face, near-horizontal rain dashing into his eyes, then peered up again. But already the window was in darkness again. Who on earth … ?

Cathy and her mother had a small place down in the village, or used to. He recalled a narrow room with pale green walls, and an uncomfortable sofa that served as a bed sometimes. An old fisherman's cottage, strange objects decorating the mantel and walls, carved driftwood and feathers. It could not have been her at the window.

Dumping the bags in the hall at the foot of the stairs, Lawrence stooped to unlock one of the cases, deciding to liberate the book he had brought his father as a present: a leather-bound edition of Frazer's *The Golden Bough*. But when he turned round with it in his hand, his father was nowhere in sight.

'Dad?'

Perhaps he had gone upstairs to dry off.

He slipped the book back inside the suitcase, then straightened to see Cathy standing in the open archway that led to the kitchen.

He did not recognise the housekeeper at first, it had been so long since his last visit. He remembered a shy local girl with a thick fringe hanging over her eyes like a moorland pony. Manx as the hills, his father had described her once, but good at her job. Cathy had never been curvaceous, not in those days, besides being a good head shorter than Juliet. But she'd been young and had a way of walking that turned heads. Turned his, anyway.

He wondered if she still had that walk, noting a thickened waist that had blurred into solid hips and thighs under her corn-yellow blouse and flared jeans.

'Hello,' he said awkwardly.

Cathy met his eyes, a hard look that spoke of neglect and long years of resentment. Then she turned and disappeared back towards the kitchen.

He slicked back wet hair, his heart thumping. *Fuck.*

'Hello, darling. Is that all the luggage in now?'

He turned, startled. Juliet was standing in the doorway to the living-room, damp blonde hair curling attractively about her face, her clothes dishevelled yet somehow sexy. Her mascara was smudged and she was wearing what he thought of as her 'brittle smile,' the one that meant trouble. Had she witnessed his encounter with Cathy? He no longer knew how to read her face. Was it too late for them? He refused to believe it was too late.

She held out a steaming mug, her voice breathy and over-loud. As if she wanted Cathy to hear. 'Has your dad gone up to bed? I'm not surprised; he looked shattered, poor thing. But his housekeeper waited up for us. She made cocoa too. Wasn't that thoughtful of her?'

'Yes,' he said automatically, and took the mug of cocoa. It smelt rich and chocolatey. 'Very thoughtful.'

He followed her into the living-room. Floor-length red velvet curtains had been drawn against the storm; he recalled a sweeping vista over the tiered gardens and the wide blue bay below. Rain battered noisily against the windows, unseen. The place looked essentially unchanged, though his father's high-backed armchair was a little scruffier, and his mother's old chaise longue had gone, replaced by a modern sofa with brown leather seats.

Lawrence stared at himself in the large gilt mirror hanging over the mantelpiece, and saw his wife come to join him, her familiar reflection meeting his eyes.

Juliet lowered her voice. 'I think she lives in,' she whispered, still smiling her brittle smile. 'His housekeeper. What do you make of that?'

Chapter Two

Lawrence stirred, vaguely aware that it was morning and Juliet had moved from his side. He turned his head, still drowsy, adjusting to his new surroundings.

The bedroom curtains had been partially opened to let in light. Outside he could hear birdsong in the unseen garden, and recalled the flat green stretches of lawn tumbling down in carefully constructed terraces towards the sea, hemmed in on one side by spindly trees, dark with rooks' nests, and luxuriously over-grown hydrangeas on the other. He remembered flights of steps running down the centre of those terraces, headed by squat stone lions ruined by lichen and decades of bird droppings, ending in a gate at the far end and a rough path beyond it which led directly to the beach.

His mother had loved this rambling old house, thinking it would be a wonderful place to spend her retirement. And the garden too, its endless hiding places and surprises. He thought of the new flower beds he had seen last night, planted up with lupins, red-hot pokers and delphiniums. Cathy's handiwork, for sure. These yellow roses too, arranged tidily in a vase on the mantelpiece. She had always loved flowers.

He turned over in bed, pushing that troublesome thought away. The island had seemed such a magical place when he first came to stay here, steeped in grief at his mother's death and open to anything which suggested that life went on, that nature always found a way. Now he knew that for a comforting illusion. Some things went on; others shrivelled and died. Not everything was magical, not everything found a way.

Juliet was sitting up nude on the edge of their bed, her back towards him, plaiting her hair in the dusty sunlight. She was humming softly under her breath. The long fingers danced in their mesmerizing rhythm, up and over, between and above, weaving both halves of neatly gathered blonde strands together into the plait.

Lawrence lay still, admiring how the muscles in her back and shoulders moved delicately under the skin as she worked. She was still a beautiful woman at thirty-nine, her waist almost as neat as when they had first met, hips curving in that slim boyish way. Following the taut fishbone of her spine with his eyes, he felt the weight of his failure pull him inexorably towards depression.

It was years now since he had persuaded Juliet to try for a baby. She had been reluctant at first, saying they could not afford to lose her income from the small accountancy firm where she worked. Then finally she had agreed, perhaps worn down by his insistence, and Lawrence had been overjoyed, promising to take on extra teaching work at the college if she fell pregnant. Yet each month she bled lightly as a young girl, shaking her head whenever he asked that familiar tentative question, her belly flat and smooth as ever. Somebody up there must be laughing at them, he thought, watching her rise gracefully from the bed and cross the room. His only true desire in life had been for a child of his own, and yet it seemed the one thing impossible to achieve. He longed to hold his wife's thickening waist in his hands and feel the baby inside kick at the thin surface of her abdomen, gripping her hand as she strained to push his child out into the world, tiny and red-faced.

She was dressing in silence now, turned away from him as she fastened her gold silk top and reached for her jeans. He had been taking wedding photos and teaching adult evening classes in North London when they met, scraping a living while he worked towards his first photographic exhibition. Juliet had signed up for his basic photography course, so vibrant and attractive that Lawrence found himself unable to take his eyes off the sensuous young woman in the bright blue kaftan.

They had shared a few drinks in the pub with the rest of the class before he finally gathered the courage to ask her out to dinner, stumbling over the words like an idiot, convinced she would refuse him. But she hadn't.

He was lost within seconds of their first kiss. Lawrence had known what he wanted as a compass knows to point north. It had kept him awake at night, his unswerving desire to marry Juliet and give her children. To fill her with them, until they were spilling uncontrollably out of her body. It had seemed such a small thing to ask at first, to become a father and watch his child grow inside her, and yet the only thing of any real significance in his life. All over the world, babies were born every day with apparent effortlessness, handed to their fathers like fruit plucked from a tree. Yet for him the days had dragged into years and still the branch was bare.

'You look beautiful in that. Ethereal.'

He had slipped out of bed and now came up behind her, putting his arms clumsily about her waist. She said nothing but leant back against him, her skin warm under the thin gold silk. They hung there in the sunlight for a few moments without speaking. He could hear her heart beating, light and rapid, as if she already knew what was on his mind.

'I want to make love to you.'

'I'm dressed now.'

'You could get undressed.'

She sighed. 'Not like this, Lawrence. Not here.'

'Why not here?'

'Your father's house. He might hear us.'

Lawrence slid his hands up to her breasts over the diaphanous fabric, unable to resist a smile at her prudish attitude, though he knew she couldn't see him.

'So what if he does? It's not against the law. We're a married couple in the privacy of our own bedroom.'

'I'm not in the mood.'

His hands dropped at her abrupt change of tone. Chastened, he let her move away. He immediately wanted to say something in return, protect himself from the sting she had driven into his flesh, but everything that came into his mind was worthless and beneath him, so he said nothing.

Lawrence picked up his shaving bag from the dressing-table and made for the door. She said his name quietly but he ignored her.

Part of him knew he was being ridiculous and unfair. It wasn't the first time she had rejected him, and it wouldn't be the last. He ought to be inured to it by now, relaxed about the fact that they made love so infrequently, yet at the back of his mind there was always the agonising knowledge that she was nearly forty. Time was running out.

Climbing the stairs to their bathroom on the upper landing, Lawrence stopped dead at the sight of a girl curled up in a shadowy alcove, a paperback book spread open in front of her. She was silently mouthing the words to herself as she read, head bent to the page. He thought at first she was a teenager, then realised she was younger, maybe eleven or twelve years old.

He wasn't entirely sure if she was real, there was something so still and other-worldly about that dark passageway; there was only one window, its long dusty curtains drawn, shutting out most of the sunlight. But then the girl glanced up as he approached and hurriedly closed her book, keeping one finger inside as though to mark the page.

'Hello,' he said rather self-consciously, aware that he was wearing nothing but pyjama bottoms.

'You're Lawrence Cardrew,' she replied, unsmiling.

'That's right. And you must be ...' He hesitated, suddenly unsure.

'Miranda.'

He waited, still not understanding.

'My mother's the housekeeper,' she explained, and there was something awkward about the way she paused afterwards, as though expecting a question that never came.

My mother's the housekeeper. He was too busy unknotting that statement to focus on her anxious air. 'Cathy? You're Cathy's daughter?'

The girl kept the book tightly closed on her finger, like a bookmark. She had her chin up, her look inexplicably confrontational. 'You were watching me last night,' she said.

He frowned, then remembered how he had looked up into darkness as the car pulled up outside the house. One window lit up, a face staring down at him through the rain.

'Only because you were watching me.'

She raised thin brows, her voice oddly precise for someone so young. 'That's no excuse. I was in bed.'

'Sorry, did we disturb you?' He managed an apologetic tone, deciding she must be angry about their intrusion. She was probably used to being here alone much of the time. 'The last ferry was the only crossing we could get at short notice. I did tell Dad we should stay in a hotel last night and drive over this morning, but he wouldn't hear of it. I hope it didn't take you too long to fall asleep again.'

When she said nothing in response, he added, curious and uncertain, 'So you live here? You and Cathy? Not in the village?'

'Not in the village,' she agreed.

He wanted to ask about her father too, but something in her expression stopped him.

'I suppose it's a big house just for one person.'

She still did not smile.

So his father's housekeeper had a daughter now, and she lived here with her mother. A strange arrangement. And a very strange little girl, he thought, with short dark hair and huge expressive eyes that watched him implacably across the landing. Her clothes seemed mismatched, a faded green dress that fell almost to her ankles coupled with a scarf tied bandana-style around her head, and what appeared to be hefty brown hiking boots on her feet. If the child hadn't seemed quite so at home in the outfit, it might have looked as though she had been delving into some theatrical costume box.

'What's that you're reading?' he asked.

'A book.'

He smiled, then tried a different approach. 'I used to do something similar when I was your age, you know. Find some dark corner of the house to hide in, so I could read in peace.'

'I'm not hiding.'

Lawrence tilted his head and slowly deciphered the title of her book.

'*I Capture the Castle*,' he read out. 'Any good?'

'It's about a girl with no money whose father's a failure.'

'Oh.'

The girl checked her page number, then snapped the book shut. He had the distinct impression that he was being dismissed.

'We're going out walking in Dhoon Glen today,' she said coolly, and for the first time he heard her mother's accent in the lilting way she pronounced the Manx place name. 'I hope you brought boots. The glen can be very muddy after a rainstorm.'

'Right.'

She glanced at his shaving bag, then pointed along the landing. 'The bathroom's the third door along.'

'I know. I've been here before.'

'Oh.' She looked surprised at last. 'Well, the bathroom lock sticks.'

'I'll remember that, thanks.'

Miranda turned and went downstairs with the book tucked under her arm, her back very straight. Her disembodied voice floated up to him from below as he headed for the bathroom. 'Don't worry if you forgot to pack boots. Gil keeps tons of spare wellies in the garage. They'll be full of spiders though, I expect.' Her voice seemed to mock him. 'Not afraid of spiders, are you?'

Smiling, he continued on along the landing. She was an interesting kid; he could see why his father might have asked them to live up at the house. And she called him Gil, not Mr Cardrew. Not much awe there. Gil would probably like that.

As he reached the bathroom, someone whispered softly behind him, 'Lawrence?' He thought he knew the voice.

Lawrence turned, but the landing was empty. And from downstairs he could hear the girl singing.

Chapter Three

The house was oppressively silent once they had all gone out, noisily and at the same time, car doors slamming and windows shivering in their frames. Lawrence had borrowed his Land Rover to take Juliet and Miranda out for the day, to 'make the most of the glorious sunshine,' and Cathy had taken herself off into the village to do some shopping for tonight's dinner. And somehow Gil now found himself outside his wife's bedroom, standing there on the landing as though by pre-arrangement.

He took the ornate brass key out of his pocket and, with the gentlest of turns, unlocked the door. He hadn't visited her room for several months now. Stale air struck him as the door creaked open, then a smell of damp from the disused fireplace. He really ought to light a fire.

He took a few tentative steps inside the room, careful to leave the door slightly ajar behind him. It was a rather childish superstition of his, not wanting to shut himself in there completely, as though Gil feared he might never get out again once the door had been closed.

'Dora?'

Usually she would be there to greet him, eyes huge as ever and shining with excitement. Today there was no sign of her. The bedroom stood cold and empty. On her bedside table, The Great Gatsby, open and face-down, as though she had just laid it aside before settling to sleep. He checked the page, then closed it softly.

Crossing to the sash window, Gil pushed it up to let some fresh air into her room. Feeling ridiculously old and lonely without her, he stared out towards the blue-grey stretch of sea. Dora had loved this view. That was why she had chosen this particular room when they first arrived, its windows facing full east so that sunlight streamed in during the long mornings and his wife could sit in this deep window-seat, watching the yachts pass across the bay. 'Yes,' she had exclaimed. 'I shall have this room. And you can be next door. And when we sleep together ... Well, we can decide that later.'

Today there was no wind for sailing and the sea lay calm to the horizon. The bay was deserted, only a lone catamaran putting out from the harbour with its white sails slack.

Gil became aware of a change in the room, catching a suggestion of his wife's perfume on the air as he turned.

'Dora?'

The floorboards creaked and there she was at last, standing beside the open wardrobe door, holding up one of her favourite blue dresses against herself. She still looked about twenty-five in the mirror, her skin pale and immaculate, golden hair gathered in a chignon above the slender neck.

His breath went out in a great sigh. At the sound, she turned towards him with an accusing look.

'You really should clear this place out, Gil,' she insisted, hanging the dress back in the wardrobe. The clothes hangers rattled gently against the metal rail. 'Turn it into an upstairs study or something. You could write your memoirs in here. Or take up watercolour painting. It's utterly pointless keeping it like a shrine, hanging onto my old clutter like this. People will think you're mad.'

'I can't bring myself to throw anything away.'

'Ask Cathy to sort it out for you. She won't find it difficult.'

'I refuse to have that awful woman poking about in your things.' Lawrence sat down on the edge of her bed to watch her flick through the other clothes in the wardrobe. He loved the familiar scent of her perfume, trying to absorb it into the very pores of his skin. 'You missed the bluebells again this spring. They were incredible. Like a deep blue sea under the trees.'

'I'm not coming back, Gil.'

'Never?'

She smiled at him gently and he could not help smiling back. 'There's a string of pearls on the dressing-table. In a small ivory box. I want you to give them to Miranda once she's old enough to wear them.'

'Not the pearls. I gave them to you on our wedding day.'

'They're no use to anyone locked up in here.' Dora lifted a black fur coat out of the wardrobe in mock horror. 'Oh good grief, did I really ever wear this? I must have looked ridiculous, lugging half a bear around on my back. The poor old thing must go to a charity shop now. That little place in the village. Tell them it's fake or they'll think we're monsters.'

Gil located the small ivory box on her dressing-table and dusted it off with his sleeve before lifting the lid. Sure enough, inside were her pearls. A long elegant string of them coiled up like a snake that he shook loose into his palm, each individual pearl heavy and luminescent.

Once again, he saw her face light up as she unfolded the tissue paper in their hotel bedroom. The bridal suite. 'Oh darling. Not real pearls, are they? They must have cost you a fortune.' The warmth of her mouth later as he fumbled with the seemingly endless silk of her wedding dress. 'Not yet, Gil. Hush, wait.'

It had been an agony of waiting. Not their first night together but certainly their first time as legitimate lovers, tied together for the rest of their lives by the vows they had so solemnly made that day.

Gil had lain there on the bed and watched his bride slowly undress, unable to believe she belonged to him at last, until there was nothing left to remove except the pearls.

'My wife.'

'Until death parted us, yes.' Dora was at his shoulder, gazing down at the pearls in his hand. 'Why don't you remarry, Lawrence? I wouldn't be angry.'

'Who could fill your place?'

Her gaze flickered away from his, gazing out at the distant line of the sea. 'You weren't always so loyal, Gil.'

'There's not a day goes by – '

'You hurt me.'

His hand closed on the necklace as he finished softly, 'That I don't regret what I did.'

Downstairs, the front door opened with a clatter of keys and Gil sat up on the bed to listen, his expression suddenly distracted. Cathy must have got back from her shopping trip. He could hear the housekeeper moving briskly about, calling his name as she opened door after door.

What did the bloody woman want now?

Probably her wages.

Gil sighed, struggling back to his feet. He should never have kept Cathy on after Dora died. Nor allowed her to convert the boathouse into her own private flat. But then he would not have been able to see Miranda. It meant a great deal to him, to have the child in the house every day, to let her sleep in the little attic room when she wanted. She brought new life to what was, essentially, a dead house. *La vita nuova.* It sounded trite, but the older he got, the more he believed love might just be the answer to everything, after all. Or at least a step in the right direction.

Cathy's heels clicked across the tiled floor below, inexorably nearing the back staircase as she searched the house for him.

Soon she would continue the hunt upstairs.

The string of pearls hung cold and hard from his fist. Miranda was still too young for such a gift, surely?

Gently, he unclenched his fingers and coiled the pearls back into the small ivory box. There was a cold draught on his face from the window when Gil turned to bid goodbye to his wife, finding the bedroom empty.

Chapter Four

Lawrence crossed the tram lines at the Dhoon Glen station and stood at the head of a long descent, staring down as Miranda and Juliet disappeared through the undergrowth into dappled sunlight, yelping and whooping like savages. He heard them hallooing his name in the glen below and forced himself to move.

The lichened steps were slippery under his ill-fitting wellington boots as he too descended, listening to the hoarse whisper of a river hidden somewhere at the bottom of the glen. The too-bright sunlight blinded him through the trees. Lawrence lowered his head to avoid it, trying to hurry as their voices called him again from a lower path.

He thought of that voice on the landing, whispering his name. It had sounded like his mother. An illusion, of course. Water cooling in the pipes; it was an old house. And he missed her, that was all. The mind liked to play tricks like that on the unwary. His mother had been gone well over a decade though. He ought to be over it by now.

They were waiting for him at a bend in the path, peering over the wooden barrier at the river below. There were lush green ferns everywhere, spilling out from the high banks onto the stony ground and brushing his ankles as he walked.

'You've taken absolutely ages,' Juliet cheerfully accused him. 'But isn't this fun? There's even a waterfall down there.'

Her mood had changed since they left the house. Lawrence wondered why Juliet had never really shared his enthusiasm for having children, when she herself was so much like a child, jeans tucked into the tops of her wellingtons as she grinned up at him and swung precariously back and forth on the barrier.

'Can we swim under the waterfall, darling? Say yes, please say yes!'

He smiled, captivated by her playful air. 'It's entirely up to you.'

Down on her knees with a look of fierce concentration, Miranda was edging a blue-backed beetle she had found onto a fern leaf, ignoring Juliet's noisy pleas. When her hair fell across her face, she tucked it back behind her ears with an irritable sigh. There seemed to be a slightly gloomy tension about her now, as though she couldn't bear to be parted from Gil even for a few hours. She was the sort of child who would have suited the Victorian age better than the twentieth century, Lawrence thought, watching her fumble for a jam jar in her rucksack and slip the unfortunate insect inside.

It must be Gil's influence, her incessant desire to explore and examine. He remembered being urged to collect insects and butterflies at roughly her age, and feeling nothing but a vague disgust at the thought, much to his father's obvious dissatisfaction.

Cathy's daughter.

He wondered again who her father was. Some bloke in the village, perhaps, clearly no longer in the picture. Or the two of them would hardly be living with Gil. Had Cathy ever married? Surely his dad would have mentioned it.

'Don't worry. I usually let them go after a few days,' Miranda said, noticing his interest. 'The ones who don't die, that is.'

'Ugh,' Juliet said.

They reached the waterfall within a few more turns of the path, a deserted greenish pool continuously struck and sprayed by a glorious white cascade from above. Miranda had run ahead and was already on her knees beside the water, searching for her swimsuit in the rucksack. The ferns were much thicker here, delicate tapering fronds protruding from every crevice, some even managing to gain a foothold on an outcrop of rock immediately beside the waterfall, shivering under the endless onslaught.

Her cheeks mottled pink from the unaccustomed exercise, Juliet bent to splash some of the icy water onto her face and shivered, instantly changing her mind about going for a swim. Instead, she found a nearby rock to perch on while she smoked her ubiquitous cigarette. Her slim thighs looked like a teenager's in those faded blue jeans, bare feet wiggling against the rock as she removed the clumsy wellingtons and drew up her legs provocatively beneath her. It had been a long time since Lawrence had seen his wife like this, out under the open sky instead of inside a house or at some restaurant, a few wispy strands of hair escaping from the neat plait lying against her shoulder. He had forgotten how beautiful his wife could look, seductive as a mermaid on her rock, cigarette and all.

For one crazy moment Lawrence was almost tempted to ask her to walk on alone with him, to find some secluded corner of the glen where they could lie together in the shade and pretend that none of the hurt between them had ever happened.

But now that her initial excitement had died, chased away by the reality of freezing water and too many flies, Juliet seemed to have grown bored with their expedition. 'Actually, look, you go and swim,' she told Miranda, crushing an errant red ant between finger and thumb. 'I'll sit and watch. Or sleep. That walk tired me out.'

Seconds later, with a practised flick of her lighter, a thin trail of smoke rose from her lips and Juliet fell silent at last, head tilted back in the sunlight.

He watched her, disappointed. There had been a light about her at the head of the glen; now it had gone out.

'It's not here!'

He glanced down at the kid. 'What isn't?'

'My swimsuit,' Miranda said, looking a little panicked. She dragged a muddled assortment of things out of the rucksack onto the damp ground beside the pool, sounding genuinely distraught by her mistake. Her fingers scrabbled hopelessly through them again and again. 'I'm sure I packed it, or at least, I remember laying it out on the bed. Here's the towel. But I forgot to put the swimsuit in. I must be the stupidest person alive. Now I can't swim and the water looks so wonderful.'

'Just swim in your underwear.'

She looked shocked.

'There's nobody else in the glen, and I won't look. In fact, I'm going to carry on a little way along the path and see if I can't catch sight of this beach you keep raving about.' He smiled at the girl, amused by her small-town prudishness. 'I promise not to come back for at least twenty minutes. Will that be long enough?'

'He's right, you mustn't let something like that stop you doing what you want. Lawrence will go off and you can swim in peace,' his wife muttered with her eyes closed, waving her cigarette in the air.

'You could come with me, Juliet.'

'Spend twenty minutes trekking along that path to the sea?' Her disdain was deliberately wounding. 'No thanks, I'm fine where I am.'

He hesitated, then let it drop. What was the use? He had tried to invest his words with deliberate meaning, unable to be any more direct with the child there listening, but Juliet was no longer able to hear him. This sunlit place, the cool green water with its iridescent bed of pebbles and rocks, meant nothing to her except a break on the path for a cigarette. So why bother asking her to step back into the light, back towards intimacy? For that too had dropped away, slipping over the edge into the shadow zone they had both learnt to inhabit.

She flicked her cigarette into the pool, her face averted.

Lawrence took the lower path towards the beach without saying goodbye.

He thought again of his father's house, a rambling warren of strange rooms with rafters and sloping ceilings and its endless, confusing corridors, and how happy he had felt there this morning, waking up with the sun streaming in through its broad windows. For a few moments after waking, he had believed a reconciliation with Juliet might still be possible. He had felt at peace with himself. Now though he was convinced that, like his mother's voice on the landing, it had been mere wishful thinking. Sleight of mind.

Still, he refused to relinquish hope. This place was special; perhaps it could achieve miracles. Not just the house but the island too. It had been like stepping back in time, driving his father's Land Rover. Not because the bodywork was so rusty, but because the island seemed a hundred years behind the mainland with its quaint Victorian shops and old-fashioned ways, the locals polite and unhurried.

'*Traa dy liooar*,' one smiling old villager had remarked when Lawrence stopped to ask for directions, irritated by the length of time it was taking to negotiate the narrow country lanes.

'*Time enough*,' Miranda had translated for them, before coolly pointing out there was a map of the island tucked down the side of the driver's seat.

After his father's phone call, Lawrence had initially been reluctant to come back to the island. Juliet even more so. But perhaps it was the perfect place to bury the past and start again. Though he and Juliet only had a few weeks before work would drag them back to England. *Traa dy liooar* was all very well when time was not an issue.

But would a few weeks be long enough for them to find each other again, when the way had become so dark and confused?

Persuading herself this was an adventure, to be embraced and not shirked from, Miranda dipped one naked foot into the freezing water at the edge of the pool and then stepped deliberately forwards without giving herself time to adjust to the temperature. There was no point being half-hearted about it. Behind her on the rocks, in a puddle of faded green, lay the dress she had tentatively slipped off before entering the pool, revealing a flat bare chest and white knickers to the astonished ferns.

She checked over her shoulder again, but Juliet seemed to be asleep on her rock. So there was no one to see her balance precariously over the slimy pebbles until the water was at her knees, so incredibly cold that her skin tingled and burnt until it was almost numb. It was much deeper further in towards the high ravine, maybe even up to her stomach where the waterfall came crashing down with its rain-like spray, already peppering her bare arms at this distance. Beyond that was the endless chute of white water under which she planned to stand for at least thirty seconds, if she could bear it.

She felt naked in nothing but her knickers, her chest completely exposed. But it was her own fault and she was determined to reach the waterfall.

Lawrence had long since disappeared along the lower path to the sea. She had revised her estimate of his character a little that morning, though not too much, since he was still too wooden and adult to be of any interest. But at least he had shown a little spirit by heading off to discover the beach, whereas Juliet had merely fallen asleep in the sun.

Miranda felt the childish quiver of disappointment starting again in her lip and bit down hard. It was an adventure, she reminded herself firmly, and adventures are never easy. The knickers clung to her wet buttocks as she waded further out, finding larger and more difficult to negotiate rocks under her feet now, their smooth surface slippery with green weed. Tiny fish-like creatures darted away at the touch of her shadow. She had to make the most of this day in the glen, with the sun warm on her back and the smell of salt on the air. It was nearly the end of the holidays and she would be going back to school soon.

She stopped to catch her breath as the cold water reached her stomach. Perhaps Gil wasn't well again, which would explain why he had decided to stay at home today.

There had been a few weeks earlier that spring when she had thought – they had all thought – he was going to die. He had fallen over in his study one afternoon, his mouth dragged down at one side afterwards and his left arm useless. Miranda hadn't been able to sleep while he was in the hospital, walking restlessly around her room most nights. She had even slipped out into the dark garden once and climbed into the lap of the great sycamore, staring up through the leaves at the stars, praying to whoever might be up there to make Gil better.

Someone must have heard her prayer, because he came home from hospital a few days later. And though at first he was slower than before and his words sometimes a little slurred, he seemed to grow stronger every day until now he was almost back to normal. But perhaps he hadn't fully recovered yet, as her mother kept insisting. She was always trying to stop their long walks together and telling Miranda to let the 'old man' rest.

It was strange to think of him as 'old'. In spite of the scare he had given them, Gil had always seemed indestructible to her – like one of the ancient Norse warriors in the books he loved, battling dragons and giving rings to his followers, then springing back unscathed from the brink of death. She could not lose him. Gil was like a father to her, especially since she had no father of her own, or not one who had ever wanted to be around. She had asked her mother once where her father was, but had been answered with nothing but silence and a cold stare.

'*Hwaet! We Gardena in gear-dagum,*' she muttered, quoting the first few words of *Beowulf* as she waded through the freezing water.

She could not remember the rest of the old poem, but it had started with Scyld Scefing's funeral, the mourners laying his body in a ship, then placing golden treasure around him. After they had pushed him onto the tide, they stood and watched as the high-prowed boat drifted slowly out to sea. Gil had read the poem to her in Anglo-Saxon over several nights, translating as he went, then let her keep the book afterwards. 'To be read aloud at my funeral,' he had told her, and she had guessed he was only half-joking.

Now she stood within touching distance of the waterfall, staring up at the rushing water and the black ravine, hung with creepers and shivering green ferns. It was much colder and darker here, out of the sunlight, goosepimples rising on her skin like braille. Miranda could barely feel her legs and feet now, they were so numb from the water. But she was not going to turn back. She had come to stand under this waterfall, however terrifying the great chute of water seemed, its force exploding into the pool with a thunderous crash mere inches from her outstretched palm. Her hair was already wet through from the spray and she could taste its clean electricity on her tongue.

Miranda took a vast lungful of air and pushed forwards into the living roar itself, deafened and blinded, her body jerking in shock as she passed through a solid wall of water to the cool stillness beyond.

Caught in that tiny room behind the waterfall, her back against the wet black rock, she stared through the endless curtain with its racing white beads of water across the pool to where she could see Juliet lying on her rock, and the winding path from the car park that led on to the sea.

Suddenly she realised they were no longer alone in the glen: a shadowy group of teenagers grew clearer as they descended the path, all of them boys, in shorts and cut-off jeans, with rucksacks like her own on their backs and fishing-rods for the beach. They stopped at the edge of the pool and tested the water. Juliet still appeared to be asleep, one arm dangling from the rock and her head back in the sunlight. They had not seen her yet. Then one of them looked up towards the waterfall and pointed, his arm flung out with excitement.

They stared at first, and then started to jeer, the tallest jumping into the pool with a cry and wading out in his shorts towards Miranda. She stood and waited in a breathless silence, still imagining herself invisible behind the curtain of water.

'Hey you! What are you doing behind there?'

His aggression made her tremble, shrinking back against the cold black rock as she realised the boys could actually see her through the waterfall, naked except for the sodden white strip of her knickers.

'Come out. We won't hurt you, honest.'

There were hoots of derision from the others at the pool's edge and the boy turned, angrily waving his hand. His voice was muffled through the great roar of the waterfall.

'Don't pay any attention to those prats. You must be bloody freezing. This isn't the Amazon rain forest, you know.'

'G ... go away!'

'Now don't be like that.'

Miranda put her hands up to cover herself, but it was useless. He was so close now, his own shoulders gleaming with the water's sheen, that he must be able to see everything.

It was at times like this when she wished desperately for a father, someone who could step in and save her. But Juliet didn't appear to have stirred and there was nobody here to rescue her except herself. She was alone as usual, just as she had been the day some of the other village kids cornered her out on the rough ground near the golf course, pulling her hair and calling her a witch, 'just like your mother!'

Her legs were cold and shaking uncontrollably. Miranda told herself it was from adrenalin, not fear. She raised her chin and stared out at the boy through the rushing waterfall. She knew the words, even if she had never used them aloud to anyone.

'Why don't you piss off?'

'Piss off?' The boy made a face and turned round to the others, raising his voice. 'Not very polite, is she? If you ask me, I think this one needs to be taught a lesson.'

The others started shouting something but their words were lost under the rush of water as the boy pushed abruptly through under the waterfall, making a grab for her arm. She flailed against him, losing her footing on the slimy rocks, and falling forwards against his chest. They struggled there a moment, blind in the freezing cascade, then suddenly she was free of the waterfall. They had dropped clean into the pool together like a stone, legs and arms entangled. It was horrible. She fought to get loose, then wriggled past him to the surface. She had about three seconds to drag air into her aching lungs before he caught up with her again, grabbing at her shoulder.

For those few seconds she thought she could hear a woman screaming. Then the boy tangled his fingers in her hair, using her like a ladder to stand up as she was forced down again into the sunlit water.

Gasping and choking, Miranda dropped to her knees on the rocky edge of the pool, held down by the boy. Huddled in mute humiliation, she waited for his laughter, his insults.

Miraculously though, the boy was suddenly plucked away by an unseen hand, and she found herself alone, clutching at the rocks to stop herself slipping back into the water, hair streaming with water.

She looked round at the other boys on the bank, but they had magically disappeared, leaving only their friend behind.

Lawrence stood blocking out the light, his trousers soaked, the boy lying on his back in the shallows. 'What the hell's going on here?' he demanded, staring down at the boy.

'Nothing. Bit of fun, that's all.'

The boy's voice was sullen. But he scrabbled backwards as Lawrence took another step towards him. He might be defiant but he was scared too. There was a darkish blonde wedge of hair falling over his eyes; he pushed it back irritably, glaring up at her rescuer.

'Don't you touch me, I'll have my dad on you. He's a black belt.'

'Go on, get out of here.'

The teenage boy picked himself up and loped away through the ankle-deep water, tripping and falling, his sun-tanned back lean and muscular.

Juliet was standing at the edge of the pool with her arms folded and started to say something in a sharp voice as the boy climbed out, only to fall silent and step back as if his expression had alarmed her. He grabbed violently at his rucksack, abandoned on the path, before trudging back up towards the car park in the direction his friends had taken. At the very top of the path, turning for a second, the boy made a brief obscene gesture at them and broke into a run as he vanished through the trees.

Lawrence came back towards her, his boots squelching heavily with water. 'Did that little idiot hurt you?'

'No.' Miranda didn't look at him.

'What happened then?'

'It doesn't matter. I'm all right now,' she insisted.

He held out his hand to help her up, but Miranda shook her head and stayed there on her knees, arms folded protectively across her chest, wanting to conceal her nakedness for as long as possible. She didn't need his help anyway. She could have handled that boy, there were dozens like him at her school, jeering and trying to upset her simply because she was different, because she knew things they didn't and actually enjoyed school. Miranda knew how to deal with that sort of situation without needing to run to some adult for help.

Now that it was finished though, her legs were trembling and she thought she might even be sick, the ultimate humiliation. Luckily, Lawrence was looking at Juliet, not her, so she put a hand quickly to her mouth and struggled out of the water.

'Where's your towel?' he asked curtly.

'In my bag. But I'm fine, I don't need any help.'

Lawrence made an angry noise under his breath. 'Come on,' he said, and before she realised what was happening, he had scooped her up into his arms and carried her to the bank.

Miranda lay there, feeling weak and trapped and acutely aware of her nakedness, cradled against his chest like a small child. His wife watched them both with concern, her voice high as she asked where the boys had come from and apologised for staying asleep so long. It had been the sun, she explained, and the long walk down through the glen that had knocked her out.

Lawrence laid her gently on the bank, then turned away to find her towel. Miranda shivered beneath it while he fetched her green dress from the rocks, wishing the earth could swallow her up. Her knickers were dirty with weed and pool mud, and there was a thin weeping cut on her ankle where she must have scraped it in the struggle.

Why had Lawrence chosen to come back at that precise moment? She had never felt so embarrassed in all her life. She tried not to cry, hiding her face under the towel, but it was impossible and hot bitter tears were soon streaming down her cheeks.

The expedition had been ruined, utterly ruined, and they had not even reached the sea.

Chapter Five

There was a terrible fragility to Miranda's face tonight, Gil thought, a pale translucence he had never seen before. She had always been such a child of the moon, happy one moment, sad the next, her emotions constantly in flux. Dora had been like that too, though she had been more fiery in her youth, like a star blazing across the night sky. Of course this was Cathy's child; her ancestors were earthier, more prosaic. But he could not recall having seen quite this air of brittle vulnerability in Miranda before, and it shook him. Had he made the right choice after all, keeping the child so close?

It was some hours since his son and daughter-in-law had brought the girl back from the glen, wrapped in a plaid travelling blanket like an invalid, her expression miserable and shamed when Lawrence insisted on carrying her up the stairs to her bedroom. But Gil still sat on the edge of her bed, listening to Miranda as she held up the jam jar and tilted its trapped occupant to the light, the shiny blue-backed beetle scrabbling uselessly at the glass.

Her voice seemed so vulnerable after the incident at Dhoon Glen. But he had been assured by his son that nothing too disturbing had happened to the child, she was just a little shaken up.

He hoped that was true, watching Miranda's smile fade occasionally as they spoke, her gaze somewhere else at times, slipping back over his shoulder to the waterfall perhaps and the boy who had nearly tried to drown her. What on earth had possessed the little idiot? It didn't appear to have been a deliberate attack, Lawrence had told him in private, just some practical joke that had gone wrong. But deliberate or not, it had left an unhappiness in the girl's eyes that Gil found disturbing.

'Goodnight, Miranda,' he said at last, bending to kiss her forehead. 'Sleep well.'

She pulled the covers up to her chin, staring up at him. 'Night.'

He left Miranda to sleep and went back to the house for dinner, which he had asked Cathy to serve outside in the gardens since the weather was still so fine.

A wooden table had been set on the terraced back lawn overlooking the sea and covered with his wife's favourite damask tablecloth, citronella candles sunk into the grass alongside to discourage the flies. He and Dora had taken to dining al fresco on summer evenings during her last years, though it had not been easy for either of them. Dora had not been entirely herself at times. After dinner they had often walked together down the steps which ran between the terraced lawns, his wife more interested in her beloved roses and hydrangeas than in his company. He still remembered feeling stung by that, and almost resentful of the flowers, jealous of their gaudy, short-lived beauty.

The lawns were empty now, the sun slowly descending below the horizon as Gil made his way around the west side of the house, its reddish light staining his face and the rows of darkening windows above.

There was no putting the task off any longer. He would have to tell Lawrence tonight.

Dinner was a subdued affair. Juliet sat a few feet apart from both of them, smoking relentlessly while they waited for Cathy to bring out coffee and dessert. Her slender, red-tipped fingers tapped at the table as if she were burning to get away. Lawrence glanced at her occasionally without speaking. They had clearly argued at some point earlier in the day and were now struggling with the aftermath of that row. But a silent atmosphere suited Gil quite well. He was completely absorbed by the task ahead of him, eating his fresh fruit salad without much interest as the light eventually failed and the table was lit only by a single lamp, flies gathering compulsively about its metal hood.

'This is all rather unBritish of us, isn't it?' Juliet said suddenly and inexplicably, as if continuing a conversation from earlier, and flicked her cigarette ash carelessly over the damask tablecloth.

Gil waited for more, but nothing else was forthcoming. Her mobile mouth fell into repose as she scanned the darkened gardens, her point apparently made.

'Why unBritish?' Gil was puzzled.

Juliet waved her hand over the wine glasses and half-eaten bowls of fruit salad. 'Eating *al fresco*.'

Then she made a sudden despairing noise under her breath, noticing a broken fingernail and held her finger next to the lamp to examine it. The spiral of tiny flies there scattered, lifting to a higher orbit above the table, only to return almost immediately to the metal lamp and its fascinating yellow light.

Lawrence pushed away his bowl and leant back in his chair, watching Juliet with a look almost of dislike. They had definitely argued.

'The British aren't natural outdoor eaters,' Juliet continued. 'I remember my mother telling me off once for daring to sit out on the lawn with my strawberries. You'll catch a chill, she said, and that was June or July.'

'Talking of which, I was wondering … ' Gil hesitated, uncertain of his ground but determined to seize this opportunity while he could. 'Have you and Lawrence thought about having children yourselves?'

The couple looked at each other in silence. Lawrence finished his coffee unhurriedly before replying for both of them.

'We've been trying. Without any luck, so far.'

'I'm sorry.'

His son shrugged. 'There are some tests we could have, but Juliet isn't particularly keen on that idea.'

'Because it's too soon for tests!'

Juliet shot her husband a brief resentful glance, then leant forward over the table to emphasise her point, speaking to Gil as if he was the only one there. By the strange yellowish glow of the lamp, he could see how flushed she was. 'Far too soon for any of that, for God's sake,' she continued, tapping the tablecloth with her broken fingernail. 'And if it does turn out there's something wrong, then the person with the … problem … is going to feel like they're being blamed for it. Do you see what I mean?'

'I didn't mean to upset either of you,' Gil said stiffly. He realised now, belatedly, that his daughter-in-law must be nearing forty, and her failure to conceive was clearly a matter of serious concern. 'I apologise. It's none of my business.'

Juliet picked up her packet of cigarettes and stood up unsteadily from the table, knocking her chair sideways onto the grass. Her hands trembled slightly as she picked it up and it was obvious she had drunk too much wine. But if she had been angry before, now she seemed merely exhausted.

'I'm going to bed. That walk up the glen, and those appalling boys ... '

'I'll come with you,' Lawrence said promptly.

'I'm fine, I don't need any help. Stay and talk to your father. That's why we came here, isn't it?' She looked across at Gil, enunciating each word slowly and clearly as though to emphasise that she was not drunk. 'Thank you for dinner. It was utterly delicious. Cathy is such a good cook, you're lucky to have her.'

'Not at all. I hope you sleep well.'

Once they were alone together at the table, Lawrence avoided his father's curious gaze for some time, staring out over the lawn and the indistinguishable tangle of hydrangea bushes to where the steps descended into darkness. He seemed to be struggling internally with something too difficult to say aloud, lips moving occasionally as if he wanted to speak but never quite managing it.

Gil thought it ironic that they should both be so reticent tonight. But the events of the day had brought his own problem to the fore and it could not be kept secret any longer.

The person with the problem is going to feel like they're being blamed for it.

That was what his daughter-in-law had said, unaware of the truth ringing remorselessly behind her words. But how could he go about it?

Little by little, perhaps, working piecemeal towards a full confession which, once dragged into the light, would surely destroy his already tenuous and uneasy relationship with his son.

Gil poured a very small amount of wine into his glass, cleared his throat, and prepared himself for the inevitable. Then something stirred inside him – a sudden fear perhaps that he might be about to lose his only son – and Gil swerved at the last moment, knowing as he began to speak that he was going to say something rather different to the confession he had intended.

'There's something I have to tell you, Lawrence.'

'Mmm?'

'I had a minor stroke earlier this year. Now it was nothing serious, no need to look so alarmed. But the doctors have warned me ... That is, I understand that if ...'

Gil paused, struggling for the right words. He disliked the way his son was staring across the table as though he expected him to collapse and die at any moment. But he had to be told.

'I have to watch my diet. They've given me some ridiculous sheet – not that I follow it – and told me to give up butter and cream and all those fatty breakfasts like sausages and bacon. They say having another stroke might not be such a good idea, if you see what I mean.'

Lawrence seemed pale. 'But are you all right now? When was this?'

'April.'

'Why didn't you ring me, for God's sake?'

'It didn't seem important at the time. But I thought you should know, Lawrence, just in case I ... ' He rearranged the salt and pepper mills absentmindedly, avoiding his son's gaze. 'There are some legal issues to take into consideration. The terms of my will, you know.' He forced a laugh. 'I want my ashes scattered over West Kennett Long Barrow, for instance.'

'Good grief.'

'No hurry, of course. It's near Avebury in Wiltshire. So not exactly local. Whenever you're passing would be fine.'

Lawrence seemed bemused, which was hardly surprising. 'Why there?'

'Call it an old man's whim.' He shrugged, trying to slip the most important thing under the wire while his son was distracted. 'After my stroke, I made a discreet arrangement with Cathy that I'll provide for her and Miranda after my death. So I'm afraid that's in the will too.'

Lawrence was frowning now. He said slowly, 'I see.'

'I thought it only fair to let you know in advance, so there won't be any unpleasant shocks when the contents of the will are read out.'

'It's entirely your decision.'

So there, the deed had been done. Or part of it, at any rate. The part that mattered for now. There was a strained silence for a while, then Gil finished his wine and stood up from the table.

'It's past my bedtime, I'm afraid.'

'Already?'

'These days I rarely last much beyond ten o'clock at night. I'll see you in the morning.'

Lawrence stood up. 'I'll go back in with you.'

'No, stay. Finish your wine. I'll probably take a quick walk before I go up.'

'I meant to say thank you for inviting us. I'd forgotten how special this place is.'

'Your mother loved this house.'

Lawrence was looking at him oddly. 'Yes,' he agreed, then hesitated. 'Dad, do you ever …I mean, I thought I heard her voice … '

So that was it.

Gil smiled. 'She loved this house,' he repeated, and put down his napkin. 'Goodnight.'

Relieved to be on his own at last, Gil strolled across the dark uneven lawns, whistling an old tune under his breath as he made for the front porch. He had meant to say far more to his son, but that could wait for another evening, another time. It had been a tiring day for all of them and he was not yet ready to admit how far his deception stretched.

It's entirely your decision, Lawrence had said. So the blame for it must lie squarely on his own shoulders.

Not for the first time Gil wondered whether he had made the wrong decision after Cathy came to him in tears, explaining about her pregnancy. But who could ever tell which was the right decision and which the wrong? His wife had only recently died at the time, and he had still been lost in pain, unable to cope with the potential aftermath of such news becoming public.

It was easy to look back now and see the whole pattern lying clear before him, to follow the events through in his memory, how one mistake had inevitably spawned another. But at the time he had been drawing threads together in the dark, weaving a spell like those old witches in the tower at Castletown, doing what he thought was best for everyone concerned.

Now everything was different. Gil felt too weary to carry on with the deception any longer, though its final unravelling would have to wait until he had the strength to pick up that last loose thread.

Chapter Six

Once again, Lawrence appreciated his father's collection of spare wellies, even if they did provide a home for grotesquely huge spiders. Going down to the harbour at Port St Mary was like stepping back into the nineteenth century, its dark stone walls mossed and slimy with centuries of salt water, and he suspected some wading might soon be required, by the look of the seaweed-covered slipway ahead. There was a brisk wind that morning and the high ringing song of wires against metal masts seemed almost relentless. A small huddle of fishing-boats leant drunkenly on the harbour wall, the tide having pulled slowly out to reveal long stretches of mudflats dimpled with worm casts. Left stranded in the middle, up to its shoulders in silt, an ancient houseboat sat and waited uneasily for the tide to return, paint peeling from its exposed timbers. The more expensive-looking modern yachts were few, though the white hull of a catamaran shone brilliantly in the sunlight only a few hundred feet from the slipway of the tiny harbour.

He stopped to take a few photographs. Harbour scenes were perennially popular in magazines; he might make a few good sales from the work he was compiling while here in the island.

'Morning!'

Lawrence nodded politely to a man and his young son who were climbing down a narrow ladder onto the soft harbour mud, armed with several lidded buckets, presumably for gathering bait.

A little way ahead, Miranda had given up waiting for him to take his photographs and was skipping along the path that ran from the old harbour to the rock pools. She seemed more cheerful today, and more like a child in her flared jeans and white tee-shirt than she had appeared when he first met her.

Juliet had kept to her bed that morning with a 'sick headache' and he had readily agreed to accompany Miranda on her outing to the beach, partly out of sympathy for the girl but also in order to escape the claustrophobic atmosphere up at the house. It had been a rough night for him, unable to sleep as he went over and over what Gil had told him and tried to imagine what the future might hold.

Now the sun on the water and the fresh tang of salt were helping to clear his mind of those unpalatable shadows, his hands sunk in his pockets as he strolled along without urgency or purpose after the child.

He recalled his father's bitter smile. *She loved this house.*

Lawrence knew what his father was trying to insinuate, but it would not work. Not with him. He did not believe in ghosts. Though he did believe in the power of suggestion.

Beyond the harbour lay a series of even smaller inlets and jetties, some with rowing boats moored to rusted wall rings, others deserted except for a tangle of broken lobster pots awaiting repair. Past them the path narrowed and grew dusty with blown sand and the strange dry sticks and ribbons of seaweed thrown up there by many storms.

Miranda stopped and pointed ahead to where the path rose on metal stilts above the rocks and the tide, twisting away out of sight towards the wide blue arc of the bay.

'Not far now,' she announced, then vanished abruptly through an opening in the sea wall only to reappear a few seconds later, running down a flight of steps to where a network of concrete paths had been set into the rock, culminating in a single jetty beside which a mass of jagged rock had collected the outgoing tide in innumerable shallow pockets.

'Wait for me,' he called after her, but Miranda ignored him. Or perhaps didn't hear.

The sun warm on his back, Lawrence followed as she ran along the jetty and, without even appearing to hesitate, leapt nimbly across onto the rocks, threading a precarious path along the weed-slick edges of the pools with her net and bucket swinging.

Inches from her feet, a low tide was pushing itself limply back and forth against the jetty wall. Miranda paid no attention, arms outstretched as she balanced across to where the rocks were the most slippery and darkest with weed.

Convinced the child was about to slip and fall, Lawrence took the last few steps at a run, poised to call her back from the brink of danger. Then stopped, realising she must have done this many times before as Miranda dropped to her knees with practised efficiency and bent close to the water, oblivious to his panic. Her short dark fringe flopped over her eyes and she pushed it irritably back, reminding him of her mother. Cathy had the same dark fringe, the same impatience. But that was where the resemblance ended, he thought. For this girl was no Cathy.

For a moment, he felt like a fool, unused to children and their ways, and wished he had never agreed to accompany her. Then she lifted her head and smiled at him across the rocks, so sunnily that he forgot his sense of incompetence and allowed himself to be pleasantly surprised instead by his desire to protect the girl.

That look in her eyes, the familiar tilt to her head, were so like his father it almost took his breath away. Surely she could not be ... ?

But no, that was impossible. Gil had clearly spent time with her and Cathy over the years, inviting the two of them to move into the house with him, treating Miranda almost as if she were his own child. Something of his character must have rubbed off on her like pollen dust from lilies, curiously indelible. And Lawrence had to concede she made a better protégé for the old man than he himself had ever done.

He had found his father a little frightening, always pushing him into situations where he felt uneasy and no longer in control, his disapproval tangible whenever Lawrence failed some challenge which had been set for him. Miranda seemed to revel in that high-pressured atmosphere, just as she had bounced back from yesterday's unpleasant incident without any obvious scars, running excitedly to change her clothes this morning when he had agreed to accompany her on this expedition.

Now he stood motionless on the jetty and watched her scoop aside the slimy green weed with her fingers, intent on her search for unusual new creatures to add to her collection. The rock pools glistened around her like treasure. He thought she seemed nothing less than a child of the sea and sky, completely at one with them, the knees of her jeans dark with water as she leant over the edge of the pool with her net to retrieve some tiny splashing jewel-like thing. It evaded her at first, darting swiftly between the tangled weeds, but once she finally managed it, there was a cry of pure delight.

Lifting the dripping net clear, she sat back on her heels and carefully deposited her catch in a bucket of pale brackish water. He had expected some sort of boyish pleasure from her in capturing something so helpless but Miranda spoke gently to it, bending over the bucket to stroke the spiny creature with a calming finger, the look on her face one of consummate satisfaction.

'What is it?' he asked, lowering himself from the jetty and taking a few tentative steps across the slippery rocks towards her.

'I'm not sure. Gil will probably know.'

He wanted to get closer but his shoes weren't right for the surface and his left foot slithered awkwardly into one of the rock pools as he tried to keep his balance. Irritated by his own clumsiness, Lawrence swore and pulled his foot out, shaking drops from the sodden black leather.

He stared across the interminable distance between the jetty and where Miranda knelt, watching him with what was clearly an amused expression. It was salt water in these pools. His shoes would be ruined if he tried to reach her.

'Okay. How on earth do you do it?'

'Do what?'

'Get across here without slipping in. I should have worn trainers.' He prodded the thick slimy weed that covered the rocks. 'This stuff's lethal.'

'I'm used to it. You just have to pick your way. I fell a few times when we first started coming down here. Scraped my knee really badly once and Gil had to carry me home.'

'So you're not immortal?'

She giggled, looking pleased but surprised. 'Did you think I was?'

'I was beginning to wonder.'

Rather more carefully now, he edged his way back to the weed-encrusted jetty and, after a few abortive attempts, finally managed to pull himself up onto the wall again. Now there was a dark green smudge on his shirt sleeve, but once he had rolled them neatly up to his elbows, it was no longer visible.

Giving up on the idea of staying clean, Lawrence levered himself into a sitting position on the damp stone and gazed out across the bay. He was still trying to adjust to the revelation that his father had suffered a stroke. The old man had seemed so strong when he came to visit them at Berkhamsted a few years ago, getting up at the crack of dawn every day and insisting on dragging him and Juliet out for a morning walk along the canal or for a ramble over the castle ruins. There had certainly been no suspicion of weakness then. But perhaps his father had deteriorated quite suddenly, like a car running out of fuel.

The wind ruffled the waves in the bay, pushing a slender white yacht far beyond the line of buoys that seemed to mark deeper waters. One lone seagull swung and wheeled above the churning wake, its plaintive cry reaching back to him on the jetty.

He watched the gull thoughtfully. Too far away to make a good picture? Then fumbled for his SLR camera, hanging on a strap round his neck, and removed the lens cap.

His father was getting on in years, yet somehow Lawrence had never considered the possibility that he might die in the near future. He had always imagined a fluid departure for his father, something that was being constantly pushed back, like a boat trip in uncertain weather. It was a shock to realise that an end date might be nearer than anticipated.

He took a few photographs of the windswept bay, adjusting the aperture size once or twice to take account of the strong sunlight. Without his light metre, he had to guess which settings to choose. They would probably turn out okay. He could always make adjustments in the darkroom once he got home to England.

The child appeared to have finished her hunt through the rock pools, wandering barefoot back across the rocks, swinging her bucket carelessly and with her trainers laced about her neck. The salt water sloshed over the rim of the bucket at each step but she didn't seem to mind. 'They're all hiding today,' she said. 'I only caught three of the spiny ones and a couple of anemones.'

She was an attractive child, flushed with the sun, her hair in her eyes. Lawrence considered snapping a photo of her with her rock pool spoils, then thought better of it.

He put the lens cap back on his camera, and let it dangle from his neck again. 'Let's see, then.'

Miranda held up the bucket for him to hold while she climbed deftly onto the jetty and sat beside him to catch her breath. 'Pretty, aren't they?'

'Extremely.'

'I've got a glass bowl for them at home. I keep it in the cellar, it's much cooler down there and they seem to like the dark.'

'Won't they die if you keep them out of the sea?'

She cocked her head to one side, forcing the trainers onto her damp feet and lacing them up again. 'Sometimes they die. But I usually only keep them for a few days. Then I put them back into the rock pools and find more.' She thought for a bit. 'Do you think it's cruel to catch them?'

'I'm not sure,' he said seriously. 'Do sea anemones have feelings?'

'Oh yes.'

'Then it must be.'

Miranda stood up and peered into the bucket, stirring the water with the end of her fishing net. There was a note of guilt in her voice. 'Perhaps I should let them go straight away.'

He was sorry then, both for having spoiled her fun and having introduced a shadow of guilt into her little expeditions to the rock pools. Time enough for guilt when she was older, he thought bitterly.

'But then you wouldn't be able to show my father.'

'That's true.' Her face brightened. 'I tell you what, I'll only keep them for one night this time. Then we can come back tomorrow morning and let them go. That wouldn't be cruel, would it?'

Lawrence agreed and struggled to his feet, brushing down his trousers and checking the soles of his shoes. As he had suspected, there was now a fine sandy network of weed drying on the shoe which had slipped into the pool earlier. He felt in his trouser pocket for the Swiss army knife which he often carried but rarely had the chance to use. The girl watched with obvious fascination as he opened one of the small sharp blades and scraped his shoe clean with it.

'My grandfather used to say every man should carry one of these,' he said. 'They're phenomenally useful. Have you never seen one?'

'Yes, Gil's got one.' She checked her trainers too, standing awkwardly on one foot to examine each sole. 'Oops, weed attack here. Could I borrow your knife for a minute?'

He handed it over immediately, amused by her intent expression. The girl opened the blade with his own seriousness and wiggled it meticulously around each groove on her trainers, oddly flamenco-like as she balanced one-legged on the edge of the jetty. Damp mud came flying out in satisfyingly large gobbets, weed and pieces of shingle from some previous beach trip embedded in it. Afterwards, she polished the blade on her jeans until it was clean and held the knife out reluctantly. 'Thanks.'

'Keep it for a while,' he said on impulse, surprising himself. 'You can let me have it back at the weekend.'

'Are you sure?'

Lawrence could see that she too was surprised by the gesture and realised the child thought little of him. He would have changed his mind but Miranda had already slipped the Swiss army knife into her pocket. No longer meeting his eyes, she thanked him with an air of uncertainty.

Suddenly the salt wind felt chill rather than bracing. He rolled down his shirt sleeves and refastened the cuffs, turning his back abruptly on the harsh curves of the bay.

'Come on, I promised my wife we wouldn't miss lunch.'

Chapter Seven

It was never easy, trying to decide what the dead would have wished. But it was even more difficult when they still seemed to be there at your shoulder, or facing you across the dinner table, or drifting back in from the garden with great armfuls of cut flowers as if they had never left and nothing could be more natural than to see them arranging chrysanthemums for the hall table.

Some things have to be taken on faith, Gil reminded himself. And what constituted the 'real' world anyway? There were always times when it was the unseen and the unspoken that mattered most. If what Dora said to him from beyond the grave came merely from his memory of the woman, from long years of intimacy and understanding, did that make her words any the less real or valid? There was no real question in his mind though. It was all decided. Now that the child was old enough, his wife would have wanted Miranda to have her long-forgotten jewellery. It certainly had no place locked away in a box on this dusty dressing-table.

Gil slipped the lustrous white pearls into his pocket and turned to leave his wife's bedroom, only to stop dead when he realised that Cathy was standing in the half open doorway.

'You're not allowed in here,' he said. 'Get out.'
'I need to speak to you.'
'Downstairs, in my study.'

But Cathy didn't move from the doorway. Her eyes were busy scanning the room over his shoulder.

'There's so much dust. Why don't you let me come in and hoover? And those curtains will fall apart if nobody washes them.'

'Please leave my wife's room.'

She looked at him, a sullen look on her face, then shrugged and left the room. He felt an unfamiliar weight in his pocket, put his hand in, and frowned. Why had he put the pearls in his pocket?

Bewildered, he folded them back into the box on his wife's dressing-table, then replaced the lid.

Cathy was waiting outside on the landing when he emerged. She stood to one side while he locked the door again, and then followed him downstairs, her lips pursed tight. He knew what she must be thinking. The old man's mad. He keeps his wife's bedroom exactly as it was the day she died and won't let anyone else in to see it, to witness his insanity. But Cathy could think what she liked. She knew nothing of the shadows gathered around his bed at night, of the voices that constantly punished him for his past mistakes. He only kept her in the house under sufferance, because Miranda was her daughter and he didn't want to lose contact with the child.

'Now,' he said, closing the study door so they couldn't be overheard and crossing heavily to his desk. 'What did you want to say to me?'

'What do you think?'

'Don't play games.'

Cathy looked surly, slipping her hands into the front pockets of her apron. Gil could not understand what had once made him consider her attractive. Of course, as a young woman, she had been rather sweet and pliant. She had worn her hair loose and made jokes, and done the housework in hot-pants and white knee-length boots. In the sunlight flooding through his study windows, her face was hard and lined, twisted by years of watchful calculation. She had been a smoker for a while, back when Miranda was a small child, and now had fine lines about her eyes and mouth. Crow's-feet, he thought they were called.

He guessed she must be hoping he would die soon and that his will would favour Miranda. Which of course it did, but in such a way that Cathy herself would be bypassed and the money left in trust until the child was twenty-one and with any luck beyond her mother's influence. It was a miracle that Miranda had grown up with such an open and sunny disposition, constantly exposed to this woman. Sometimes it seemed to Gil as though they were at opposite ends of the human spectrum, one created entirely of light, the other of darkness. But that would be to invest Cathy with almost mythic qualities, when she was nothing more than an unscrupulous and rather stupid woman who had discovered a way to satisfy her greed.

He glanced at his watch. 'I can only give you five minutes. I'm going out with my son this afternoon.'

'That's what I want to talk to you about. Your son.'

'We've been through all this.'

'No,' she said and took a step forward, then stopped as if unsure what she had intended to do. 'Things have changed.'

'What things?'

'Your health.'

'I'm not about to die, if that's what you're trying to insinuate.'

His voice was deliberately steady, though it took all his effort not to show how anxious this conversation was making him. As soon as she had brought Miranda to visit him in hospital, he had seen that the woman was excited by his brief encounter with death. There had been a change in her face, as if she could already smell the money. It was what she had been waiting for all these years, after all.

'Nothing has changed,' he continued firmly. 'I had a minor stroke, that's all. Though I fail to see what it has to do with you.'

'Miranda?'

'Please lower your voice. They're still eating lunch.'

'He ought to know.'

Gil shook his head. 'It would destroy his marriage.'

'So he's never going to know he has a daughter?'

He sat back in the black leather swivel chair and looked hard at her. Cathy shrank from that gaze and he knew she was still under his control. But how long that situation would continue was not so certain. Since his son had sent word that he was coming back to the island, she had started to pull away, to show signs of restlessness with their arrangement. Perhaps she hoped to interest him again, as she had done once when he was at his most vulnerable.

'Lawrence will be told,' he told her firmly. 'But not yet, not until I think the time is right. My own marriage...'

Gil stopped, unable to finish the sentence. She was not the sort of woman who would respect or understand a natural desire to protect his only son, so he didn't bother elaborating.

His voice hardened and he stood up. 'That's all I have to say on this subject. Except that I should never have changed my mind about sacking you once my wife had died. You've caused nothing but trouble for this family.'

'I'll tell him myself then,' Cathy said defiantly. 'It's past time. What's the point in waiting any longer?'

Gil faced her, his hands trembling as he placed them on the leather-top desk to support himself. He had given in to her blackmail before, but he was not interested in making the same mistake twice. On the wall behind her, the afternoon sun glanced brilliantly off a black and white photograph of his wife. He experienced a vague sensation of faintness and the photograph blurred, oddly out of focus for a few seconds. Then the room steadied around him again. It was time to call her bluff.

'Fine,' he said lightly. 'Perhaps this is the right moment. You must do as you see fit, Cathy. I won't try to stop you.'

'What do you mean?'

'Tell him Miranda is his daughter, if that's what you think is best for the child.'

Her pale eyes had narrowed on his face. She took a step backwards, clearly confused by his abrupt change in tack. 'Best?'

'Yes. Then he can begin to support her financially.'

'But I thought...'

'That I would continue to keep you both on here once Lawrence knew the truth?' Gil watched the changing emotions on her face and knew that she was beginning to comprehend the delicately balanced nature of her position. 'As you have pointed out, he is the child's father. Once he is in full possession of the facts, it will be his responsibility to look after Miranda and our little arrangement will be at an end.'

Her lips moved silently for a moment, then she managed to say, 'Well, I'm still going to tell him.'

Gil shrugged, sitting back down at the desk and pretending to flick idly through the book which lay open in front of him. His contempt for the woman knew no bounds. How he had borne her insolence all these years was beyond him, except that everything had been done to protect Lawrence. And later, Miranda had been a reward in her own right.

He had expected her to make a scene. But Cathy unfolded her arms and left the room, closing the study door behind her with surprising self-control.

Now that he was alone, he realised his knees were trembling, with fatigue as well as rage. He had not felt this old in a long time, not since he had woken in that narrow hospital bed to be told that he had suffered a serious stroke and might not survive another. He had told no one except Lawrence what the doctors had said, of course. It had been passed off as a minor incident, nothing to cause alarm or make people fuss over him like an invalid. He had felt the girl should be spared that worry, at least, aware of her affection for him.

Instead, he had carried the knowledge of his own mortality about with him like a talisman, a word he could come back to when he was alone, something which reminded him to live every moment as fully as he could and not yield to that woman's cheap blackmail.

Gil put his head in his hands, rocking back and forth like a child, a tide of guilt rising darkly inside him. 'Dora.'

Chapter Eight

Miranda had first discovered this secret hideaway as a small child, following Gil down into the cellar once to admire his rows of dusty wine bottles. While he was bent over some ancient crate, she had decided to explore, tottering around the cellar until she came across this low narrow space tucked away under the stairs. It had seemed magical to her, just the right size for a child to crawl into, a place satisfyingly hidden from the grown-ups, waist-deep in that musty smell from damp wood and walls running with condensation.

    Right from the start, she had made this place her own, forcing an empty crate in sideways, covered with an ancient yellow cot blanket to make a comfortable seat. Her place, her magic territory. Sometimes spiders had to be evicted with the use of a glass and a piece of paper, but she sang to them as she removed them, 'Hoorah, and up she rises!' and they did not seem to mind so much. Gil had taught her some sea shanties that were especially useful for charming the huge hairy ones with extra-long legs.

    Once she was older and able to come and go as she pleased, Miranda started keeping her large glass bowl down here, originally bought for some long-dead goldfish whose name she had forgotten but now specially reserved for whatever tiny creatures she caught in the rock pools. Filled with salt water and unusually-shaped pieces of rock, the glass bowl teemed with life in that dark space under the cellar stairs, continually changing as the summer wore on, sometimes mysteriously alive with strange pink anemones and their waving fronds, then bright with those spiny dappled rock fish who loved to dart under rocks and through weed as soon as her shadow fell over the water.

Today it held both, the spiny fish still exploring their new glass bowl home while the anemones clung sleepily to the bottom, unaware of her fascinated gaze, no doubt imagining themselves safe in the cloudy water.

She had come hurrying down into the cellar after lunch to check they were settling in okay. Gil had not yet seen them and Miranda felt certain he would be impressed, especially since one of the spiny fish was the largest she had ever caught. Sitting on the crate under the stairs, she looked up through the loosely fitting floorboards above her head to where tiny cracks of light showed through directly beneath Gil's study.

On quiet days she could sometimes hear him on the phone up there, his deep familiar voice easily audible to her through cracks in the cellar ceiling. Once or twice Miranda had even overheard him having a conversation with the empty room, asking questions and then pausing before answering them himself, but she often did that too. Sometimes it was the only way to make sense of things.

She was just lifting the glass bowl to admire her most gigantic spiny fish, when she heard her name being mentioned above. The floorboards creaked and Miranda knew that somebody had moved up there in the study. Then she caught her mother's voice and Gil's quiet reply.

They must be talking about her.

Standing perfectly still in order to hear them better, Miranda craned her neck towards the nearest crack in the floor and listened hard. The glass bowl was heavy and slippery in her arms but she needed to hear what was being said. Perhaps she was in trouble again and that was why her mother sounded so unusually angry.

Her heart beat a little faster and she tried not to feel scared. Her mother was always threatening to send her away to live with her aunt out in Spain. That might be what she was saying now. But Gil wouldn't agree to anything like that.

She really hadn't meant to stay out so late the other night; she'd just forgotten the time, he knew that.

He wouldn't let her mother send her away, surely?

It was Gil's voice she heard first, low and strained. 'You must do as you see fit, Cathy. I won't try to stop you.'

Miranda thought he sounded more serious than she had ever known him. Her mother said something but she couldn't quite catch it. Gil spoke again, his voice ringing clear through the floorboards this time.

'Tell him Miranda is his daughter, if that's what you think is best for the child.' Miranda felt her legs almost give way beneath her, her stomach clenched as though someone had punched her there. Her hands shook on the glass bowl as their voices dropped for a second. 'Then he can begin to support her financially.'

Her mother sounded confused now. 'But I thought...'

The glass bowl was beginning to slip from Miranda's numb fingers and she knew she couldn't hold onto it much longer, but she didn't dare move to put it down. She desperately needed to hear the rest.

'That I would continue to keep you both on here once Lawrence knew the truth?'

For a few bewildering seconds, Miranda didn't understand what he meant by that, until the truth hit like a huge dark wave crashing over her head. Gil had lied to her.

Her mother had lied to her. Her father was not dead, as they had always told her. He was right here in this house, the man she had laughed at this morning for not wanting to muddy his shoes. But it couldn't possibly be true. It must be some kind of mistake. It couldn't be him, not someone like Lawrence. He could never be her father. Her father would be someone quite different, she knew it instinctively.

Miranda's calves ached from being continually on tiptoe and she was forced to drop down onto her heels a little more. Their voices continued above her, slightly muffled. 'He is the child's father. Once he's in full possession of the facts … his responsibility to look after Miranda… arrangement will be at an end.'

She could hardly breathe, she was hurting so much. Why had they lied to her like this all her life? What was wrong with her that she had to be hidden away from her real father?

There had been a time when she had secretly hoped Gil himself might be her father, he was so like her and it would have explained so many things in her life. But now Miranda realised he had only helped bring her up because he wanted to keep her safely away from Lawrence, as if he was ashamed of her, as if she wasn't good enough for his son.

The glass bowl slipped from her fingers and smashed on the stone floor. Miranda jerked back instinctively; her jeans were soaked as water poured swiftly out from the broken bowl towards the dusty rows of wine.

She cried out in horror as she realised what she'd done, dropping to her knees despite the glass. Her beautiful creatures!

She tried to stem the flow with her hands, but it was too late. There was already a mess of pink like a melted sweet where the anemones had stuck together, and her glorious spiny fish lay on the stone floor, helplessly flipping themselves backwards and forwards as the last of the water trickled away. Miranda scrabbled tearfully at the largest spiny, cradling him in a rounded shard of broken glass where half an inch or so of salt water still remained, but it was no use. There was not enough water there to keep him alive, and the desperate flipping gradually slowed and then stopped altogether, his tiny body heaving in her hands once or twice before lying still forever.

'I'm sorry,' she whispered, crying bitterly as the shiny eye dulled and stared motionless. 'I'm so sorry.'

Miranda wiped her face on her sleeve, sniffed one last time, then stood on tiptoe. She dragged the sleeping bag down from on top of her wardrobe and threw it onto the bed. Stuffed tightly into its carrying bag, it just about fitted into her rucksack along with the other essentials: map, water bottle, folded anorak, torch, box of matches, the tin of toffees her aunt had given her last Christmas and a packet of biscuits she had stolen from the kitchen. She had absolutely no idea where she was going, all she knew was that she had to get away from the house as quickly as possible.

Perhaps she could make for the other end of the island where there were fewer people to see her. She could live wild on the coast, sleeping on the beach at night and catching fish or rabbits for food. She need never bother coming back at all, in fact. None of them would miss her anyway and it would solve all their problems if she simply disappeared.

Miranda checked feverishly through the rucksack, removing the anorak because it took up far too much room, and adding *Teach Yourself Astronomy* which Gil had lent her and Ursula Le Guin's *A Wizard of Earthsea* as an afterthought. She loved books, and could not make it through without at least something to read. She also had some money saved in a box on her bookcase, from birthday and Christmas presents. Emptying it out onto the bed, she realised how little was actually there.

But she wouldn't need much money. She was going to take her battered old bicycle and everything else she might need was in her rucksack. The money would be strictly for emergencies only. Miranda tried to imagine what sort of emergencies might occur in the wild, but her mind was blank. She was in too much of a hurry to worry about any of that. All she could focus on was getting out of the house without being seen and stopped.

As she pushed her old bike out of the garage, rucksack weighing heavily on her back, there was the sound of footsteps behind her. It was Lawrence, strolling across the lawn towards her.

'Going out again?'

She nodded, not meeting his eyes, and swung onto the bike. It was so strange to think that he was her father. She kept darting little looks at him and making comparisons – eyes, hair, the shape of the face – but not seeing any resemblance. Maybe the eyes.

'We're going out soon,' he remarked. 'Just for a drive.'

Miranda didn't say anything in return, but pedalled hurriedly out of the gate and onto the narrow high-banked lane above the house. It was usually hard work from a standing position, as the drive was on a slope, but she seemed to have enough energy for ten men today.

Lawrence raised his voice to call after her. She thought he sounded a little surprised. 'I'll see you when we get back then.'

Not a chance, she thought, still not replying, and pedalled even harder once she was out of sight of the house. It was not that she blamed him for being her father. But he felt like an irrelevance to her. It was Gil she was angry with. Gil and her mother. They had lied to her. For years. And she had no idea why.

Once she had swept down past the houses of Fistard and through Port St Mary itself, Miranda pedalled at great speed along the coast road with the sun on her face and a cool breeze at her back. Gansey Bay looked almost copper-coloured that afternoon, the sea lying bright and flat with a few white yachts in the distance, apparently motionless, as though glued to the horizon.

Now that she was this far from home, she started to worry that someone would realise she had run away and come after her. Lawrence might say in a puzzled tone 'I saw her cycling off with a rucksack on her back' and Gil would instinctively guess the rest. Each car that whizzed past made her head turn nervously, but it was never them. Anyway, they would probably search the village first. Or drive up into the southern hills, away from the holiday traffic on the coast road, and miss her completely.

The rucksack dragged terribly at her shoulders and she began to wish she'd left the non-essentials behind. Those ancient sticky toffees were probably too disgusting to eat anyway. But she set her teeth determinedly and kept going. If she couldn't manage this part of running away, how would she cope with living out under the stars?

She reached Fisher's Hill and pedalled even more fiercely as she climbed its near-vertical slope, gripping the handlebars with whitened knuckles, her thighs working harder and harder to turn the wheels as she approached the high summit. Bees droned past on their way to somewhere fragrant, and she only narrowly avoided swallowing one as she struggled and gasped, mouth wide open. That would not have been pleasant. Finally she reached the top, her thighs burning and trembling. On the other side, released from her labour, she lifted her feet off the pedals and let the bike freewheel down at a violent pace, faster than she had ever gone before. The wind tore through her hair and ripped her tee-shirt clean out of her jeans. For one wild moment, it felt like she was flying.

Then something hit her back tyre, probably a small piece of rock or metal embedded in the road, and the bike jumped crazily sideways. The handlebars were wrenched from her grasp by the abrupt change of direction, and she cried out, fumbling for them. But it was too late, she had lost control. Skidding sideways for what felt like forever, Miranda ended up huddled against a dry stone wall at the bottom of the hill, her whole body shaking from the impact and her left knee in agony.

'Oh no! Poor bike!'

Aching and embarrassed, she hobbled round to examine the back tyre. The rubber had been partly slashed by something sharp and the frame was bent. It would be impossible to ride it any further.

Sitting down at the side of the road to cradle her hurt knee, Miranda could have burst into tears again at her own uselessness. The rucksack was killing her shoulders and she angrily dragged it off, propping it up behind her and leaning back against it in the sunshine. She dragged up the leg of her jeans and examined her knee. It was bloodied and grazed, but not as bad as she had thought. Still, with the tyre ruined, she would not be cycling any further today. This was not how she had imagined it when she first decided to run away. She was barely five miles from home and the journey already seemed to be over.

Just as Miranda was thinking about getting up and beginning the long trek back home, a small red van pulled up beside her.

'Need a lift?'

Miranda looked up at the young man leaning cheerfully across the passenger seat to get her attention. He had a nice smile and protruding ears, one of which was pierced with a gold sleeper. He did not look particularly threatening. But then, attackers on the prowl were hardly likely to go round looking grim and dangerous, or girls would ever speak to them. And she knew better than to get into a car with someone she didn't know.

'No thanks,' she said politely. 'I'm okay.'

'Bike knackered, is it?'

'I hit something.'

He laughed. 'The wall, by the look of it.'

'And my knee.'

'Ouch, I bet that hurts. Come on. I'll give you a lift home. You'll have to leave your bike, but your dad can probably come back for it later.'

'I don't have a dad,' she said irritably.

'Oh.' The young man paused, looking embarrassed. 'Sorry to hear that. But I can't just leave you here in this state.'

Miranda rubbed her knee and considered the weight of that rucksack on her back. She didn't want to waste all her money on bus fare either.

'Are you going to attack me if I get into your van?'

'No, of course I'm bloody not.'

The young man sounded angry at first then stopped himself, looking down at her and beginning to laugh again. He had a round cheerful sort of face with freckles all over his forehead and short sandy hair. It really didn't look much like the face of a murderer, she considered. Even if he did wear a stud in one ear, which was the kind of thing Gil didn't approve of.

'Though you're right to be suspicious, I suppose. Sensible girl. Perhaps you'd rather I just phoned your mum or someone to come out for you instead?'

'No thanks.'

She threw her rucksack into the back of his van and climbed into the front seat. The cracked plastic of the seat was shiny and hot, and when she leant her forearm along the window the metal was tacky to the touch. There was a sweet, aniseed smell in the van, like he had been eating boiled sweets or perhaps liquorice. She would love a boiled sweet, she reflected, looking about at the neatly kept van. There were some used envelopes stuffed down beside the seat, and what looked like an old spanner half-wrapped in sacking on the floor near her feet. But no paper bags that might contain sweets. Her knee still stung like anything, and sugar was good when you had suffered a shock.

She considered asking the young man if he had any sweets in the van, but decided to wait until they were safely on the move. Now that she had done the dangerous thing and accepted a lift, all she could think about was putting more distance between herself and home.

Her mother would murder her if she could see what she was doing but Miranda didn't care anymore. She was going to make her own decisions now.

'What's your name?'

'Pete,' he said, reaching across to shake her hand. His palm was clammy. 'How about you?'

'I'm...' She hesitated, then lied, thinking of a girl she knew at school. 'Emily. My name's Emily.'

The young man didn't seem to notice any hesitation though, putting the van into gear and pulling noisily away. 'Nice to meet you, Emily.'

She stared back over her shoulder, seized too late by a moment of regret. Her rusty old bike stood slumped against the wall with a dejected air as if it knew it had failed her. Perhaps she ought to have asked if he could put the bike in the back of his van.

But soon the bike was lost to view, and she looked forward again, enjoying a new-found and unexpected freedom. The fields and houses flashed by, miles faster than she could ever have managed on the bike. In the distance she could see the dark shape of Witch's Tower rising above the road into Castletown. For a moment everything had seemed to be ruined and suddenly here she was on the road again, a warm wind in her hair as she leant out of the open window, stretching to brush against hedgerows with the tips of her fingers.

Pete turned on the radio and hummed along to the music. 'So where do you want me to drop you, Emily?'

'As far away as possible,' she said.

Chapter Nine

'Gone?' Gil put down his book and lowered his reading glasses, staring up at Juliet with a perplexed frown. 'Gone where?'

'Nobody knows. But apparently she's taken her sleeping bag.'

'Good God. When was this?'

'Just before we went out this afternoon. Lawrence actually saw her cycling off, but he didn't think anything of it at the time.' His daughter-in-law gave a delicate shrug. 'It may be completely innocent, of course. But I don't think a child of her age should be out this late without anyone knowing where she is.'

'Didn't she leave a note?'

'No, and her bedroom's in a bit of a state. Cathy says it looks like she may have left in a hurry.'

Gil stood up from the armchair, carefully marking his page before closing the book and laying it aside. He had an uneasy feeling in his stomach, but there was no point becoming agitated before they were sure that Miranda wasn't merely out a little later than usual. It wouldn't be the first time she had defied her mother's curfew of nine o'clock, and the child had common sense enough not to put herself in danger.

'Where is Cathy?'

'Outside, searching the gardens. Lawrence has just taken the car down into the village, to see if he can spot her cycling around.'

'Has anyone checked the house?'

Juliet followed him out of the study. 'That was my first thought. That she might be hiding somewhere indoors. But I don't think she's here, Gil. It's been hours since anyone saw her. Do you think there's any chance she might have run away?'

'Why on earth would she want to run away?' Gil laughed, a little irritated by the old-fashioned look on her face. 'Miranda is far too intelligent to play that sort of game. There's bound to be a logical explanation for her absence.'

It was already getting dark outside.

Gil stood in the front doorway and looked up at Miranda's unlit window. It wasn't something he would readily admit to his daughter-in-law, but he was genuinely concerned by the girl's absence.

Where could she have gone?

He thought immediately of her usual haunts: the beach, the rock pools, that little cave of hers. Those were the places to try if she didn't come back within the next half an hour. He certainly could not believe she had run away. If Miranda was upset about something that badly, she would have come to him first and asked for his help, not simply disappeared into the night. He felt that vague faintness again and leant against the porch wall, breathing in the sweet heady scent of honeysuckle as it curled around the entrance.

He peered out through the dark but there was no small figure wandering in through the open gate. Why had nobody noticed before now that she was missing? Her mother hadn't even mentioned it when she was serving dinner, though she must have been aware that Miranda had not come home.

Juliet hurried out into the garden as Lawrence pulled up on the drive, dipping his headlights and getting out of the car alone, their conversation low and concerned. So he hadn't found her in the village.

Gil shivered, drawing the edges of his cardigan closer together. It was getting distinctly cold now. Perhaps Miranda was feeling neglected and had vanished in order to teach him a lesson.

Lawrence didn't meet his eyes as he came back into the lit circle of the porch, his voice carefully neutral as if Gil was an invalid who might shatter at the first hint of bad news.

'No sign, I'm afraid. What next?'

'I think we'd better call the police,' his wife said suddenly.

'The police?' Gil was bewildered by the speed at which this was turning into a serious matter. 'Is that strictly necessary?'

'It's been eight hours since anyone saw her, Gil.'

Lawrence too seemed hesitant. 'But what about friends? Could Miranda be sleeping over at someone's house tonight and not have told us?'

Gil didn't know the answer to that. He shook his head, helpless. Miranda did have school friends, he seemed to remember her mentioning one or two other girls in the past, but she had never invited them to the house and he had no idea of their names or where they might live. Her mother would probably know. Maybe she even knew the telephone numbers of some of the other mothers. They could call round them all, see if Miranda had gone to a friend's house for tea and forgotten the time.

As they stood there in the porch, debating whether or not it was the right time to involve the police, there was a rustling sound from the dark garden and they all looked up in sudden expectation, hoping to see the child herself standing there.

But it was only Cathy who appeared around the west side of the house, still in her plastic apron, her face white and curiously owl-like as she blinked under the porch light.

'Have you found her?' she asked.

Lawrence shook his head. 'We were wondering whether she could be out with a friend. Or maybe she's gone to someone's house for tea. Is that possible?'

'I don't think so. The other kids don't like her very much. She's too clever for them.' Cathy put a hand to her mouth. 'Oh God, where can she be?'

Gil turned back into the house, simply unable to stand there and do nothing while they talked. The pain in his temples had returned, stabbing at him relentlessly, but he ignored it. There was no time to worry about that now. He would get some rest later, when they had found the child.

Dear little Miranda. He thought of her rounded face, grinning up at him day after day, so wonderfully innocent. What could have happened to prompt this sudden disappearance? Had she genuinely run away, as the others seemed to think? But why would she do that? He had always made her welcome at this house, treated her as one of the family, which indeed she was, unknowingly.

For the first time he felt real fear for the girl and clamped down hard on that sickening anxiety. He would be no use to anyone if he allowed his imagination to run away with him.

The others had followed him inside and were standing about in confused silence. Someone had to take charge.

His voice was deliberately brisk. 'I'm going to put my boots and overcoat on, and go down to the beach. Miranda sometimes plays in a little cave down there. It might be worth a look.'

'You should take the car,' Lawrence told him firmly, as if he was incapable of making such decisions himself.

'No, you take it and keep driving round the village. Look in playgrounds, parks, the shops, maybe even the harbour. I can walk to the beach. It's not far and we've got more chance of finding her if we split up.'

Juliet followed them and stood in the narrow passageway with her hands on her hips. 'But what about the police?'

Gil paused, forcing his feet into the old wellingtons as he tried not to succumb to their air of collective panic. There was still every chance that the girl was simply out rather later than she had intended and would reappear at any moment, astonished to have caused so much mayhem. He remembered a similar incident with his own father when he was a young child and that mixture of anger and grateful relief with which he had clipped Gil round the ear on his return.

'If she isn't back within the hour, then we must definitely call the police. Until then, we keep looking ourselves. There's no need to make a fuss until we're sure that …' He hesitated, then repeated, 'Until we're sure.'

'Cathy?'

'Another hour, yes.' Cathy nodded at Juliet. She untied her apron and hung it up on one of the coat pegs. 'I'll go with you in the car, Lawrence, if that's okay? There's still the park to check and that covered area under the promenade. It's mainly the older kids who hang out there, but you never know. One of them might have seen her.'

Gil buttoned his coat in preparation for the walk. Juliet lit a cigarette beside him, watching silently from the porch as her husband's car pulled away with a flash of headlights. He had decided to take the shorter way to the beach - down the terraced steps to the rear of the house - even though it was unlit. At least his back appeared to have stopped aching now, thank God. Probably the adrenalin. There was a nagging fear at the back of his mind that Cathy might take this opportunity to tell Lawrence the truth about the girl. But the car had already disappeared out of the gate and the situation was beyond his reach.

'Are you okay?'

Gil glanced up at Juliet, suddenly realising that he was having trouble buttoning his coat. 'I'm a little tired, that's all.'

'Perhaps I should go instead.'

'You don't know the way. No, you stay here and hold the fort, Juliet, in case she comes back while everyone's gone.'

Gil muttered a peremptory goodbye and set off across the garden, frowning at the pain in his head. It was hard to block out, though he was soon comforted by the familiar gnarled wood of the walking stick under his hand and the hope that he might yet find Miranda in that tiny cave on the beach, crouching amongst her collection of glass and driftwood. There was nothing he could do about the other matter.

But as Gil turned his face towards the dark, he wondered fleetingly what Juliet would do once she discovered the truth. The woman was not stupid, and once

Lawrence knew he had a daughter, it would only be a matter of time before his wife did too.

Chapter Ten

It was just after ten o'clock at night and Port St Mary had the air of a village getting ready for bed, sleepily drawn curtains in most living rooms, lights burning at bedroom windows, the occasional man walking his dog along the deserted High Street. As most evenings around this time, the benches above the sandy bay were inhabited by teenagers, girls sitting in tight groups and the boys circling slowly on bikes or playing chicken in the road with their skateboards. This was their time and they knew it. Shouts and cackles of laughter broke the dusty silence as one of the boys slipped off his skateboard in the middle of the road and picked himself up with a wry shrug.

'Skateboarders,' Lawrence murmured, glancing at Cathy.

'She doesn't like them. Horrid, dangerous things.'

'But maybe some of her friends do. I'll do a loop, just in case.'

Lawrence crawled past them in the car, Cathy leaning eagerly forward to look for her daughter amongst them, but there was no sign of her. The kids stared back at them curiously, one girl sticking two fingers up at them before collapsing into giggles, face buried in her friend's coat.

'She's not with them,' Cathy muttered, gripping her hands together in her lap. 'She wasn't at the park and she's not here. I don't know where else to look.'

'Could she be down on the beach?'

'Maybe.'

Tired of cruising the streets without any success, Lawrence swung the car into a parking space further up along the kerb. He tried to sound positive, even though he was seriously beginning to doubt that the child was anywhere in the village.

'Let's park, then walk down and check the bay for her. There's no point guessing without looking. If she's not there, we can always drive back to the house and see if she's turned up yet.'

It was a cool evening, the moon rising above the terraced houses as they wandered back along the High Street towards the bay. When they came level with the group of teenagers, Cathy stopped and questioned a few of them while Lawrence waited, poised at the head of a steep flight of steps which led down towards the sea.

There was a small rookery on the wooded slope to one side of the steps. He remembered standing here as a boy, watching the rooks flap heavily in and out of these branches. Their cries had always seemed strangely sinister on sunny afternoons, as if the birds belonged in a graveyard rather than high above this blue bay. Now their nests lay blackened and silent above the street lights, cradled in smoke drifting from a nearby chimney. He had not ventured this far down into the village the week of his mother's funeral; too many people here had known her and might have wanted to stop and commiserate with him. Instead, he had made a bloody fool of himself, then sailed back to England with his self-respect in tatters.

Cathy finished talking to the kids and came over, shaking her head when he glanced up enquiringly.

'None of them have seen Miranda at all today. But they've promised to keep an eye out for her.'

'Shall we check the beach anyway?'

Without replying, Cathy stood beside him and stared blindly down at the dark curve of the bay below them.

With both hands gripping the metal barrier at the top of the steps, she suddenly seemed so vulnerable that he began to regret his behaviour towards her yesterday. He had only seen her as a threat then, not as a real person. But her concern for her daughter was humbling, reminding Lawrence that he had no real concept of how it felt to be a parent. Perhaps Juliet had been right to stall him for so long. He did not feel ready for this crushing weight of responsibility. Not yet. Perhaps never.

'I don't know what to do,' she said simply. 'I mean, what if something's happened to her? What if she never comes back?'

'It's a bit early to start thinking like that. Let's look at the facts, okay? The kid's got a sound head on her shoulders and she's only been gone since this afternoon. I wouldn't be surprised to find she's been with a friend all day and just forgot the time.'

She did not reply.

'Why don't we just check along the bay, and then head back to the house?' he suggested lightly. 'If nothing else, the fresh air and walking will do us both good.'

She nodded automatically, but he could still feel tension singing between them in the silence. It had never really gone away, he supposed. Just been put on hold for her daughter's disappearance.

He hesitated. 'Cathy, have you ever seen or heard anything unusual at the house?'

'You mean, like a ghost?'

He was taken aback by her blunt reply. 'Yes.'

'No,' she said sharply, looking at him sideways. 'Though your dad's always talking to himself in your mum's old room. He won't let me clear it out neither, nor even dust in there.' Cathy shrugged. 'I don't say nothing about it. My take is, if it gives your dad comfort to keep hold of her things and pretend she's still alive, why kick up a fuss over nothing?'

'I agree.'

They descended the narrow, steep flight of steps one after the other. To their left at the bottom, there was a spring issuing noisily into a stone-tiled well which trickled erratically across the path and down a conduit onto the beach. From there they turned along a path built on metal stilts above the water level, which fetched nearly all the way round towards the harbour mouth.

As they walked along the bay, they searched the rocks below in the hope that Miranda might be hiding on the beach. But everything was still and silent in the moonlight and the rocks were deserted.

'It was worth a try,' he said awkwardly. 'But this is a dead end. There's nobody down here. Let me drive you back to the house.'

'Wait,' she said suddenly, and he could tell by the high pitch of her voice that she was scared. 'There's something I have to tell you first.'

Lawrence turned slowly. He knew a moment of dread on seeing her expression. But he forced himself to stay calm. 'Okay, what is it?'

'It's about Miranda,' she said, watching his face.

'What about her?'

Cathy's mouth quivered. 'She's your daughter.'

It was like a slap in the face. He had been expecting her to confess to having slept with his father. 'My daughter?' he repeated blankly.

'I'm so sorry, Lawrence. When I first realised I was pregnant, I tried to get in touch with you but your dad wouldn't give me your address. He didn't want you to know about Miranda. He said it would ruin your marriage, and maybe your career too. You know how funny people can get about things like that. And then he gave me some money.'

He was staring like a fool. 'Money?'

'It was more than you could have given me. Your dad knew that. He wanted you to stay married to Juliet, but he also wanted to make things right for me and Miranda.' She shrugged, as if it had been a simple choice. Nothing important. Just the difference between one path and another. 'After she was born, he asked us to move in with him. My mum didn't have room for a baby too, and that was about the time she got sick anyway. It was for the best.'

His feet were rooted to the path. Why had he not guessed as soon as he saw Miranda up at the window on the night they arrived? She was the right age to be his child, after all, and so excruciatingly like Gil at times that he had often found it hard not to stare. Perhaps that was the reason why. Because in his heart he had suspected Gil himself was the father. It seemed an outlandish idea, but it would certainly have explained his father's initial hesitancy whenever Cathy or the girl were around.

Now he realised that his father had merely wanted to avoid any contact between them, in case Lawrence noticed the family resemblance and asked awkward questions. The girl was his daughter. His daughter, for God's sake. But why had the old man concealed it?

She looked at him. 'What's the matter? Did you think she was Gil's?'

'It crossed my mind.'

She looked offended. 'At his age? There was never anything like that between us. Your dad was going to sack me after your mum died. He gave me notice, said he didn't want me around after the funeral. But he changed his mind when I told him I was pregnant.'

'Is that why you did it?' Lawrence drew a sharp breath, suddenly understanding. The old man had been going to sack her but she had found an ideal way to keep her job. 'Did you sleep with me deliberately, hoping to get pregnant? Because my father wouldn't dare throw you out if you were carrying his grandchild?'

'It wasn't like that,' she said sharply.

Her lips quivered again, and he had a vivid memory of kissing those lips, the two of them alone together in the dark, smoky living-room of her mother's house in the village. Lawrence had been drunk after the funeral, rambling endlessly about his mother, his guilt about not being there for his parents, while she said nothing, merely listened to his outpourings. Then Cathy had looked at him through that heavy dark fringe, and he had known what she wanted. They had made love clumsily and with no thought of contraception, right there on her mother's sofa. He remembered the strange carved piece of driftwood displayed above the fireplace, and the cloying smell of incense in her long hair.

What a fool he had been.

'You're so quick to judge people, aren't you?' she was saying in her singing Manx accent. 'But you don't know how it feels to be caught in a trap.'

He rather thought he did, actually. But Lawrence did not trust himself to answer her civilly, even though it was his own guilt that stung most. He had betrayed his wife with this woman, and afterwards had never thought to check ...

He turned and walked back along the pathway, not bothering to look back over his shoulder to see if Cathy was following. Emerging at the top of the steep steps, he found the high street dark and deserted. The kids with their bikes and skateboards had gone home at last.

He glanced down at his watch and was shocked to see it was already after eleven o'clock. Juliet must be getting ready to call the police by now, assuming that Miranda had not yet been found or returned to the house of her own volition. It was almost impossible to think of her as his 'daughter', yet he had no reason to disbelieve Cathy's story. If anything, it rang so true he could hardly believe that he had not already guessed the truth on his own.

Eventually reaching his parked car again, Lawrence leant on the bonnet to wait for her. He knew the truth had to come out sooner or later, there was no way to stop that now, but he needed time to adjust to it himself first. If he went back to the house in this state, Juliet would be bound to start asking questions. And he was not ready to answer them yet.

By the time Cathy appeared beside the car, Lawrence had got himself back under control. He coolly opened the passenger door and watched her climb in, ignoring her look of surprise. She had evidently imagined that he would be furious about the situation. But he suspected the real culprit to be his father. For some reason which was still unclear to him, his father had paid her off and left him in the dark about it.

'I couldn't keep the secret anymore,' she said simply, as though that were some sort of apology.

Lawrence pulled away from the kerb, staring straight ahead as he drove back to his father's house through the dark silent streets.

'I don't want to discuss it.'

Up at the house, it was like a scene out of some amateur production of *An Inspector Calls*: the unsmiling policeman with his pocket notebook, and the family watching him uncomfortably from chairs and sofas as they answered polite but searching questions.

The room was over-warm, and Lawrence soon got to his feet to open a window.

It was long past midnight but there was still no sign of Miranda returning. Outside in the moonlit garden, an owl hooted from somewhere amongst the trees and the young constable paused appreciatively to listen to it, painstakingly reading his notes back before continuing. He seemed to want to know everything about the girl: her usual haunts, the type of bike she was riding, how many friends she had, even the colour of the socks she had been wearing when she left. In between questions, the constable would glance down surreptitiously at his watch.

They were all waiting for the detective sergeant to arrive, who was apparently dealing with some other police business in Douglas and would not be able to get here much before one o'clock in the morning.

Lawrence sat up and accepted a cup of tea from Cathy without meeting her eyes, conscious of Juliet's scrutiny from the cushioned window seat. His wife had the unsettling ability to know whenever he was nervous or upset, and though she had said nothing so far, he could hear the unspoken questions in his head almost as if she were whispering them to him telepathically.

'But there's been nothing unusual before this?'

Cathy shook her head, stirring two sugars into the constable's tea before handing him the cup. Even though it was her daughter who had gone missing, Lawrence thought she seemed vaguely uneasy at being here in Gil's living room.

'And there's been no arguments? No particular...' He hesitated, looking round at them all. 'Disagreements?'

Gil frowned, instantly defensive. 'She's always been very happy here.'

'I'm sure, sir.' The constable nodded respectfully and wrote something down in his notebook. Then he shook his pen and discarded it on the coffee table, hurriedly fishing for another in one of his uniform pockets. 'Sorry, the ink ran out. So your son and daughter-in-law arrived two days ago? How did Miranda take to them? Any problems there?'

Juliet looked irritated, lighting another cigarette. 'Are you suggesting it's our fault she's disappeared?'

'Not at all, madam.'

'Because it's not. We get along perfectly well with the girl. In fact, we took her out for a long walk on our first day here, and my husband went down to the beach with her only this morning. Well, yesterday morning now.' Juliet flicked her ash out of the open window. She was clearly impatient with this process now, dying to get all the questions over with and go up to bed. 'They were down there for hours, messing about in the rock pools. Weren't you, Lawrence?'

The constable turned towards him. 'Sir?'

'Yes, I went down to the beach with her. She caught some little spiny-looking fish with her net, and then we came straight back home again.'

'How did she seem to you?'

'Fine.'

'She didn't mention that she might be going out again later?'

'No.' Lawrence paused. 'Though I did see her leave.'

'When was that, sir?'

'Just after lunch. Maybe about one-thirty? I was in the garden and saw Miranda taking her bike out of the garage. I said something to her, nothing in particular, just chatting. And then she left.'

'She didn't say where she was going?'

'Of course not. Or I would have mentioned it already.'

The constable nodded slowly, scribbling something else in the notebook balanced unsteadily on his knee. His fair hair fell over his forehead and he flicked it back absent-mindedly.

Lawrence watched him with mild dislike. The constable looked about thirteen and it seemed to him that the police couldn't be taking Miranda's disappearance very seriously, sending this boy out to get the details. He found himself wondering drily whether the attending detective sergeant would be old enough to shave before realising with a shock that he was starting to sound like his father. His laconic replies to this boy's ridiculous questions, the way he had crossed his legs at the onset of the interrogation, even the tilt of his head as he listened, these were all his father's mannerisms – not his. Yet he had adopted them without even noticing, as naturally as breathing, while his father himself sat to one side like an old man whose views were no longer relevant to the discussion.

'Then you would have been the last to see her, sir.'

'I suppose so.'

'What were you doing in the garden?'

'Stretching my legs.'

'I see. And whose idea was it to go down to the rock pools?'

'Hers.'

The constable hesitated, looking at him. 'I wouldn't have thought it was your sort of thing, sir.'

'What exactly do you mean by that?'

'Nothing, sir. I'm just trying to build up a picture of what happened today. There's no need to get upset.'

Gil stirred at last, having remained silent and somehow distanced for most of the interview. Lawrence got the impression that his father had dragged himself back from some other place, not quite the past, nor entirely imagined, but somewhere quite different from the living room where this unlikely constable scribbled notes under a fringed standing lamp. He had changed so much since Lawrence had last seen him, over that hurried lunch in Chelsea, even though it was only a few years ago.

The old man seemed to be pulling back into himself, like a snail into its shell, as if he had given up on the world and found somewhere more familiar and comforting to live out his last years. It was a painful process to watch. That strong and imaginative man he remembered from his childhood was being gradually replaced by this introverted figure, shambling about the house and gardens in his ancient cardigan, having whispered little conversations with himself as if there were some invisible friend at his shoulder.

Now his father sat forward to confront the policeman, his voice shaking with some deep emotion. 'This is ludicrous. My son has nothing whatsoever to do with Miranda's disappearance.'

'It's just routine, sir.'

The front door bell rang and Cathy jumped up, her expression wild. He had not thought her very close to her child, but perhaps maternal instincts were kicking in at last. Either that or she saw her daughter as a precious possession that had been snatched away from her, and this was a very lively desire to have it back again.

'Do you think that's her?' she gabbled, knocking over a small table. 'Maybe they've found her.'

But it was only the detective sergeant who had arrived at long last, along with a dark-haired young WPC who popped her head round with a smile, then discreetly pulled their door shut while the detective held a whispered conversation in the hallway.

Still rankling from the constable's questions, Lawrence glanced at his father to check how he was bearing up under this inquisition. Gil was staring down at his hands again in silence. Not much to read there. Juliet was still smoking on the window seat with a slightly manic air, watching his face as she tried to guess what had happened earlier to upset him.

The door opened again and all three police officers trooped back into the living room like a comic trio. The detective sergeant was a humourless and heavily-built man in his fifties, who introduced himself as DS Quine and the woman as WPC Faragher. He sat on the sofa opposite Lawrence while his colleagues stood. There was something curiously staged about this, as though he had already decided that Lawrence was somehow responsible for events.

For the next fifteen minutes the detective went laboriously over the information his constable had already garnered from them, looking at each of them carefully and assessingly as they spoke, but clearly focusing his main attention on Lawrence.

'So what did you two talk about, down at these rock pools?' DS Quine asked.

'Fish.'

His eyebrows shot up. 'Fish, sir?'

'Miranda likes to bring her catches home in a bucket. As I recall, we were discussing whether or not it was cruel to take the fish away from their natural habitat.'

DS Quine looked at him searchingly. 'And is it?'

'I think so.'

'Did she think so too?'

'I'm not sure.' Lawrence shrugged, unable to take the policeman seriously. 'Presumably not, since she brought them home to show my father.'

'So there was a disagreement between you?'

'Hardly.'

'What, then?'

'It was more a question of semantics.'

Gil stood up angrily. 'Officer, we've told you everything we know. Is anyone out there looking for Miranda? She's only a child and she's been gone nearly twelve hours now.'

DS Quine nodded at the constable, who discreetly left the room. 'We'll be circulating her description immediately, sir.'

'Thank you.'

'But in these cases, where there's been no note left behind, it's always best to know as much as possible about the missing person.'

'Of course.' Gil sat down again. He looked utterly exhausted and Lawrence thought he had never seen his father so weakly apologetic, one hand up to his forehead as he turned away from the policeman and stared blindly out at the dark gardens instead. 'I'm sorry. It's been a difficult evening.'

'I quite understand, sir.'

Taking advantage of the short silence that followed, Juliet yawned exaggeratedly and leant forward to stub out her cigarette on a saucer.

'Listen, officer, do you still need us all here?' she demanded. 'I'm sure I can't help anymore and I'm ready to fall asleep.'

'But you'll be staying here in the house, Mrs Cardrew?'

'Where else would I go?'

'Very well.' DS Quine stood up, motioning to the young woman police officer who had been standing motionless beside the door the whole time. 'Thank you very much for your patience and cooperation. You've been very helpful, but I think that's enough for now. If there are any further developments, we'll be in touch immediately.'

'You're leaving?' Cathy looked shocked.

The detective gave her an unreadable look. 'Try not to upset yourself, Miss Maddrell. We're going to do our best to find your daughter.'

Chapter Eleven

For the third night in a row, Gil found he simply couldn't sleep. By first light he grew tired of staring at the ceiling and got out of bed instead, throwing himself carelessly into yesterday's clothes before slipping downstairs to the empty kitchen. He put the kettle on and listened to the comfortable rattling hum of the fridge. The cold pale light of the garden was as wonderfully alluring to him as always, the birds just beginning their faint song.

He stood at the kitchen windows and stared out, thinking of Miranda. She was such a clever little girl, so sensitive and intelligent, he couldn't believe she had chosen to run away rather than come to him for advice. Whatever was troubling her must be serious, something she had felt completely unable to share with him. He wondered for one breathless moment whether Cathy might have told Miranda the truth about her father, imagining the cataclysmic impact of that revelation on the young girl, then shook the idea away as untenable. Cathy might be an unscrupulous woman, but she was not cruel and she quite clearly loved her daughter.

Could Miranda have overheard their conversation yesterday?

Gil poured himself a cup of tea from the pot and stirred a small amount of sugar into it. It was possible, though he doubted it. The door had been firmly closed, and as far as he knew, the girl had not even been in the house at that time.

Gil remembered the acrimonious tone of that conversation and flinched. If she had overheard, it would certainly explain her disappearance.

He was feeling older than usual this morning. His hands around the cup were those of an old man. His reflection in the kitchen window was an old man's. This loss of Miranda, even if it was only temporary, had made him realise how much he depended on the girl to keep him feeling young. Her laughter and quick wit sparked his own, and staved off the terrible deadening of old age. They were so alike, in looks as well as temperament, that Gil often found himself watching the girl with brutal apprehension, convinced she must be on the verge of noticing the family resemblance and questioning it.

But what seemed so obvious to him was still invisible to Miranda, too young to start asking that sort of question about herself and her origins.

Too restless to sit still, Gil dragged on his overcoat and let himself silently out of the house.

The grass was damp under his house slippers. He could feel the warning twinge of arthritis in his bones, but he didn't care. He wanted to stand on the lawn under the vast sycamore and listen to the leaves rustle gently against each other in the early light. The branches were green with unfurled summer leaves, the trunk too broad for him to stretch his arms around it. Dora had loved this tree, he remembered. And now Miranda loved it too. Her unoccupied swing hung on its ropes from the lowest branch, and he looked at it mournfully.

There had been another sycamore like this in a glorious back garden in Oxford, though without a swing.

He stood beneath the tree and suddenly it was Dora up there, cradled in the lap of the branches, laughing down at his expression of consternation. She let her hair fall back over her shoulders and it was the rich golden colour of her early twenties.

'Gil!'

'Dora?'

'Oh, that frown. You look so sad, darling.'

He thought of Miranda. But now was not the right time. 'I'm tired, that's all. Why don't you come down, talk to me properly?'

'You'll have to catch me,' she warned him, teasing.

Gil opened his arms in welcome and looked up. But the tree was empty and it was raining.

He looked down again and saw the cliff edge, the loose soil crumbling away where she had stood. It had been raining that day too.

Her father had tried to stop them seeing each other at first. Hers was a very wealthy family and Gil had still been a junior lecturer in those days, living in digs within the college grounds and scraping by on what little money he had saved from a summer job.

Dora had seemed like a creature from another world, beautiful and vivacious, driving herself to parties in a brand spanking new MG Midget and not giving a damn what people thought when she and her friends got drunk and jumped into the Cherwell. Although she lived in London part of the year, she had a job on one of the local Oxford rags, though it was never clear what she did there except show up and write the occasional witty column under her initials only. She said she preferred anonymity, but he suspected her real reason was a fear people would not take her seriously if they knew she was a female. Certainly she liked to act like a man occasionally.

Gil had seen her in the Turf one night, standing at the bar with a group of noisy male journalists, and had been able to take his eyes off her as she downed whisky sodas with the best of them. He hadn't thought he stood a chance with a girl like that. But when they eventually met at a party later that year, Dora had let him walk her back to her car afterwards and even kiss her, in a fumbling sort of way.

'Here's my number,' she whispering, handing him a card. 'Call me.'

He jumped off the running board just in time before her pale green MG Midget roared off into the night.

Gil stared after it entranced, his lips still tingling.

When he stumbled back to his digs that night, everything seemed to have subtly changed. He threw himself into one of the old leather armchairs and flicked restlessly through a book before getting up again, standing by the window to gaze across the moonlit quad. Some young undergraduates were still down there, talking in drunken whispers outside the lodge in case the porter heard them and came out to investigate. He meandered back across his room, black-stained floorboards creaking under his feet, and put some Ella Fitzgerald on the gramophone.

His head was spinning and he felt vaguely sick. Too much cheap bitter. Gil felt in his pocket for the crumbled piece of paper she had pressed into his hand before driving away, and repeated the phone number to himself several times.

What would he say though if he rang her? 'Would you like to come to dinner?'

He had no money to take her somewhere expensive and she didn't seem the sort of girl who would be impressed by a fish and chip supper. Something more casual then, less open to a humiliating rejection. 'Come up for a drink in my rooms next time you're in town.' Gil looked round at the bare walls and austere furniture. He imagined her crossing this room with her quick light tread, laughing at his dusty book collection, head on one side as she read through the titles. He could never ask her up to his rooms. She would see straight through to his real self and turn away in boredom.

Gil shook his head at his own stupidity, tucked the crumpled number inside one of his less interesting books, and never rang her.

It was a mutual friend who brought them together in the end. There was an end of term party in some house just off Long Wall Street. It was a rambling old building with many floors and an enclosed garden at the back. Gil turned up alone at the party and realised he knew nobody there except the boy whose place it was. Someone in the sitting room was playing the piano, some popular tune, and everyone was singing along to it. He pushed his way through a crowd of party-goers towards the kitchen, but some political types were already in there, their coat lapels too wide for his taste, arguing heatedly over a game of rummy. They looked up at him without interest, then carried on with their discussion, one of them trying to swat a fly with a rolled-up copy of The Daily Worker, another dealing cards across a beer-stained table. Gil was about to slip back out of the front door, still clutching his bottle of French table red, when a young woman leapt up from a huddle of students on the stairs and called out his name, exaggeratedly climbing over people to get down to him.

It was Dora.

'Oh don't go, Gil! Bloody hell, these heels ... ' Her voice was accusing. 'You never rang me!'

He stared. 'Dora? What are you doing here?'

'I could ask the same of you.' She shrugged, looking back at the group of snappily-dressed young men she had abandoned, some of whom were protesting in loud drunken tones. 'Some postgrad from Queens insisted I come along with him. But it's such a bore, darling. They're all so bloody young.' Her gaze fixed on his mouth. 'Not like you.'

Stepping back into an overladen hat stand, Gil knocked it to the floor with a clatter.

'I say!' one of the socialists complained, staring.

Dora giggled at the mess on the floor, and grabbed Gil's hand. 'Quick, let's flee the scene.' Sticking out her tongue at the card-players, she pulled him through the kitchen and out into the cool dark garden. 'Come on, it's lovely out here. And no piano!'

There was a vast sycamore in one corner, growing perilously close to the high red brick wall, its branches rustling with leaves. Dora clapped her hands when she saw it. 'How unspeakably glorious, I can't resist. Here, be a darling and hold my shoes,' she told him, kicking off her shoes, and immediately started to climb up into the branches.

He stood beneath her, feeling too dazed to speak, her expensive high heels clutched to his chest. Her laughter rang out over the music thudding from an open second-floor window.

'This dress is going to be absolutely ruined. I never liked it though. My mother bought it for me. I hate my mother!'

He was amazed, staring up at her bare legs. 'Why do you hate your mother?'

'Because she's an utter bitch who doesn't care two hoots for me and goes round sleeping with other men. Isn't yours a bitch too?'

He had not known how to reply.

Much later, lying back on the damp grass beneath the sycamore, Dora passed him a cigarette and stretched her arms above her head.

'Oxford's so dull at the moment, don't you think? Everyone interesting has gone home for the long vac. I want to sail to New York as soon as I can afford it. Have you ever been to America?'

He shook his head.

'Well, they say everything's happening there at the moment.' He could see the shape of her breasts as the dress lifted with her body. 'Would you like to come with me to New York?'

'Yes,' he replied, unthinking.

She rolled over onto her stomach and looked at him. 'That's what I like about you, Gil. You're so uncomplicated. Those other boys – '

'I think I'm in love with you.'

Dora reached out and squeezed his hand. 'Dearest Gil, you mustn't.'

'I mean it.'

'But how sweet you are! We barely know each other.'

'*Le coup de foudre.*'

She stared, her lips open, her eyes like saucers, and the laughter came bubbling from her throat rich as melting chocolate. 'Of course, it must be possible, love at first sight. All the best Italian poets tell us it happens. I just never thought ... But then, why the hell not? You are so *very sweet.*'

He found the way her mouth moved when she emphasised the words *very sweet* intensely erotic, the red lips pursing as her eyes looked into his.

Amazed at how easily the thing had been said, Gil said, 'I love you,' again, several times, then added naively, 'I've never been in love before.'

'How wise of you,' she said, reaching for the cheap red and drinking out of the bottle with no sign of embarrassment. Gil watched every movement she made, utterly mesmerized by the way she stroked the grass with long delicate fingers while she drank, head back and eyes closed, before handing the bottle back to him.

Did she know how much he wanted to make love to her? Gil wasn't sure, though he guessed that many men must have lain beside her like this, in many other dark gardens or on the smooth leather seats of her MG, and wondered precisely the same thing.

'How about you?' he asked, suddenly a little jealous.

She put down the wine, her smile disturbingly enigmatic. 'I've been in love thousands of times, Gil, and it never lasts.'

'Oh.'

'Ships in the night, darling. The things I've done for love. God, some of them against the law, I'm sure! But not one of those boys mean a thing to me now. Trust me.' She laughed at his confused expression and knelt up on the damp grass, one of her dress straps slipping to reveal a white shoulder. He loved the way she moved, so impulsively and without restraint. 'Kiss me then, if you're so in love with me!'

'What?'

'Kiss me,' she repeated softly. 'Or don't you want to?'

'Yes,' he stammered. 'Yes.'

They moved quickly towards each other at the same time and banged heads, Dora reeling back in riotous laughter and clutching her forehead, Gil down on all fours, dazed for a moment and bitterly aware that he must have blown his chance. He wanted to get up and walk away from this disaster, but part of him knew he would look like some ridiculous virgin schoolboy if he did, so he grabbed her shoulders without even bothering to apologise and pulled her mouth towards his.

He kissed her much harder than he had intended, his anger aimed at himself rather than at her, but she didn't struggle to get away as he expected her to do. Instead, she wriggled even closer, her fingers electric on the back of his neck.

He thought they kissed like people who were already lovers, a startling intimacy in those little sounds she was making under her breath. He had kissed girls before, of course, in unlit doorways on the way home from a dance, or briefly and furtively on the back seats at the cinema. But this was nothing like those dusty tight-lipped attempts at love. For a start, they were lying down, so it was more like the act itself, and her shoulders were excitingly bare, the hairs rising on the back of his neck as he realised how easily he could slip his hand under her dress if she let him.

There was a moment when he decided to pull away, his dignity still reasonably intact, but she had a way of silently drawing him back which left no room in his head for refusal. Giving up the fight, he concentrated instead on her lips, the taste and shape of them, how their tongues met with such a shock it seemed to sensitize his entire body, reducing him to nothing but breath and urgency.

The groan he gave when she touched him was purely organic. It grew out of the darkness tinged with red behind his tightly closed eyelids and passed into her blood system until they were both part of the same fierce creature.

Deaf to the music from the house behind them, sheltered by the sycamore and the surrounding darkness, they lay there on the grass as though it were the most natural thing in the world to be pressed together like this, lost in the tiny pulsing of blood under every inch of skin as their bodies touched.

She ran her fingers down the length of his spine and back up to his neck again, clutching him closer. 'Dearest thing.'

With great daring, Gil stroked her small breasts through the thin fabric of her dress, saying her name softly under his breath, afraid that she might pull away in anger or disgust. But to his astonishment, Dora took his hand and slid it inside her dress, shifting slightly to undo the catch on her bra for him.

Gil had never felt a naked breast before and for a moment he thought he was going to jerk back, terrified by what she was asking and by his own inexperience. But she whispered something encouraging and he found himself pressing the warm skin as if he had done this many times before, feeling her nipple come hard and erect under his searching fingers.

She pulled his head down and suddenly Gil was kissing her breast, suckling like a baby at her nipple, imprinting every inch of her pale skin on his memory so that he would never forget this moment.

He had loved a few girls before, in his own way, watching them from a distance or sometimes talking to them clumsily at parties, trying to catch their attention before they turned away, rapidly losing interest in a boy whose only topic of conversation seemed to be dead civilisations and their half-forgotten myths. But he had known from the first instant he saw her – wearing a tight skirt with a provocative little split up the back, drinking whisky with her journalist friends, her head thrown back in uncontrollable laughter while the others in the bar looked on disapprovingly – that Dora would be different. When she had looked at him so intensely just now, discussing love while they shared her cigarette, Gil knew she had seen something in him nobody else had ever done.

She understood him, that was it.

So she forgave the occasional stammer, the clumsiness, the sexual inexperience, because she could see beyond them and didn't care what lay on the surface. She was touching his chest now, her hands flat as she drew them down over his stomach. Then she mouthed his name and he kissed her, catching the silent word on his tongue.

Every part of his body seemed connected to that kiss; it was a lynch-pin that held them together, her body too arching against his in reaction. Gil raised his head and stared down into her face, studying the flushed cheeks and bruised-looking lips, pale now and denuded of lipstick.

'Do you want me to stop?' He had shocked himself with the way his knee had begun to push between her legs and felt sure he must be frightening her.

'No.'

Far from pushing him away, she rolled slightly to make it easier for him and he was on top of her in the same movement. Then she was fumbling with his trousers, undoing the belt, giggling with a sudden disarming embarrassment when it caught for a moment before releasing. His whole body was alive and trembling, the desire to enter her almost unbearable.

That he didn't have to think about it surprised him. The dress came up easily under his hands, sliding over the narrow bones of her hips, and then he was touching her thighs while she whispered, 'Yes,' and 'Yes,' again, in quite a different way to how she had said 'No' before. He had been worried, not wanting to ruin it with his usual clumsiness and make a fool of himself, but there was no difficulty in the end. They might have been making love for the thousandth time, not the first.

Gil thought of all the nights he had dreamed how it would feel to be this close to a real woman, to look into her eyes as he pushed himself inside her, and knew that no amount of imagination could compare with this sheer physical shock, his nerve-endings stretched raw with the voltage.

Her breath was warm on his ear as she kept watch over his shoulder, both tacitly aware of those brightly-lit windows only a few hundred yards from where they were lying, the party still going on into the early hours. He raised his head and chest, straining to keep his weight on his hands. There was a sudden cool breeze and a few curling leaves fell from the sycamore above, but Dora didn't bother shaking them away.

She lay beneath him, nymph-like, leaves in her hair and between her naked breasts, the dress still draped about her waist in a glossy ribbon of silk. Her fingers touched his back through the shirt he had kept on, her eyes closed and breathing rapid, the warm thighs wrapped around his hips as if she too wanted them to merge and become one.

Gil concentrated on the branches gently rustling above and the sound of the music still streaming from the open windows. It was a mellow late-night tune he vaguely recognised, though the name kept slipping out of his head. He glanced down at her breasts and then instantly away, scared to finish too soon and disappoint her. She was the most beautiful and mesmerizing woman he had ever seen in his life, and Gil could scarcely understand how any of this had happened.

You're going to ruin it, nagged the voice in his head. You'll ruin it and she'll never see you again. Then somebody was groaning and he realised belatedly that it was him.

Dora opened her blue eyes wide and he couldn't resist, lying against her fully as they kissed again, his body soaring up into the branches of the sycamore.

'Pull out,' she said urgently in his ear, but only part of him heard the command, shifting slightly too late.

When she sat up afterwards, pulling the dress up over her breasts and wriggling the rest down to cover her thighs, Gil knew she was angry and cursed himself inwardly. 'I'm sorry.'

Dora reached for the bottle of wine and drank a little, flashing him a quick irritated smile. 'Don't worry. Let's cross our fingers!' This time Gil did as he was told, watching as she crossed her own fingers too and held them up like a talisman against bad luck.

'And I thought Oxford was dull!'

Her laughter was a little wild as she handed him the wine and collapsed again on the damp grass, arching her spine with languorous pleasure, her anger forgotten.

'If we both cross our fingers,' she told him confidently, 'I can't get pregnant. That's what they say, anyway. Do you fancy another cigarette before we go?'

Chapter Twelve

It had been too easy to expect an endless sense of the idyllic from this place, Gil thought, standing at his study window with his hands behind his back as he followed a row of graceful white yachts across the turbulent blue expanse of the bay. But then life is rarely predictable and more often than not a disappointment. The yachts shone milky as opals under the pale sunshine, tiny figures of yachtsmen almost lost in the spray as each yacht skirted a line of red marker buoys almost out of view of the house. Gil had always dreamt of owning a yacht and sailing along the wild and beautiful Manx coast each summer, but he supposed it was too late for that now.

Reluctantly, he turned his gaze away from the sea and surveyed his study instead. Cathy had been in here again tidying, he decided. His desk was not as chaotic as it had been when he left it yesterday, and someone had picked up the tipped-over chair and set it neatly back into place.

The house itself was an intriguing honeycomb of passageways leading to rooms with quaintly sloping roofs and unusual angles, but it was the bluebell wood that had decided it for Dora. They had viewed the house in early spring and soon discovered the little cluster of ancient gnarled trees to one side of the terraces, rife with bluebells and snowdrops at that time of year and delightfully hidden behind a vast yew hedge.

Dora had clapped her hands and instantly darted into the little wood, ankle-deep in its thick sea of flowers, her whole face reflecting their blue light. 'This is the place,' she had told him. 'I want to retire here, to spend the rest of my days in this place.'

She had used an inheritance from her late father to buy the house, putting their semi-detached in Oxford up for sale, but it had not seemed real until Gil announced his retirement from the lectureship. They moved over to the island later that year, and it was not long after that, as they had suspected and the doctors had warned, that Dora's condition began to rapidly deteriorate and Gil found himself alone with a wife who needed to be reminded daily of his name. And even her own, after a while.

Though he had never regretted their hasty and discreetly arranged marriage, back in their early twenties, not one second of it. Lawrence had arrived like a gift from the gods – the image of Gil's own father and aptly named after him – and the family line had been preserved for another generation. But the long series of miscarriages that followed the war had shattered Dora's confidence, each one harder to accept than the last.

'Why can't I carry any of these babies?' she would cry whenever the bleeding and the pains started. 'I carried Lawrence for nine months. Why not this one?'

Gil had looked on aghast, helpless to halt the inevitable loss, wondering if it was something he had done wrong that was causing this horror.

In the end, they had simply stopped trying. Lawrence was their son and that would have to be enough. But when Dora reached the menopause and her periods stopped altogether, she had wept silently for days, and he knew it was for all the children she had so longed to bear and now never would.

Gil sat down at his desk and began to sort through the chaos of papers in front of him. He could not leave it any longer to organise his estate, however much he wished to deny his own rapidly failing health. The bulk of it would go to his son, naturally, but there was also Miranda to consider now. Should he leave her something beside that money in trust? His books, naturally. Lawrence had never been a great reader, he had always preferred drawing and photography to books as a boy. But what else?

His hand paused, hovering above the long-sealed envelope of his previous will. He had been trying to avoid thinking about Miranda this morning, feeling a little more frail than usual after a sleepless night. But her disappearance continued to prey on his mind. The police seemed unable to find her and the island had been put on a full scale alert for the missing girl. He did not know what he would do if something appalling had happened to her.

Miranda's bike had been found yesterday morning, leaning against a wall near the Castletown bypass, clearly damaged in some collision and then abandoned, but there had been no sign of Miranda herself.

A house-to-house enquiry in the area had turned up a possible sighting: a young girl, matching Miranda's description and in the right place at the right time, had been driven away by a man in a red van the previous afternoon. But the farmer who had seen all this from his tractor was uncertain about the vehicle's make and couldn't even be sure that the van had been red. The potential interpretation of his story was desperately worrying though.

Cathy had been wild with hysteria when she heard this latest news, first blaming herself, then him and Lawrence for failing to look after her properly. 'She's dead! I told you she was dead!' she kept crying, her face ravaged by tears. 'My little girl's dead, and it's all your fault!'

Gil had not known how to comfort her. He could only hope that the farmer had mistaken some other girl for Miranda.

He tore open the envelope, his hands trembling, and read briefly through the contents of his previous will to see what needed to be changed and what could remain the same. It was important to keep busy, for life to continue as usual.

His mind insisted on wandering though, even as he began making notes on the necessary changes to his will. He told himself there must be plenty of girls out there of the same height and colouring as Miranda, and his granddaughter knew far better than to accept a lift from a stranger. It was only two days since she had disappeared and he stoutly refused to assume the worst unless presented with somewhat harder evidence. Her mother might be utterly frantic, telling everyone she met that Miranda had been abducted by some madman, but he at least intended to carry on believing in the girl. Miranda was his flesh and blood too, and made of sterner stuff than her mother realised.

The knock at his study door ten minutes later was an unwelcome intrusion. Gil barely raised his head from his papers. 'I'm busy.'

'This is important.'

It was Lawrence in the doorway. His son came in without waiting for permission and shut the door behind him. The look on his face told Gil that this could not possibly wait, so he painstakingly removed his reading glasses and placed them on the papers in front of him.

Lawrence did not sit down, even though he waved him towards a chair, standing instead by the window and staring out at the wind-torn bay.

'I wanted to speak to you last night, but it wasn't the right time, not with the police round here again. That detective rang Cathy this morning, you know.'

'Any news?'

His son shook his head. 'They're going to talk to some of the other kids in the village today. In case somebody knows something but isn't telling, if you see what I mean.'

'Do they think it's some kind of conspiracy?'

'Most child victims know their attacker, apparently.' Lawrence must have seen his father's expression, because he made an apologetic sound under his breath. 'I know, it's inconceivable even to consider that. I'm merely repeating what Cathy told me.'

'It's complete and utter nonsense.'

There was an uncomfortable silence. The child was safe and well, and hiding somewhere, Gil was convinced of it. This obsession with her abduction was nothing but scaremongering. These policemen didn't know what they were talking about. They were wasting time on telephone calls and interviews when they should be out there, on the ground, physically looking for her. Miranda was an intelligent child who knew the island intimately and would never knowingly put herself in harm's way. Everything else was mere conjecture.

Gil felt his head buzz slightly, as though something inside his brain was tingling and fizzing. Immediately afterwards, a vague sensation of nausea and faintness swept over him. It was happening again. He laid his palms flat on the leather-topped desk and tried to stay lucid.

'Now, what was it you needed?'

Lawrence turned away from the window and stuck his hands in his pockets. His voice sounded odd and Gil looked up at him, sensing that something must be badly wrong.

'The other night, when Cathy and I went out in the Land Rover together ... We had a chance to talk, and she told me about Miranda.' Lawrence swallowed, staring at him. 'Why did you insist she kept quiet about her getting pregnant? Bloody years, absolutely desperate for a child, and Miranda was here all the time, growing up without me.'

He made an obvious effort to pull himself up short, presumably not wishing to descend into ranting. In the momentary silence that followed, Lawrence stared at his mother's photograph on the far wall.

'I didn't even know she existed until now. I would have acknowledged her. Looked after her financially. You must know that.'

Gil didn't know what to say. 'I'm sorry.'

'Is that it?'

'I did what I thought was best at the time.'

'For you or for me?'

Gil had always known this moment would not be easy, but now that it was here, he was afraid: afraid of losing his son and afraid that he had made a terrible mistake, that he could no longer justify his actions, even though everything had seemed so clear and defensible to him in the beginning. What had changed to make his motives suddenly so suspect? The passage of time, perhaps, and the accompanying benefit of hindsight. Lawrence was perfectly right to be angry, of course. It had been an outrageous deception and harder to justify as the child grew up and began searching for answers to the inevitable question. He had lied to her too, and that was unforgivable. Something moved away from him in the sunlight, leaving him empty and saddened.

'For you, Lawrence. I wanted to save your marriage.'

'It wasn't your marriage to save. You should have told me the truth and let me deal with the consequences'

Gil looked down at his hands, mottled and greyish at the knuckles. 'You don't know what you're saying, Lawrence.'

'And you do?'

'I've had to deal with those consequences myself, yes.'

Lawrence made an impatient noise under his breath, opening his mouth to speak, and Gil held up one hand to silence him. He hadn't finished yet. The doctors' warnings came back to him, their stark words in that sterile hospital clinic leaving him in no doubt of his mortality. However appallingly difficult, this thing had to be done now, it had to be brought out and cleared up, before his chance to confess was lost forever.

'You won't be aware of this, but before your mother ... ' He struggled with the weight of what was to come, terrified of his son's reaction but forcing himself to continue nonetheless. 'It was a mistake, a stupid unforgivable thing to do. I knew that as soon as it happened. But you saw how your mother was, walking around in a dream state, barely able to recognise any of us, not even responding to her own name. I was lonely. I was frustrated.'

Gil looked up at his wife's photograph on the wall opposite his desk and caught a hint of accusation behind her eyes. This was his penance and he must go through with it.

'Your mother wandered into the kitchen one day and found me with Cathy. No, don't look at me like that. It wasn't an affair. It was a moment of madness. I was exhausted and unhappy, and Cathy was there. I kissed her.

That was all, I swear it. But Dora saw us and although she didn't seem to understand what was going on, I'm sure she must have done at some level.'

Lawrence was staring. 'When was this?'

'About a week before she died.'

There was a terrible silence. His son put a hand up to cover his face. Gil waited for his contempt, for the anger and loathing which he was sure was about to follow and which his wife had been unable to express, her mind lost in some other world where such things had ceased to have any meaning. He would have to face them without flinching, for they were his accusers and his guilt was undeniable.

He added in a whisper, 'Ever since she died, I've been trying to make up for it. To change what happened. To live that day again and stop her from – '

Lawrence stirred at last, interrupting him. 'Is that why Mum did it, do you think? Wandered out to the cliffs that day? She was confused, of course, and the coroner ruled it was an accident. But I always wondered.'

'I don't know. I'll never know.'

His son put his hands back into his trouser pockets and blew out a long breath. 'What a bloody mess. And I thought my life was complicated.'

Gil watched him, unable to understand his son's calm acceptance. He had betrayed the boy's mother with another woman and possibly prompted her to commit suicide, yet Lawrence seemed relieved more than anything else. It was almost as if Gil had merely given him the solution to a long-standing puzzle.

'You're not angry?'

'I am angry, yes. But what good would it do to show that? Perhaps you'd prefer me to drag you outside and beat the hell out of you?'

'Perhaps.'

'I'm guilty of making a similar mistake myself though, and with the same woman, which is worse.' Lawrence smiled tightly. 'Perhaps we should beat the hell out of each other instead.'

His son's humour, so inexplicable at a moment like this, seemed to lighten the darker corners of their conversation. Gil felt himself gradually emerge from that grim wasteland where he had lingered for days now, fearing to move forward but unable to turn back. He felt it easier to speak too, as though an iron weight had finally been lifted from his tongue.

'Yes, it was a similar mistake. That's why I asked Cathy to keep her pregnancy quiet. I was shocked when she told me about it, of course, but I understood how it might have happened. You looked so broken at the funeral,' he explained, his voice cracking on the word broken, 'and Cathy has a certain way of listening.'

His son looked at him drily.

'Besides,' Gil continued, avoiding his gaze, 'Juliet would have left you when she found out, and I wanted to prevent that at all costs. I knew how much you loved her. I didn't want to see your marriage fail. It would have destroyed you, so soon after your mother's death.'

Gil thought back to the day when Cathy had come to him in tears and begged for his son's address. The idea of offering her money instead had arrived so easily in his head, it had felt almost trivial, a quick-fix solution to some temporary problem. It was only much later, when the child was a pretty little toddler stumbling about his garden, her resemblance to his dead wife striking and undeniable, that Gil realised the problem would not go away. It would merely grow with the child, year upon year, demanding greater and more complex acts of deception to be concealed.

'I didn't think it through properly. I didn't look ahead to the future. It never occurred to me that you and Juliet ... '

'Wouldn't produce a child ourselves?'

'Exactly.'

Lawrence threw himself into the green leather armchair and sighed, staring up at the ceiling. His entire body seemed to exude defeat, the large-lidded eyes closing wearily. There were flecks of what seemed to be grey in his short-cropped hair and his face was heavily lined from that look of frowning concentration, so comical in his infancy. Now it was the face of someone who had been quietly and consistently disappointed by life.

For the first time Gil saw his son as an individual separate from himself, no longer a child to be protected and gently excused for any failings, but a man who needed to be held accountable for his actions, if only to jolt him at last into a long-overdue adulthood. It had been an appalling mistake to keep Miranda's existence a secret from his son. But it had seemed so unlikely, back then, that his marriage to Juliet would be a childless one.

How could anyone have foreseen such a thing?

Gil watched his son, guiltily aware that he robbed him of something no career success could replace. It was fatherhood that forced the greatest changes in a man: to keep Lawrence from his responsibilities as a father, to trap him forever in an uneasy adolescence, had been an unforgivable act of hubris. But perhaps it was not too late to make amends.

'We must find her,' Gil said suddenly, standing up.

Lawrence opened his eyes and stared, momentarily confused, almost as if he had fallen asleep there for a moment.

'Who?'

'Miranda. We must find her ourselves, there's no point waiting for the police to do it.'

'But where would we look?'

'Anywhere,' Gil said impatiently, slipping his documents back into the top drawer and locking it. 'Everywhere.'

'Yes, absolutely.' Lawrence dragged himself upright in the armchair and rose to his feet, waggling his neck first to loosen it and then shaking his fingers out as if they were stiff. Fully awake now, he seemed exhilarated by the idea of this impromptu rescue mission, like a drowning man who had suddenly been thrown a lifeline. 'So where do we start?'

Gil turned to his map of the island which hung on the wall beside his desk. His finger hesitated over Spanish Head, a few miles west of his house: a wild and desolate tract of land, smothered in ferns and deep-sprung purple heathers at this time of year and only accessible via a rambling network of coastal paths. Just below Cregneash, adjacent to Spanish Head and the last village at the southern end of the island, the land fell away sharply until it reached a mass of chasms which hung above the sea like giant marbled teeth. It was precisely the sort of place Miranda might choose if she wished to avoid capture, knowing how hard it would be for anyone to find a child in all that wilderness.

'How about starting with the Chasms and Spanish Head? They've already searched that area, of course, but it's worth another try.'

'Good idea.'

'You and Juliet can take my car. I'll try the other side of the peninsula, starting at Bradda and working my way round to Fleshwick. Oh don't worry, I don't intend to walk the whole way myself. I have a friend there who can help, and probably give me a lift back too. We'll rendezvous here at ...' Gil glanced at his watch, invigorated by this renewed sense of purpose. He would have gone mad eventually, sitting like a spider in the silent room, waiting for a phone call that never came. At least they were moving now, doing something constructive. 'Six o'clock?'

'If you're sure you're fit enough?'

'I can manage.'

'Take it easy though. I'll drop you off in the Land Rover.'

Gil reached over and shook his hand, a sudden awkward gesture which nevertheless cemented the moment for both of them.

'Thank you,' he said.

Chapter Thirteen

The sun imprinted itself on the eye with its pale glare, imbuing the mist with an unearthly light as Lawrence and Juliet stood – two still figures – at the gate barring the way to the chasms.

DANGER CHASMS, warned the small board tacked to the gate in front of them, once white with bold red lettering but now battered by the elements to a murky grey.

Beyond the warning sign, the path ran towards the cliff edge for a few innocent yards and then split in several directions, each sub-path weaving in between the white and grey marbled rocks jutting out of the earth and just missing by inches each deep crevice that dropped straight down to the beach below. Tiny flowers grew there, a purplish flourish of thrift and saxifrage, dotted attractively amongst the rocks. The ground itself simply vanished, rather than stopped, at the ends of these paths and became the sea instead, a barely visible yellow and blue layer of chiffon floating under the mist.

In this uncertain weather, it would be difficult to see anything up here, let alone a child who was determined not to be spotted.

Lawrence unlatched the gate and they went though, Juliet clutching her red jacket in silent protest. It was cold and damp on the cliff, rather like being inside a cloud, and he knew she had not wanted him to drag her all the way from the car park above Cregneash. 'I'll wait in the car,' she had said as he parked up alongside what looked like a radio mast, producing one of her glossy magazines from the floor. But he had insisted and now her unspoken fury lay between them like a third person in the mist, shifting restlessly as she struck out along one path and left him alone on the other.

'Watch out for the chasms,' he called after her. 'If you fell down one, you might not survive. They drop all the way to the sea.'

But Juliet was already moving away through the white air, her only response a contemptuous flick of her hand. Lawrence stood for a moment and watched her, afraid that she had not taken him seriously, but to his relief she seemed perfectly aware of the danger, lifting her feet clear over some of the thinner slits in the ground and neatly jumping the wider ones.

The sun came through the cloud for one startling second, and he turned, shielding his eyes as he faced the vast blinding acres of sea beyond the cliff edge. Then it was gone and the waters disappeared again as if they had never been there. Juliet was almost out of sight now, a pale reddish figure far to his right, bending to peer down one of the chasms. She had been so distant these past couple of days, even turning her cheek away this morning when he tried to kiss her. It was almost as though she already knew the truth about Miranda, though that was surely impossible, even taking into account a woman's instinct for these things. He could hear her call 'Halloo', faintly over the crashing waves, and realised she must be listening for the echo.

Lawrence stared along the cliff edge in the mist, searching for any signs of his daughter's presence, but the place held nothing but rocks and tiny flowers ruffled by the wind.

What had he expected to find? Some carelessly discarded item of clothing, perhaps, or a rough shelter somewhere beneath the dry stone wall that enclosed these chasms. But if Miranda had ever been here, she was long gone now.

Nevertheless, he continued to follow the path a little further along, in case he had missed something in the thin light. The wind buffeted him violently as he came closer to the edge, making his jacket flap like a ship's sail and almost dragging the woollen hat from his head. He stood on the rock with his arms outstretched for balance, nerves tight as catgut, aware that he would have to make his confession to Juliet when she came back. It had to be done somewhere and this place was as good as any. The thought of telling her back at his father's house this evening filled him with horror. Her first reaction might be to confront Gil and he simply couldn't allow that to happen. The old man was too fragile at the moment.

No, it had to be here, and now. Let her rage at him in the strange privacy of this mist and wilderness, overheard by no one but himself and the seagulls.

As he thought that, the sun flashed out of the blank whiteness again and the whole cliff was lit up in a burst of glorious sunshine. Lawrence felt his spirits lift with the weather and he ran back along the path between the yawning chasms with the impatience of a schoolboy, needing to tell his wife now, immediately, before he lost his nerve.

But Juliet was nowhere in sight.

There was a great gash in the ground quite near to the gate, and Lawrence stood above it for a while, staring down into its slowly diminishing tunnel of stone. The rock was quite damp higher up, glistening with a strange black light, presumably rain that had clung to the sides during the night and never evaporated. It was too high to be sea spray, the entrance several hundred feet above the water mark, which he could just see by crouching lower and peering right inside - a dark tide mark staining the walls in a distinct line at the far reaches of his vision. Beyond that the chasm narrowed to a grim slit as it plunged to the sea, though he could still hear the faint hiss and boom of water as the tide moved restlessly against the unseen lower walls.

He picked up a pebble and dropped it down the crack, waiting for the clatter or splash at the other end as it hit either rock or water. But the sun had vanished back into the mist again and there was that curiously muffled sound to everything, so he couldn't quite hear which it was. He suddenly remembered some garbled myth from his childhood, about a man who had fallen down one of these and been stuck for more than a week, unable to move in either direction, and was only found when someone heard his dog barking and came to investigate. But by then, the man was so thin with lack of food, he had simply slipped through the gap when they tried to shift him and broken his neck on the rocks below.

Lawrence knelt on the edge and shouted Miranda's name into the whispering darkness, but there was no response. Only a vague whispering echo from damp walls.

'Wonderfully eerie, aren't they?' a voice asked. 'These chasms, I mean. They're everywhere, all these bloody huge cracks in the ground.'

He looked over his shoulder to see Juliet standing behind him in the misty sunshine, a little cluster of wild flowers in her hand.

'I don't think you're meant to pick those,' Lawrence said, recalling some law his mother had been forever drumming into him, about the preservation of wild species and never picking flowers outside your own garden, but regretted it instantly when her smile faded. 'But I don't suppose it really matters. There's no one around to see you.'

'Can we go now? She isn't here.'

'I know.'

'It's a waste of time anyway. The police can look for the girl.'

He stood up, dusting his knees. He had never really noticed before this week how incredibly selfish Juliet was. He felt anger rising inside him at her petulant attitude and checked it, aware that he had to go at this gently. Counting to ten in his head, Lawrence stepped over the chasm and stared blindly out to sea.

'Look, Miranda's only a kid. She could be lying hurt somewhere. Don't you think it's worth a few hours of our time to help look for her?'

'I wanted to go shopping today.'

'Juliet!' The wind yanked at his woollen hat again and he clamped it down with his hand. 'I'm sorry things aren't going to plan, but this is rather more important than shopping.'

'I'm not a fool. I can see that.'

'In my family, we pull together when there's a crisis. We don't pull in opposite directions.'

'But that's just it. Miranda isn't family.'

Juliet looked at him angrily, her cheeks flushed and her loose hair whipping about in the wind. Behind her back, he could see the mist beginning to lift at last, the hills a deep shiny bottle-green as they rose through sunlight towards Spanish Head.

'She's your father's housekeeper's daughter,' she said, emphasising each word sarcastically. 'So explain to me why we should run about the island in such a panic, looking for this stupid bloody girl, when she's obviously only doing this in order to get attention.'

This was the opening Lawrence had been waiting for. He opened his mouth to speak – to lay it all before her with the flourish of a magician – and felt the words dry in his throat. It ought to have been easy, letting the words fall naturally into that gap so they would fit with no visible seams, no excess or deficiency, and no need to elaborate any further. But it wasn't easy. His words would be a slap in the face, however they were spoken.

'She's my daughter.'

Juliet's impatient tone did not change. 'What did you say?'

'She's my daughter,' he repeated tersely. 'I had an affair with Cathy. Well, I'm not sure it really qualifies as an affair. More of a one-night-stand. If it helps, I was not sober at the time.'

'What the hell are you talking about?'

'It's quite simple.' Lawrence felt his face burn, forced to spell out his infidelity. 'I had sex with my father's housekeeper while I was over here for my mother's funeral, and Miranda is the result.'

'You're not serious?'

'I'm afraid that I am.'

There was an electric silence. 'You *fucked* that woman?'

'Yes.'

Juliet jumped over the chasm like a wild animal and caught him hard across the face before he could say any more. Lawrence reeled back in a flash of agony, swearing incoherently. He almost slipped on the edge of the chasm and fought to steady himself.

Why were women so unable to strike a clean blow? His cheek was bleeding from something sharp, presumably one of her rings, and his whole head was ringing with the impact of furious uncoordinated knuckles.

Gingerly, he took a few steps back for safety's sake and felt along the bone, but his nose didn't appear to be broken. He watched his wife as she swayed there on the uneven lip of the chasm, fists by her side, apparently blind to the danger she would be in were she to step back even so much as an inch.

The look on her face was one he had never seen before; an ugly light in her eyes, her skin glowing with rage and some other emotion he couldn't decipher, Juliet stared back at him across the abyss like a maniac on the verge of some dreadful act. It had gone much as Lawrence had imagined so far: the brief stark confession, the animated fury, even the physical reprisal. But now he was at the point where imagination had failed him. This was where he discovered what the true cost of his infidelity was to be. He hadn't really cared before, assuming that he would deserve whatever punishment she meted out.

But the blow had sobered him and the slightly mad look in her eyes worried Lawrence. He said, 'Look, I didn't even know Miranda existed until this week. It was a complete shock to me too.'

'But presumably you're aware how she was conceived?'

Her sarcasm was reassuring. 'I know, I know. It was unforgivable of me. But I didn't intend any of it to happen. I was drunk ...'

'Oh please!'

'I'd only just buried my mother. Well, cremated her, to be accurate.' He struggled, horribly aware of the ridiculousness of it all, the schoolboy nature of his stammering explanation. 'My dad locked himself up in his room and wouldn't come out. You were hundreds of miles away at that bloody gardening exhibition. There was no one to turn to.'

'Except Cathy.'

'That's about it, yes.'

'Boring, simple-minded Cathy. Cathy who wears clogs to do the dishes. Cathy who – '

'Now you're just being nasty,' he interrupted her.

Her eyebrows soared, her tone suddenly brittle and mocking. 'I wonder why?'

'I deserve your anger. Cathy doesn't.'

'She knew you were married.'

'Okay, that's fair enough. She knew.' He stuck his hands in his pockets. 'And I know it's no consolation, but I regretted it immediately. I didn't want to lose you, Juliet.'

'How many times?' she demanded.

'Sorry?'

'How many times did you sleep with her?'

'Only once,' he insisted, then frowned, adding, 'I think.'

'You think?'

'I told you, I was drunk.'

Juliet stared at him in disbelief, then made a furious noise and spun abruptly on her heel. Tiny blue-grey splinters of slate shifted in the dust behind her and slid into the chasm, hitting the rock wall in a thousand places, the sound of their falling ominously lost within seconds. He wasn't sure how it happened afterwards, but her foot just seemed to slither on the loose scree and everything changed in that instant, like a London cabbie turning neatly on a sixpence.

Juliet tried to right herself, made a surprised sort of face, eyebrows raised and mouth flying open, then slipped directly into the chasm itself. Her momentum was such that he almost believed the chasm to be sucking her in.

Everything seemed to move in slow motion as Lawrence dived towards his wife, suddenly realising the danger she was in. He caught her just in time, one foot dangling into the chasm, the other twisted in the earth as she fought for balance. Her body felt warm and heavy in his arms as he dragged Juliet back out of that dark empty space and onto solid rock again.

Yet more slate fragments dislodged by their struggle dashed themselves down the walls, a strange crashing echo audible from those unseen depths, the chasm crying out like some prehistoric creature deprived of its prey.

In the bewildered aftermath, they sat together on the dusty marbled rock, listening to the sea and contemplating what had so nearly happened.

He thought of his mother. That was how she had died.

She said, 'Lawrence, I don't want to have a baby.'

'I realise that.'

'No, you don't understand. I've been lying to you for years.' She hesitated. 'I've been on the pill since the first year we were married.'

'What?'

'You were so hung up on having a son, all that next generation crap, I couldn't bring myself to tell you how I felt about it. Just the thought of dirty nappies and baby sick and getting up at three in the morning ... Maybe it's a hang-over from my name, but I always thought love and marriage would be more romantic than that.'

Juliet shrugged, her tone becoming defiant. 'So I went on the pill and just decided not to tell you. It seemed easier than having a row about it.'

He wanted to say something, but his mind was blank.

She made a face, banging on the rock as if to loosen the dirt beneath them. 'Okay, you're looking shocked. But if we're going to play truth or dare, perhaps we should talk about Cathy. You slept with her behind my back. You got her pregnant, for God's sake.' She shook her head in disbelief. 'Your dad's housekeeper, of all people. That flat-footed nobody. You lied to me first, Lawrence, and you can't deny it.'

Lawrence lapsed into silence. All those years of trying for a baby, and she had been on the pill without telling him. He thought back, piecing odd little details together until they made sense at last, those times she had disappeared to the clinic for a 'routine check-up', how her periods had been scant for months on end, and her lack of surprise when pregnancy tests proved consistently negative.

He studied her profile, stung by the realisation that after so many years of marriage, he barely knew his wife at all. He had mapped her body over the years, every smooth astonishing inch of it: that soft sensitive skin at the back of her knees; the tiny indentation at the base of her spine; her inverted navel, the ticklish well of her belly, which sent her giggling whenever he kissed it. But her mind was still a foreign country. He had no idea of the processes that went on behind that high shuttered forehead, what she thought of him, the plans and decisions she made without him.

Abruptly she asked, 'Do you even love me?'

Lawrence hesitated, surprising himself by having to seriously consider the question before answering. Did he still love his wife? Only a few days ago, he would have said, 'Yes,' automatically and not doubted it to be the truth. In fact, in their comfortable place in Berkhamsted, facing her across the breakfast table, he would have found the question absurd. Irrelevant, even. But here, on this desolate cliff top, his grasp on solid facts seemed to be slipping away.

'I'm not sure anymore.'

There, it had been said, and the sky had not fallen.

Lawrence looked at his wife's face, trying to gauge her reaction. Her lips pursed in a long silent whistle, clearly taken aback by the bluntness of his answer.

He asked, 'Does that bother you?'

'To be honest, it helps.'

'Is there more?'

Juliet understood instantly what he meant, giving him a tense little nod, her tongue caught between her teeth as she searched for the right words.

'I haven't been happy for a long time. I'm too restless to be anyone's wife. I can't stand the bloody routine of it. Day in, day out, always the same things in the same order.'

'In other words, you want a divorce.'

'I really don't know,' she said. 'I haven't decided yet.'

Lawrence stood up from the rock they had been sitting on, surprised by his sudden anger, and pushed through the small battered gate without looking back to see if his wife was following him. He was suspicious that Juliet had been jerking his strings for her own amusement all these years, and that hurt. The wind lifted his hair under the woollen hat as he began the steep climb back up to the car park at Cregneash. But at least it had blown away the mist and there was a pale sunshine on his back now, the sweat of exertion creeping between his shoulder blades under the borrowed anorak as he kept climbing.

From below him on the rock-strewn path, he could hear Juliet calling his name in a weary fashion, as if she considered his behaviour an over-reaction, but he didn't wait for her.

It seemed oddly appropriate to be here when his marriage fell apart, on this little island in the Irish Sea, so familiar from his childhood but still somehow alien; a place he only knew in snatches, details misplaced or rehashed by his memory as time passed, like parts of a poorly overheard conversation that he was struggling to remember years later.

Had he always known it would end like this?

Lawrence tried to remember the first impulse that had driven him into marriage; walking down a street, arm in arm with Juliet, and seeing some pregnant woman or a baby in a pushchair perhaps. Something as simple and unthought-out as that.

It had never occurred to him that Juliet might have missed both those 'signs' and seen only her own reflection in the shop windows.

Chapter Fourteen

The noise of wind rattling at the glass woke Gil with a start. He was propped up on his elbow in an armchair and the room was dark. For a moment he was confused, thinking his dream had come true, that he was back in the living-room of that small house in Summertown, waiting for his wife to give birth upstairs, then he looked up and saw the moon over the sea and remembered where he was. He must have fallen asleep at some point earlier in the evening and it had grown dark while he slept. His body was stiff from the unnatural position and Gil forced himself to stretch, wincing a little as he got unsteadily to his feet and fumbled along the wall for the light switch. The clock on the mantelpiece told him it was a few minutes past midnight.

'Where are you, Miranda?' he muttered, staring up at the moon, which looked back at him dispassionately.

He secured the old sash window, which had been left slightly open, and poured himself a small brandy from the decanter on the sideboard. Lawrence and Juliet must have gone to bed without saying goodnight. He was not surprised. The couple had been subdued tonight after coming back from their fruitless search for Miranda, heads down, not looking at each other. He suspected they must have argued while they were out. He knew the signs of a marriage in trouble only too well. And right now, they must be under tremendous stress. He and Dora had never had to weather anything so terrible as the loss of a child. Though they had still found plenty of occasions for argument.

Smiling drily, Gil thought back to that memory of his wife in the early stages of labour, her irritable snapping when she discovered there was only a little coal left in the bunker and their bedroom was bitterly cold. Dora had certainly known how to make him suffer when she was angry.

When the midwife arrived on her bicycle, resplendent in a huge red woollen coat, she had even suggested he borrow some coal from their elderly neighbours. 'You can't seriously expect your wife to give birth in these arctic conditions? At the very least, we need a warm room for when the baby comes.'

Gil had refused point-blank, too embarrassed to go begging for hand-outs in the middle of the night.

The midwife rolled up her sleeves and brutally repeated her request, a plump business-like woman in a starched white apron and low heels, 'Do you want your wife and baby to die?'

Pricked into action by such dire warnings, Gil had stumbled out into the pitch-black garden in boots and mackintosh, and gathered as much dry wood as he could find, piling it into the grate in the front bedroom and padding it out with twists of old newspaper. That was the best he was able to manage under the circumstances. Dora's father had rejected her completely after their marriage and they were surviving on his meagre income as a university lecturer. It had been barely enough to pay their rent, let alone stock up the coal bunker for winter. His makeshift fire had burnt merrily enough for the first half hour, then died to a sombre flickering glow, the midwife slipping her coat back on for warmth and Dora huddling under several layers of blankets. It had not been an easy night for any of them.

Gil sipped his brandy, glancing over the rim of the glass to see Dora curled up in the deep window seat, shaking her head at him.

'We nearly froze to death that night! You were such a boy.'

'I loathed that woman,' he said.

'She was just doing her job. You should have bought more coal.'

'What nonsense. You and Lawrence survived, didn't you?'

'Only just,' she reminded him gently.

But it had been typical of Lawrence to be born at such a desperate time, the early hours of a February morning, the streets outside their window slick with black ice and the pipes almost frozen. Gil had waited downstairs most of the night, pacing the floor in time-honoured fashion or sleeping fitfully in an armchair, trying not to listen to the terrible groans and cries from the bedroom above.

It was hard, not being able to hold Dora's hand. But the midwife had bustled him out of the room once the fire had caught and whenever he put his head round the door, disturbed by his wife's obvious difficulties, she shooed him away like a disobedient child. So he wandered about the house instead, making himself tea and trying to wash the dishes from last night's dinner in icy water. Dora had been ill for the last few weeks of her pregnancy – confined to bed with swollen ankles and a blinding migraine that came on in a flash whenever she moved – and Gil had been forced to look after the household himself, becoming quite adept at boiling down a ham bone for soup and not leaving his shirts to burn under the iron. Once a week, he even mopped the kitchen floor and scrubbed round the bath, and hoped to God none of his colleagues at the university even caught him with his pinny on.

Housework was not something Gil particularly resented. Dora was carrying his child and to him that was worth the frustrations of cooking and cleaning that followed his daily work at the college. But coal was expensive, money was scarce, and he could hardly be expected to produce a roaring fire out of thin air.

Exhausted by the long wait, Gil had only intended to sit down for a moment but had fallen asleep instead, still clutching his dishcloth.

About three o'clock in the morning, he heard a shout from upstairs and jerked guiltily awake. Dora had been calling his name in a high frantic voice for some minutes and he hadn't heard her. He leapt out of his chair and took the stairs two at a time, nearly falling several times in his hurry. The door to their bedroom was slightly ajar and he burst in, ignoring the disapproving tirade of the midwife and taking his wife's hand.

She stared up at him wildly, her eyes bulging and her face covered in a fine sheen of sweat.

'The baby's stuck, Gil. I can't push it out.'

He looked at the midwife, who avoided his eyes. 'What's happening? Is the baby all right?'

'Of course it is, Mr Cardrew. But the cord's wrapped round its neck and I need your wife to stop pushing until I can free it.'

'You hear that, Dora? The baby's going to be fine. You must do as the midwife tells you though.'

He kissed her and felt her hand grip his until he thought his bones would break under the pressure. She was obviously afraid and he seemed to catch that panic too, though he didn't dare show it on his face, his skin clammy as he straightened up. He didn't know what they would do if the baby died; it had been the centre of their world for so many months now, their only topic of conversation, the knot that had bound them irrevocably together. The midwife had pushed his wife's legs further apart under the heaving blankets and Gil suddenly thought he might disgrace himself by being sick.

He tried not to look at the blood on the midwife's hands, fixing his eyes on Dora's face instead.

'Don't push, do you understand? You mustn't push.'

But Dora seemed lost to his voice, her head thrashing on the pillows as she moaned, 'No,' and strained downwards with her eyes shut tight, her forehead creased and her cheeks bright red.

'Don't push!' the midwife repeated urgently, crouching between her legs. Her hands disappeared into that dark mysterious space under the blankets and she made a tutting noise under her breath as Dora grunted and squeezed his hand, arching her spine so far that her body weight was resting on her shoulders and feet alone. The midwife looked up irritably, her back hunched, strangely demonic in the reddish glow of the fire. There was a steely edge to her voice. 'You really must be patient, dear. It won't be long now, the cord's almost free.' She bent and fumbled under the blankets again like a Victorian photographer. After what seemed an interminable interval, she said sharply, 'Now. Push hard now.'

Dora screamed and suddenly the midwife was stepping back, lifting something in her arms like a trophy, a tiny scrap of flesh, its skin streaked with blood and a waxy substance like Brylcreem. The face contorted in a terrible grimace and then there was a thin piercing wail.

'Well done, dear.' The midwife lowered the baby in her arms, showing it to Gil as if it were a wine he had ordered. 'It's a boy.'

He looked, dazed, then the baby was gone, whisked away to the fireside where a neat pile of sheets and towels lay waiting. The midwife busied herself with them in the firelight, her movements ruthless and practised. The baby's wail intensified for a few moments as she rubbed him clean, then died to a disconsolate whimper, leaving a tightly-swaddled bundle of white cotton where his tiny face peeped out, red-raw and wide-eyed.

Gil felt his hand squeezed weakly and glanced down at Dora, concerned by her breathless pallor. 'Are you all right?' he whispered, bending close to her face, then felt a rush of emotion that almost threatened to overwhelm him. His voice sounded embarrassingly choked. 'It's a boy, Dora. Did you hear what she said? You've given me a son.'

She nodded and managed a thin smile, her fingers tightening slightly in his. When the midwife brought the baby back and arranged it in Dora's arms, Gil stared down astonished at his son's strong nose and tiny cleft chin, the huge violet eyes fixed on his mother's face. It was a face he knew intimately and his voice was high with amazement.

'My God, he looks just like my father. Look at that chin...and even his ears! It's incredible.'

The midwife smiled indulgently down at the baby, clearly satisfied with her part in the birth. She wiped her hands on her white apron, leaving reddish-brown streaks from the blood. 'I don't think we'll need to call the doctor out. He's healthy enough, considering the problems we had. Do you have a name yet?'

Dora glanced up at Gil, uncertain. 'Darling?'

'Let's call him Lawrence,' he said impulsively. 'Since he looks so much like my father, he might as well share his name.'

'Yes, that will please your parents.'

'Unless you'd rather ... ?'

Dora shook her head, 'Lawrence is perfect.'

Then the midwife clapped her hands and asked him to leave the room so she could clean his wife up and help latch baby on for its first feed. His task was to make a fresh pot of tea and a few slices of buttered toast, and bring them up on a tray when he was called for. There was no room for argument, the midwife stern again as she poured warm water into a basin from the jug on the hearth and shook out the clean towels briskly. He had played his part, but the crisis was over and a husband was no longer welcome here.

Feeling a little out of place, Gil bent to give Dora a quick reassuring kiss on the forehead before he went downstairs, then hesitated, unable to resist pulling aside the cotton wrappings to stare down into his son's face once more.

'Hello there.'

The inquisitive blue eyes shifted and met his. There was a shock, almost of recognition, and Gil stroked his cheek with one gentle finger, laughing when that hungry little mouth turned instantly at the sensation, a raspy cat-like tongue protruding, quite obviously searching for his mother's breast. His final whisper had been for his son alone, barely able to keep his voice level for the tightness in his chest.

'Happy Birthday, Lawrence.'

He had a son.

He and Dora had blithely thought there would be others, that day. More children to follow, sons and daughters, to give them joy. But then the war had come along, like a dark and impossible night of grief, and when Gil returned home, unable at first even to speak of what he had done and witnessed, Dora had suffered the first of her miscarriages.

For years, it had seemed to Gil like a punishment. For the things he had done in the war. The lives he had taken, or failed to save. But now, he decided it had been a blessing. Just one blessing on their house, to be passed on in a look or a smile or a whisper.

Chapter Fifteen

Miranda jumped down from the last tram at the Dhoon Glen stop, shouldering her rucksack and waving goodbye to the friendly conductor. She bent down and pretended to lace her trainer, carefully waiting until the electric tram had juddered out of sight before turning towards the entrance to the glen. The fewer people that realised where she was going the better.

    She hopped across the dusty tram lines, her throat dry and the late sun still warming her face. It had been something Pete said as he dropped her off in Douglas that had given her the brilliant idea of camping out at Dhoon Glen. She had told him how unhappy she was at home, and he'd said jokingly, 'Don't go drowning yourself now,' because she'd asked to be dropped near the sea terminal. It was not so long ago that the boy had tried to drown her at Dhoon Glen – though it felt more like centuries ago – and the two images had collided in her head. The glen was the ideal hideout. There were so many places along the path or down on the beach where she could camp out and live quite comfortably.

    The glen had seemed blissfully deserted as she began her long descent towards the beach, but within minutes Miranda could hear dogs barking ahead and had to dive sideways into the undergrowth to avoid being seen. She was scared the dogs might smell her, but the man with them chose that moment to throw a stick and the two black

Labradors were too busy chasing after it to notice her, crouched beside the path in the bushes. Once they had disappeared up the steps towards the car park, Miranda crept back out, pulling leaves from her hair. She would have to be more careful in future or she might be spotted and taken home again. Everything depended on her staying invisible, blending into the scenery.

She looked down critically at her jeans and white tee-shirt, now slightly grubby. It was hardly the sort of outfit which would blend seamlessly into the undergrowth. Why had she not changed into something less conspicuous before leaving home?

Miranda made a mental note to see what could be done about her clothes once she had established a base camp, then ran hurriedly down the steep zigzag of steps, this time keeping a watchful eye on the path ahead in case there were any more men with dogs. The rucksack bounced on her back, hurting her shoulders, but she kept her head up and tried to ignore it. It was such a beautiful afternoon. The sun filtered greenly through the high trees above and the stream at the bottom of the valley ran faster and louder than her feet. When she reached the rush and thunderous roar of the waterfall, she paused with a sudden dread, looking anxiously along the rocks as if she expected to see that boy there again, but of course the place was deserted. Greatly relieved, and feeling a little bit ridiculous, Miranda turned down along the path which led to the beach. They had not managed to get this far when she came with Lawrence and Juliet. From this point on, it would be solely her adventure, not theirs.

The path grew narrower as she approached the sea, its blue glittering just visible beyond the thick undergrowth as she dipped under trees and over rocks, balancing along a tiny wooden bridge placed across the stream, then swinging up again through dense bushes where the path climbed for the last time before dropping down abruptly onto a pebble beach, bleached white with great boulders. Here Miranda stopped dead and stared, gripping the painful straps of her rucksack. To her left, the sea washed gently up against the vastness of a rock as high as a cliff and yellowed like butter in the late sun. There was nobody else on the beach and even the horizon lay empty of boats. Hundreds of pebbles along the shallows dragged and grated against each other as the tide pulled slowly in and out, so calm and invitingly blue it seemed as though it had been created only for her.

The hurt she had been feeling all afternoon began to drain away in the astonishing silence. Without thinking twice about it, Miranda abandoned her rucksack and hot sweaty trainers at the mouth of the trickling stream, treading carefully over pale shifting pebbles to stand ankle-deep at last in those cool shallows.

This was what she had been looking for all her life, a real place of her own, where none of them could ever hurt her again.

The sun was beginning to set when she eventually made her way back up the beach, rather tired now and sometimes losing her footing, but certain in her heart that she had made the right decision in coming to Dhoon Glen. They would never think to look for her here, so many miles from home, practically at the other end of the island. She could try to catch some of those little darting fish she had seen in the shallows and cook them over an open fire after dark, when there was never anyone about. During the long hot days, she could hide from passers-by on the wooded slopes in the glen and read her books, lying idly under the trees.

She could even set traps for rabbits, though she wasn't sure she really liked the idea of killing and skinning them.

But before any of that, she had to choose somewhere suitable for a base camp. She glanced up and down the beach for a likely spot. It would have to be near this little stream, so that she had easy access to fresh water, but concealed enough to keep her safe from capture. That was the most important thing, because Miranda never wanted to go home again. Here she could be herself, living free and honest. At home she would have to face them all without letting on that she knew the truth about her father. She would have to smile and lie, just as they had done with her.

Relacing her trainers, she glanced up at a red glow spreading slowly across the rocks. It was getting colder as the sun sank lower towards the horizon, and she would really have to hurry if she wanted to find somewhere to sleep before it got dark.

Miranda stooped for her rucksack and cried aloud in horror. The bottom was sopping wet.

She stood there, bag dripping silently in her hand, unable to understand what had happened until she suddenly remembered throwing it hurriedly aside on her way down to the sea. The rucksack must have fallen too close to the mouth of the stream.

Fighting back the tears, Miranda squatted down in a panic beside the rocks and dragged her stuff out of the bag. The two books had been at the top, so thankfully they were still dry. Most of her other things were either damp or wet, but would be easy enough to dry in the morning. Her sleeping bag though, which had been packed tightly at the very bottom of the rucksack, was soaked through.

She shook it out despairingly, trying to dry the sodden nylon by wiping it against the pebbles at her feet. But it was useless. The sun had nearly disappeared and the wind felt cold now. There would be absolutely no chance of drying it out tonight and she had even crazily chosen to leave her anorak behind at the last minute. She had nothing but her jeans and tee-shirt to keep her warm tonight, which were both still damp after an hour of messing thoughtlessly about in the shallows like a child, unaware of her own stupidity.

She sank down on the uncomfortable pebbles and broke into tears. The sound echoed about the high rocks but it didn't matter how much noise she made, there was nobody to hear her. She was completely alone on this horrible beach and there was no one in the world who cared about her. No one who loved her. No one who would come to rescue her.

'What did I ever do that was so wrong?' she cried to the pebbles and the stream and the great trees rising like cold black spires above the glen.

Wrapping her arms around her knees and pulling herself up into a tight ball of misery, Miranda sobbed for her lost happiness.

Behind her, the sea crept inch by inch up the pebbled beach, its constant whisper eerie in the growing darkness.

Miranda opened her eyes in the chill half-light to see a small dark shape watching her, mere inches from her face. But after a few heart-racing moments, the shape blinked and she gasped with immense relief, realising it was nothing more threatening than a rabbit. Hysterical laughter rose in her but she managed to suppress it.

The animal had frozen nervously at her gasp. But when nothing else happened, its body gradually relaxed again, and the two continued watching each other in silence.

Delighted by this visitor but scared of frightening him away, Miranda lay like a fallen statue on the damp ground, her eyes gradually adjusting to the greyish light filtering down through the undergrowth. Out of the corner of her eye, she could just see a spider delicately spinning itself down out of the leaves. The intricate web above danced and jerked at each tiny movement.

Painstakingly, hardly daring to breathe, she slid her eyes back towards her visitor. The soft brown ears perked up high as the rabbit sat there in front of her, nibbling speculatively at a patch of grass under the thick bushes she had crawled into last thing at night, fully prepared to bolt if the human intruder so much as twitched another face muscle.

She had no watch, but by the pale growing light it was easy to guess that it must be about five or six o'clock in the morning. Everyone would be asleep back at the house, tucked up warmly in their beds while she lay here in the cold glen at Dhoon Glen, her whole body aching and with what felt like a stick pushing into her shoulder blades. She wondered if they'd realised she was missing yet and whether Gil was at all worried about her. She hoped he was. But it was his fault she had run away. He had lied to her. Her mother was always lying to her, so that didn't really matter, but she had trusted Gil. She had never imagined he could betray her like this.

The tears from last night came back easily into her eyes and she let them roll down her cheeks in a choking silence, not raising a hand to wipe them away in case she frightened the rabbit. If it was true and Lawrence was her real father, that could only mean that Gil was her grandfather.

So why had he hidden the truth from her?

The rabbit nibbled and watched her curiously as Miranda became locked into her misery, remembering how often Gil had talked to her about his dead wife and his son, and how important it was to be part of a family. Didn't he want to be her grandfather? She must have been a terrible disappointment to him as a grandchild, or he would never have lied to her. That was the only explanation she could come up with.

She must have made some involuntary movement, because the rabbit froze again, ears flat on its back, then darted away through the undergrowth. Left alone, Miranda crumbled under the weight of her own inadequacy and sobbed out loud. She was a disappointment and they were well rid of her.

Eventually, she ran out of energy for crying and sat up instead, blowing her nose on a torn piece of tissue she found in her jeans pocket. Then she crawled out unceremoniously from beneath the bushes, dragging her rucksack after her and pulling bits of twig and leaf from her tangled hair. The birds, who at first light had only been a faint occasional chirping in the background, began to sing in earnest as she made her way down the narrow glen path towards the stream. The sky had lightened and she could hear the sea again now, hidden just beyond the small sloping path ahead.

Miranda stood and stretched beside the shingled bank of the stream, looking up through the trees. She had never seen the dawn before. Not the exact moment when the sun came up. It was not beautiful and romantic as she had expected, but grey and chilly.

After splashing her face in the fresh running stream, she bent lower and cupped her hands to drink. The water was an icy shock but she was thirsty enough not to care, gulping it down anyway. Her throat had been so painfully dry during the night she had even dreamt about licking the cool green leaves that hung about her head in the darkness. It was the first time she had ever slept outdoors on her own.

She and Gil had gone camping a few times when she was younger, up in the hills in the south of the island, but he hadn't been well enough this last year and her mother had refused to let Miranda go on her own. She stared down at her face in the stream, surrounded by reflections of clouds and trees, shifting into strange unpredictable patterns whenever she dipped her fingers into the water and then steadying again into a perfect mirror while she drank.

It felt a bit odd, being entirely alone for so many hours and not having anyone to talk to. Miranda wondered if people who were permanently cut off from the world, like hermits or castaways on desert islands, actually lost the power of speech in the end.

Perhaps she ought to talk to herself every now and then, in case she forgot how to.

'Hello,' she said experimentally to her reflection. 'Did you sleep well? No, actually, I'm afraid not. I was freezing and now there are probably spiders in my hair.'

Suddenly, on the still morning air, she heard the sound of a car engine on the road high above the glen.

Miranda scrambled to her feet, wiping her wet hands on her jeans, and listened hard to the sound of the car. No one could possibly be coming to look for her yet. Though if they did, she would be ready to bolt for shelter. There was no way they were taking her back to that house.

But the car didn't stop. Whoever it was kept going on towards Douglas, the engine droning gradually into silence.

After a few minutes she relaxed again, and knelt to refill her water bottle from the stream. Then she shouldered her rucksack with a sigh and began to follow the narrow path back towards the beach. By the gradually darkening clouds coming from the west, Miranda guessed it might rain later today. She had at least an hour or so before anyone was likely to come down into the glen, and it was vital that she found a drier and more comfortable place to hide.

She had been right about the change in the weather. By the time Miranda had eaten her meagre ration of sticky toffees and biscuits, perched like a bird on one of the white boulders facing the sea, a few drops of rain had already started to fall. But she had spotted an overgrown path on her left leading away from the beach, and as soon as she had packed away her things after breakfast, she began the steep climb in search of a better hiding place.

 The path took her up beside the huge rock she had seen yesterday evening and then wound its way tightly around the cliff until it opened out onto an uneven grassy slope, dotted with small greyish-white boulders, overlooking the sea. From here Miranda could no longer be seen from the beach, and in this weather it was unlikely that anyone would come walking up such a tricky path.

 She stopped to catch her breath after the long climb, sitting cross-legged on the grass and blinking the soft rain out of her eyes. Far out on the misty line of the horizon there was a small fishing-boat, almost exactly like the ones which regularly put out from Port St Mary harbour with a flock of greedy screeching seagulls in their wake. The boat was heading north-east away from the island, making good speed in the pale early light.

 Watching it with a sudden burst of nostalgia, she decided to set up camp right there on the cliff so she could watch the boats sail past and listen to the cry of the seagulls.

Finding a narrow dryish cleft in the rock not far from the path, Miranda draped her sleeping bag over the top and weighted it down with stones. Then she gathered handfuls of long rough grasses and prickly gorse, laying them carefully over the damp sleeping bag and around the low entrance as a form of camouflage. From a distance it looked reasonably natural and she stood back to admire it for a moment, pleased with her efforts.

Her hands were still quite sore from picking the yellow gorse and she spent a few minutes pulling its tiny thorns out of her skin before gathering more of the long seed-headed grasses to make a soft bed inside her den. By the time she had finished that job, the rain had started to fall more heavily. Miranda dragged her rucksack inside and started to unpack, cautiously allowing herself another sticky toffee as a reward for such hard work. Arranging her food stores in a dry area at the back of the crevice, she realised there were only about a dozen toffees left in the tin and even fewer biscuits. She would have to be much stricter with herself from now on, because after seeing that rabbit this morning, she didn't think she could bring herself to eat one. Though she imagined her squeamishness might well disappear once she was starving enough.

She took out *Teach Yourself Astronomy* and flicked through it, hoping to find the star patterns she had seen the night before. But everything looked more difficult to understand on the page than it had done in the sky, so Miranda lay down on her stomach instead and watched the rain drip gently off the edge of the sleeping bag.

She was feeling cold and hungry now. But at least it was dryish here in her little den, and there was the constant and achingly familiar hiss of the sea below to keep her company.

After a while, she opened *A Wizard of Earthsea* to the last chapter – her absolute favourite, where Ged chases across the dead waters after his Shadow – and began to read.

Chapter Sixteen

Miranda pulled her knees to her chest and cradled herself for warmth, sitting in the mouth of the crevice as she listened to the wind drag and jerk at the sleeping-bag which formed the roof of her shelter. It was getting cold, the sun had nearly disappeared for the third day in a row, and she was utterly starving. She had finished the last of her biscuits yesterday and there was only one sticky toffee left, strictly for use in emergencies. That last toffee was even stickier than the others though, as she had already taken it out of its plastic wrapper several times and licked at it speculatively, savoring the sweet thick taste on her tongue before wrapping it up again and replacing it in the tin.

Occasionally Miranda would simply pick up the tin and rattle it, satisfied by the knowledge that the last toffee was still in there, waiting to be eaten. For she knew that while she possessed it, while she had that last toffee to fall back on, this terrible seige could not break her spirit.

'Courage, lads. Our supplies aren't out yet.' Miranda imagined their bellies tight with hunger, the starving faces of the crew gathered around her in the half-light, their eyes fixed on the tin with its tiny rattling treasure. 'A guinea to the first man to catch us a rabbit.'

They scattered in every direction to take up her challenge, tall thin shadows creeping across the cliff in the dusk and her dry mouth watered at the thought of a rabbit, stripped down to its flesh and roasted on a spit over some crackling fire, blood sizzling into the flames. But she was alone in the gathering darkness, and the make-shift traps she had set yesterday - crude little holes with sharpened sticks at the bottom - had all been empty when she checked them late this afternoon.

It was then that she heard the unmistakable sound of somebody whistling. It came from far below her cliff hide-out, high and clear, and soon she could hear feet skidding on the sharp rocky incline at the end of the glen. Miranda sat up in a sudden rush of alarm, her arms dropping from her knees and all thoughts of roasting rabbits gone. She recognised that noise perfectly well, having made it often enough herself, misjudging the steepness of that path at night. Somebody must be stumbling down through the glen towards the beach.

Miranda crawled out from under her low-slung sleeping bag, most of its ragged camouflage of gorse and long grasses lost in the strong winds that afternoon. She crouched on the rough cliff, listening to every sound from below as whoever it was approached the beach. It was unlikely, in this darkness, that anyone would tackle the narrow path that ran up beside this rock and came out close to her hiding-place, but she had to be prepared to take action if they did. What form that action might take she wasn't sure, but running for cover was probably her safest bet.

Something in the damp grass stung her palms. Miranda shifted position slightly, suspecting it to be one of those spiky little plants that grew in patches along the cliff, not quite nettles but almost as prickly. It was useless, crouching here on the cliff like a scared rabbit. The vast rock that loomed above the beach was blocking her view and she badly needed to see who it was and what they were doing before deciding how to react.

Returning to her shelter, she quickly located the long branch she had been sharpening earlier. Using the Swiss army knife that Lawrence had lent her, she had spent much of that afternoon stripping its leaves and bark, squatting at the back of the crevice and pretending to be a caveman, but she had not yet finished bringing the end to a good sharp point. It was intended for fishing in the shallows, but it suddenly occurred to her that it might make a good weapon. She wasn't certain she could actually stick it into someone, even in self-defense, but it might look threatening enough to keep an attacker at a distance. Searching for the knife again in her rucksack, she unfolded one of the bigger blades and rapidly cut a few more splinters of wood away from the tip until it felt sharp enough to break flesh.

Armed with her freshly sharpened stick, Miranda crept round the edge of the rock and followed the path down a little way towards the beach, though not so far that she was in any danger of being spotted.

In the thickening darkness, every bush and rock along the path seemed threatening, though most of them were familiar to her now and she tried to steady her nerves by greeting each one as she passed it. Thorn bush shaped like a stooping old man. 'Hello.' Odd knobbly rock to her left. 'Hello.' Strange cluster of grasses that bent in the wind with a vaguely sinister rustling sound. 'Hello.'

The moon came out for a moment, on the turn between full and waning, and she could see her way rather better. Then the path narrowed around the rock and Miranda had to squeeze through a straggling group of stunted gorse bushes, tortured by the sea winds into bizarre prickly shapes. They always looked like little people to her, crouched in the grass on either side of the path, ready to spring out and abduct her if she didn't acknowledge them. It was never wise to ignore the little people so she said, 'Hello,' and moved on politely, though their wizened shapes seemed rather less menacing tonight than usual. She suspected it was because the stick looked so strong and heavy in her hand. Even the little people wouldn't want something like this landing on their heads.

At first, she thought the beach was empty.

Then a cracking sound alerted her to the fact that someone was down there, close to the mouth of the stream that trickled down from the glen, their shadowy figure moving slowly about amongst the rocks. From the slim-hipped outline and the way they held themselves, she thought it must be a man, or possibly a boy. Miranda frowned, cautiously dropping and flattening herself to the damp earth as the cracking sound came again, louder this time.

What was he doing?

A few moments passed in silence while she lay there, then a light flared out in the darkness and she realised angrily what the cracking sound had been. He must have discovered her hidden store of driftwood near the stream and was cheerfully lighting a fire with it. She sat up, staring at his pale face lit up by the growing flames.

It was a boy. In his late teens she guessed, dressed in shabby jeans and a dirty-looking denim jacket. There was something horribly familiar about him.

Then Miranda suddenly realised who he was. Her palms grew clammy with fear, and she shrank back into the rough grass, clutching at her stick for courage. It was the boy who had tried to drown her that day in the glen, holding her head under the water until Lawrence leapt in and chased him away.

It was stupid to be so afraid. He hadn't seen her and she was safe enough here, hidden by a darkness far beyond the circle of his fire.

Miranda reminded herself that this was her secret place, her home, and he was the intruder. She grasped her stick and crept closer over the shifting pebbles of the beach, careful to make as little noise as possible. Once within throwing distance of his camp, she crouched down behind a largish white boulder and craned her neck round to keep an eye on what he was doing.

The boy had shaken his sleeping bag out on the grass bank near the stream and now, whistling to himself again, he was carrying something back down towards the smoking fire; a large backpack, from which he produced a frying pan, a packet of what looked like sausages, and a bottle of pop.

Much to her amusement, he slipped on the pebbles as he stooped over the fire, nearly losing his balance and falling into the flames. The boy righted himself with an effort and swore explosively, bending to rub his right ankle. He had obviously hurt himself. His exclamation echoed around the enclosed beach and the boy straightened, glancing straight up at the rocks where she was hiding.

Miranda shrank back behind her boulder and held her breath. She tested the point of her stick again on her finger: sharp.

The possibility crossed her mind that she could wait until he was asleep and then sneak down in the darkness to spear him through his sleeping bag. But that wasn't fair tactics, even if he had played dirty himself. For all Miranda knew, the stupid boy hadn't meant to drown her that day. It might have been a joke, as he told Lawrence at the time. Though that was no excuse. It had been a pretty pathetic joke.

He had the frying pan balanced on two large stones now, right above the flames. Then he rummaged for the little greaseproof packet and tore it open.

She watched, her mouth watering uncontrollably, as he laid one, two, three, four, five and then six fat sausages in the hot pan. The glorious sound of sizzling filled the air almost immediately and soon Miranda could even smell the meat itself, crisping in the heat. Her stomach rumbled so loudly she bit her lip and pressed down frantically on her belly, hoping he couldn't hear it from where he stood. But the boy seemed completely unaware of her presence. He was kneeling near the fire, jiggling the pan occasionally and taking long swigs from his bottle of pop. His face was lit up by the flames, almost devilish in the darkness, and he kept whistling in that irritating tuneless way.

Miranda could hardly bear to watch this feast being prepared when she was close to starvation herself, but she couldn't bring herself to move. The sight of sausages frying in a pan was simply too mesmerizing. She wished he was someone else – anyone else in the world would do – because then she could go down and politely ask to share his supper.

But he was the boy who had tried to drown her.

Then a miracle happened. The boy stood up, poked the sausages with a little stick to check how they were cooking, then picked his way carefully over the pebbles down towards the sea. Miranda watched him go in silent astonishment, mentally measuring the distance between her boulder and the camp fire.

The fool had left his sausages unattended. He stood at the edge of the outgoing tide and stared out to sea, fumbling with his jeans.

She had to stifle a little giggle, suddenly realising that he was peeing into the water.

But this was her chance.

Praying the sound of the waves would cover any noise she might make, Miranda balanced swiftly across the shifting pebbles to the camp fire. In a flash, she had bent over the six sausages in the pan and, using her sharpened stick, speared three of them in rapid succession, as many as would fit onto the pointed end before the wood grew too thick. Then she turned and ran back unevenly to her boulder, the oddly top-heavy stick waving in front of her like a trophy, pierced sausages dripping hot fat down the stick and onto her wrist.

By the time she reached safety and dropped back into the shadows, her heart thudding like crazy, the boy had finished peeing and started back up the beach.

He stood over the fire for a moment, then kicked the discarded wrapper as if checking that he had put all six sausages into the pan. His hands went to his hips, he raised his head and looked around the dark deserted beach. In the leaping firelight, the bewildered frown on his face was clearly visible.

His gaze swivelled in her direction, as though he knew she was there.

Miranda pulled back instantly, still holding the stolen sausages aloft as she flattened herself against the large boulder. Part of her wanted to giggle, remembering the boy's confused reaction - standing motionless above the frying pan, staring down at his remaining sausages as if they were about to jump up and explain what had happened to the other three - but there was no sound on the beach except the grate of waves over pebbles, and she knew he would hear if she laughed and come furiously hunting. So she stayed completely still and silent until she heard the boy muttering to himself, and then a sharp crunching of pebbles away to her right.

Thinking he had given up and settled down again in front of his fire, Miranda risked a quick look round the boulder and nearly dropped the sausages in horror when she saw him advancing on her hiding-place.

There was no time to panic. She reached down with her left hand and scrabbled about for a largish pebble. Then she threw it under-arm through the night air, awkwardly and too high to go any respectable distance, hearing it land with a clatter halfway between her and the water's edge. It was what Gil would have scathingly called a 'girl's throw', but it had the right effect. The boy's head swung at the sound and he immediately began to struggle across the beach towards the spot where the pebble fell, stumbling and cursing in the darkness, leaving her free to dart back up the narrow cliff path to the safety of her hide-out.

She nearly lost the sausages twice as she ran, even tearing her jeans on the unfriendly gorse bushes, but she reached the top without any obvious sign of pursuit. Pausing breathlessly before she was out of sight of the beach, Miranda looked back and caught a glimpse of him scouring the bushes near where she had been hiding. He must have heard her escaping. But it was clear that he had no idea which way the thief had gone.

Miranda staggered on towards her dark little shelter and crawled inside, devouring two of the warm sausages while still on her hands and knees, fatty juices running down her chin in an ecstasy of greed. She didn't think she had ever eaten something so delicious.

With a supreme effort of will, she licked her fingers clean and slipped the last greasy sausage into the toffee tin for her breakfast. Then she lay down on her side, unable to stop laughing at the thought of his fury. The stupid boy was probably still searching the beach for her. Too sleepy to worry about the consequences of her revenge, Miranda snuggled into the dry grasses of her bed and allowed her eyes to close.

He had tried to drown her and she had stolen his dinner. Now they were even.

Chapter Seventeen

It was hard not to look for Miranda everywhere he went. Pounding the stony ground in tracksuit and trainers, Lawrence turned right at the end of the unmade track and swung steadily up a path that he knew ran beside the sea for half a mile or so before turning back on itself and leading back towards his father's house. And as he ran, his gaze scoured the pebble beach below, the cliff edge, every bush and hiding place along the way.

But of course there was never any sign of her. It was as though the girl had flown away like a caged bird finally escaping its prison.

The early light was growing stronger now and his legs were getting tired, though he was pleased that he had bullied himself into going on this run. It was so beautiful here in the misty dawn and he could feel the stress of the past few days gradually loosening from his neck and shoulders. Lawrence snatched a deep breath and raised his head for one last punishing effort as the path steepened. He could remember this place from his youth, ambling cheerfully along with his mother, the path narrowing so much at times so they were forced to walk single file. After the age of about ten, their summer holidays had always been spent here, on the southern coast of the Isle of Man, far from the noisy streets he was used to back home. There had been few cars on the road in those days, the air clean and salty. The sea and sky had seemed almost indivisible to

Lawrence as a child, a blinding blue mass in which the harsh outlines of seagulls wheeled menacingly against the sun, like fighter planes from the war.

There was another track further back along the bay, overgrown with yellow gorse and leading down to a deserted cove that he remembered well. His mother would sit on the rocks there, reading a library book while he stumbled about in the shallows, trousers rolled up to his knees, throwing stones as far as he could into the dizzying water or searching for the pale formless transparencies of jellyfish.

Lawrence smiled, suddenly recalling how an unexpected wave had once knocked him head-over-heels and he had scrambled to his feet, yelling hysterically for his mother, his trousers soaked and dripping. She had come running at once, half laughing, half sympathetic. That was one of his earliest memories of the island, he realised, the panic and discomfort of that sunny afternoon; he couldn't have been much more than eleven or twelve at the time, a quiet child, often staying close to his mother.

His grandfather had disapproved of that clinginess early on, always pinching his cheek and telling him to stand up straight. 'That's not how a Cardrew acts.' But his grandfather had never come to the island with them and Lawrence had revelled in those lazy unsupervised days, able to read or sketch rough drawings of the coastline without being forced to play cricket or some other energetic game.

He reached a wooden stile bordering his father's lands and paused for breath before climbing over it and dropping down into the short rough grass. There was no one to see him take the short cut across near vertical fields to where his father's house stood, jogging more gently as he warmed down.

He walked more slowly down the drive, hands on hips, only to be brought up short by the sight of a police car outside the front door. DS Quine and WPC Faragher were just getting out, their faces sombre in the early light.

'Is there news of Miranda?' he asked, hurrying to reach them before they could ring the bell. 'I don't know if Cathy is up yet. What is it? Have you found the girl?'

'Not yet.'

'Well, something must have happened or you wouldn't be here.'

The detective looked at him. The heavy lids flickered as he took in Lawrence's tracksuit and grass-stained trainers, his tone mildly ironic. 'I didn't have you down as the athletic type. Been far?'

'Far enough to get a sweat up.' As he stared back at the detective, uncomfortably aware that he was still somehow under suspicion, WPC Faragher turned and rang the door bell. Lawrence strode past them impatiently; he pushed open the unlocked door and invited them both inside. 'Come in, we can talk in the kitchen. But please don't make too much noise. My father's probably still asleep and I'd rather not disturb him if it's at all possible.'

'Why's that, Mr Cardrew?'

'My father is not in the best of health. He suffered a stroke earlier this year. Did nobody tell you?'

'It was mentioned, sir.'

He led them through the green louvre doors into the kitchen and was surprised to see Cathy there, on the phone. She turned as Lawrence came in and looked at DS Quine over his shoulder, speaking rapidly to whoever it was on the other end. 'Look, I've got to ring off. The police are here. Yes, call me back later. Okay. Love you, bye for now.'

She hung up the phone with a guilty air. 'That was my sister, Cheryl. She lives in Spain. She rang me, of course, I wouldn't dream of making a long-distance call without permission.' Her voice became more nervous and agitated as she stared at the police. 'But what is it? Have you found Miranda? She's dead, isn't she? Oh my God, she's dead!'

'Now, don't get yourself upset,' the detective said soothingly while the pretty WPC put her arm around Cathy's shoulders and led her to a chair. 'It's nothing like that. We've had a possible break-through, that's all.'

Lawrence stared. 'A break-through?'

'You remember the red van that was seen picking up a girl of Miranda's description near where her bike was found? Well, the driver of that van came into the station last night. He claims he saw her picture on the front page of the Examiner and recognised her immediately. We spent some hours questioning him and it all seems perfectly innocent. He says he dropped her off in Douglas near the sea terminal at about three o'clock that afternoon, and he doesn't have any idea where she was going after that.'

'But he's obviously lying. Did you check his van? I mean he could be keeping her somewhere. In his house, perhaps.' Cathy had become hysterical, a rapid flush spreading along her cheekbones. 'What's this man's name? Where does he live?'

'I'm sorry, that's confidential information.'

'But you didn't let him go?'

DS Quine looked irritated. 'I can assure you, Miss Maddrell, we have no reason to believe this man is lying.'

Lawrence frowned, leaning over the sink to pour himself a glass of cold water, his mouth dry as paper from the long run.

'You say he dropped her off at the sea terminal? So you think she may have left the island?'

'Oh my God,' Cathy said shakily.

The detective pulled out a spindle-backed chair for himself. 'May I sit down? Thank you. I didn't get much sleep last night, as you can imagine.' He made himself comfortable and laid his hands flat on the kitchen table, watching them both. 'Now, let's not leap to conclusions. There's nothing to suggest that she's left the island. We've spoken to the Steam Packet staff and none of them saw her boarding the ferry either that afternoon or evening. Luckily though, we have another witness who rang in first thing this morning, a woman who says she may have seen a girl of your daughter's description boarding the electric tram in Douglas. Unfortunately, any other people on the tram would probably have been holiday makers, and we haven't been able to talk to the driver yet. He's gone to Liverpool for a few days and no one seems to know where he's staying. But we're making enquiries. Hopefully we'll get hold of him within about twenty-four hours.'

'The electric tram?'

DS Quine nodded at him. 'It runs from Douglas to Ramsey.'

'So she may be in Ramsey?'

'Possibly, sir, or she may have disembarked anywhere along that route. We're got officers checking that out now.' He turned to Cathy. 'Miss Maddrell, does your daughter know anyone in the north of the island? A friend, perhaps? Or someone in the family that she could have been going to visit?'

She blinked. 'No, there's nobody we know up north.'

'Okay.'

The detective pulled at his lower lip and made a thoughtful, 'Mmm,' noise under his breath, staring out of the kitchen window at the mist rising from the lawns. He tapped on the table for a moment, then felt in his pocket for a notebook and scribbled something in it. His large balding forehead had developed an almost plastic sheen under the strip lighting.

Lawrence watched him in silence, grimly suspicious that the policeman wasn't telling them everything he knew.

He wondered for a moment whether Miranda had already been found and that this was some sort of test, primarily aimed at himself as the potential abductor, then dismissed the idea as ridiculous. If they really suspected him, they would have dragged him off to their police station by now and grilled him for hours. They would hardly be tormenting the girl's mother like this.

Putting down his notebook, DS Quine continued, 'There is just one other thing before I go. We've been trying to establish what I like to call the whys and wherefores of Miranda's disappearance, and I'm afraid we've drawn a blank. Normally, you see, there's a pretty clear-cut reason why a child of her age should suddenly decide to run away from home.' The policeman sighed exaggeratedly as he tilted back in his chair, his expression sympathetic. 'Arguments, accidents, misunderstandings. You know the sort of thing that can upset a young girl. But in this case there doesn't appear to be a reason, and that bothers me.'

'What do you mean?' Cathy said angrily. 'What are you saying? That we drove her away?'

'I'm not pointing any fingers, Miss Maddrell. God knows, kids can be unpredictable sometimes. I've a few of my own and I'll be the first to admit they aren't always plain sailing.' He smiled. 'But just to clarify matters, you told us in your original statement that Miranda had no reason to run away from home, that she was perfectly happy here?'

'That's right!'

'Okay, understood. My problem is, it's been suggested to us that she wasn't happy.'

'Who said that?'

'That's not important right now. What's important is that we find your daughter as soon as possible. So perhaps you could cast your mind back to the day she disappeared, and try to remember whether anything out of the ordinary may have happened to upset her?'

For a while nobody said anything. The detective continued to watch them with his brows knitted together in a frown while Cathy struggled for composure, her eyes filling up with tears, and Lawrence leant against the fridge door with his arms folded. She reached for some tissues on the windowsill and shook her head, but there was something unconvincing about her hunched shoulders and defensive expression that made him wonder what Cathy was hiding from the policeman and why. As for himself, Lawrence could remember with perfect clarity everything that had happened the day she disappeared: that sunlit walk along the harbour, with Miranda skipping ahead; their solemn discussion about the ethics of fishing; the bucket sloshing salt water over his trousers on their way home; the odd look in her eyes when he caught her leaving – a look of desperate unhappiness, he realised now – poised on her bike as if it was about to carry her to the ends of the earth; Cathy standing in front of him on that moonlit path beside the bay, admitting at last that Miranda was his daughter.

But none of that could help them.

If the detective was right and something had upset Miranda, it must have happened during the two or three hour time span between their trip to the beach and when he caught her wheeling her bike out of the garage, a time he had spent first eating lunch and later wandering the gardens alone.

But perhaps Cathy knew more than he did, because she had risen from her chair in an agitated fashion and was pacing the kitchen.

'She must have overheard us talking. That's the only explanation. But the study door was shut, I swear it.' Cathy drew a shaky breath. 'I shut it myself. And we were speaking quietly. There was no way she could have overheard.'

'Overheard what exactly?'

Cathy looked at the detective, then suddenly at Lawrence, her face flushing with guilt. 'I was talking to Gil ... Mr Cardrew, I mean ... about Miranda's future. It was after lunch and we were in his study. I thought Miranda was playing outside, but she must have been in the house and heard what we were saying.'

DS Quine sighed impatiently, 'And what were you saying about her future, Miss Maddrell? Just take your time.'

Straightening up from the fridge, Lawrence stared at her, realising belatedly what she was about to confess and feeling a pulse jerk at his throat. It might no longer be a secret, his one mistake, his mindless adultery, but he was still horrified by the idea of having it spoken aloud in this room, to these strangers. He had admitted his past error, held up his hands and probably paid the price of his marriage for it, but his guilt was not for public consumption, for God's sake. This was something that should be kept in the family.

Lawrence fixed his eyes on her face, her trembling parted lips, silently willing her not to carry on. But Cathy avoided the simmering fury of his gaze, sitting down again in front of the policeman, clearly determined to lay their family bare in the false belief that this betrayal might somehow help her daughter.

'We were talking about Miranda's father.'

'But I thought ... No, never mind.' The detective opened his notebook again and nodded encouragingly at her. 'Right, go on. So who is her father?'

'He is,' she whispered, and pointed at Lawrence.

The silence in the bright kitchen was electrifying. Lawrence was unable to bear the raised stares of first the detective and then the WPC, their suspicion written on their faces.

'Excuse me,' he said abruptly, turning to leave.

'Now, sir, if you would just wait a minute – '

Angry now, ignoring the detective, Lawrence pushed through the green louvre doors into the cool dark passageway beyond. From there, he trod lightly to his father's study and rapped at the door.

There was no answer, so he assumed the old man must still be in bed. He wasn't sure what he would have said if he had found his father there anyway. 'Come and stop Cathy, she's telling on me,' would have been too petulant and child-like.

Frustrated, Lawrence wandered down the hallway into the dining area, its dark wood panelling and sombre oil paintings suddenly oppressive where they had once seemed stately and calming. The police had not followed him out of the kitchen, which meant Cathy was still talking to them, spilling the beans onto the grubby pages of their notebooks. There was nothing he could do but wait for the humiliating interrogation that would undoubtedly follow her confession.

He examined the polished surface of his black shoes, ran an experimental finger along the open keys of the piano, stared out of the bay windows towards the bluebell wood, empty of flowers now until next spring, sinking at last into the high-backed carver at one end of the dining table and resting his hands on its scrolled arms like a prisoner awaiting execution.

The heavy oak door to the living-room was firmly closed, but from inside he could hear the clock on the mantelpiece strike the hour. His father should be downstairs by now. It wasn't like him to linger in bed much beyond half past eight. In fact, during his childhood, his father had been up and dressed by six or seven in the morning most days, though he had no need to leave for the college until much later. His father had always been restless, late to bed and an early riser, his constant saying, 'Plenty of time for sleep when I'm dead.' But today there was no sound from upstairs, except the faint creaking of floorboards directly above his chair where Juliet must be wandering about their bedroom, slowly getting dressed.

He hoped Juliet would delay her entrance until at least after the police had gone. There would be no surprises for her, of course, but it would be a difficult moment for them both if he was being questioned about his relationship with Cathy when his wife stumbled down for her strong coffee and first cigarette of the day. Then he heard the rattle of the louvre doors being opened and the deep tones of DS Quine echoing along the passageway.

Lawrence jumped to his feet, suddenly desperate to avoid their prurient questions and sneering looks.

Why should he hang around like an accused man in an interview room, waiting to be grilled by the local police? He was guilty of nothing but being lied to for years.

Lawrence dived into the living-room and closed the heavy door behind him, leaning against the oak to listen for their voices. The central light must have been left on from the night before and he snapped it off without thinking, preferring the darkness. It was a slightly ludicrous position to be in though, rather like a kid playing a game of hide-and-seek. But the living-room was quiet and shady now, curtains half drawn against the early sunlight, and he felt calm returning to him as the minutes passed and the hall remained silent. They must have gone the other way, along the narrow tiled corridor towards the front porch, which meant the police had finished and were leaving. The relief was incredible.

Lawrence straightened and stepped back from the door, turning into the centre of the room. Then he became aware there was a man half-sitting, half-lying in the deep leather armchair near the window.

He was taken aback at first, thinking it must be some friend of his father's who had spent the night there and not sure whether to tiptoe out again or announce his presence. But then, his eyes gradually adjusting to the dim light, Lawrence realised it was his father. Still dressed in yesterday's clothes, the maroon corduroys with his favourite green cardigan, badly worn and with some of its buttons missing, the old man didn't respond when he discreetly cleared his throat and stepped closer to the chair.

His father seemed to be asleep. His knees were together and he had slumped forward over the chair arm, one slippered foot sticking out at an odd angle.

'Dad?'

But there was no answer. Lawrence crept to his father's side and knelt on the carpet, feeling for a pulse in the wrist dangling limply over the side of the chair. It was a moment he had always dreaded arriving, never quite sure how he would react, afraid it might prove too much for him. But now that the moment was at hand, he didn't lose control, his breathing even and unhurried, his gaze lingering thoughtfully on the man beside him as he waited for a pulse which might no longer exist. But he felt something there. Sluggish, but undoubtedly a pulse.

He knelt up and peered carefully into that unconscious face, white as paper, noting the mouth dragged down to the left and the skin around it rucked up like cold porridge. His left shoulder was hunched and it was the left foot which had turned so curiously inwards.

Lawrence said, 'Don't worry, Dad, I'll get help,' though he had no idea whether the old man could hear him or not.

He scrambled to his feet, thinking rapidly now, then made the difficult decision to leave his father alone, hoping to catch the police before they could leave. There was no sign of Juliet yet. The front door stood wide open, a warm breeze blowing through the empty corridors.

DS Quine and the young WPC were standing outside by their police car in the misty sunlight, still talking to Cathy, whose arms were folded defensively across her chest, her lips pursed as she listened and nodded. All three turned in surprise as Lawrence came towards them at a run.

'Could you call an ambulance, please?' he said urgently. 'I think my father's had another stroke.'

The boat swayed gently but relentlessly on the swell of the tide, cradling Gil as he lay swaddled in warmth. He could hear seagulls cry and the low murmur of his mother's voice somewhere far above his closed lids. It was an old lullaby she was singing, perhaps. He was asleep in his mother's arms as she paced back and forth on the deck of a small boat, waves dashing occasionally against the sides, he could hear them now, and he suddenly remembered how the bright sunlight had hurt his eyes.

'Hush, hush,' his mother kept saying, 'You're going to be fine. We're nearly there now.'

The seagulls were still screeching invisibly above, louder and louder, following the boat into harbour. It was summer, and he was still a small child, listening to the shouts of the fishermen as they heaved on the ropes, the ties of a tiny lace bonnet scratching his hot cheeks.

His mother's voice was soft in his ear, soothing him as the boat rocked against the harbour walls. He struggled to reach his mouth with his thumb, desperate for comfort, but the tight blankets had bound his arms by his sides and his face broke into misery, crying aloud. 'Poor baby. Poor little man,' he longed to hear his mother say again, but her words seemed lost in the noisy clatter and bustle of the harbour.

Then someone lifted him out of her warm arms and he was floating in mid-air, terrified that he might fall, his eyes jerking abruptly open.

The blonde nurse paused, gripping the rail of his white stretcher as they lifted it down from the double ambulance doors, and smiled at him reassuringly. Behind the neatly starched cap on her head Gil caught a jumbled glimpse of hospital signs and the dazzle of sunlight on plate glass before the stretcher tilted and they were moving again under a white and grey canopy.

'Don't worry, Mr Cardrew,' the nurse said cheerfully. 'You've been taken ill, but you're at the hospital now and we're going to take good care of you.'

His voice didn't seem to work any more but he tried the word again, watching her face, his tongue heavy as lead. 'Lawrence.'

'Your son's on his way. Now lie still and relax.'

The ceilings flickered past in a blur of white tiles and door frames. Taken ill? He struggled to remember what had happened but there was nothing there to fall back on. He had been sitting in his armchair in the living-room, not reading, not sleeping, simply watching the hands of the mantelpiece clock tick steadily through into the early hours of the morning. Then, almost seamlessly, as if one time had clicked quite naturally into another, Gil had been back on his uncle's fishing boat, his father dangling him over the sides to see the waves and his mother hysterical in the background. 'Give him back to me, Lawrence, please. He's only a baby.'

Then the white spray and the sunshine slipped away, and he was being wrapped in tight blankets, his mother's lips on his forehead under the scratchy bonnet. 'My poor baby. Poor thing. Did Daddy scare my little man?' In the fierce blue sky above, the endless cry of the gulls.

He hadn't even realised that early memory existed, locked for nearly seven decades in the treasure-house of his mind – assuming it existed at all and was not merely a fabrication of old age, some unconscious desire to see his mother and father again.

Gil felt the stretcher stop and opened his eyes to see the backs of nurses crossing in front of him. The blonde nurse said something to a white-coated doctor and vanished back along the corridor. Why was he at the hospital? He didn't feel ill, he felt tired. His limbs were too heavy to move and his mouth was oddly numb, as if he had just come back from the dentist's surgery.

He remembered that other time, finding himself on the floor of his study in a daze and Miranda standing over him, her voice strangely adult in its tones of concern, 'Are you all right, Gil?'

He hadn't been able to speak then either. They had taken him to the hospital, but the symptoms had nearly disappeared by the following evening and he had been home again within a week. *No more butter*, the doctor had said, or some such nonsense.

There was a sharp stinging sensation in his arm and he tried to jerk it away but they must have strapped him in. That infuriated him. There was no reason for him to be here. Miranda was still missing, he had things to do.

'Sharp scratch from the needle. Don't try to move, sir.'

He wanted to answer that disembodied female voice, which had come from somewhere behind his head, but a phone was ringing and he became confused again, tumbling back into the half-light.

'Dora?'

Her face swam into view, smiling under the neat brows and smoothed-back hair, and Gil felt a jolt of recognition.

He said thankfully, 'Take me home, darling. There's nothing wrong with me, I'm just a little tired,' and only realised afterwards that his mouth had not moved. But he still knew it was his wife, standing there in the immaculate nurse's uniform. He met her eyes pleadingly.

'Hush,' she said. 'Don't wake the baby.'

Gil looked down and suddenly saw the little bundle in her arms, stirring slightly as she rocked him to and fro. The perfect hands opened and clenched back into fists at the sound of her voice. The baby could only be a few months old, blue veins showing through the fine dark hair on his scalp, the image of his grandfather, sleeping now with those huge pale lids closed over his violet eyes. The tiny chest rose and fell in regular, almost imperceptible motion.

Lawrence Cardrew, Junior. His whole life lay ahead of him like an open road: no mistakes yet, nothing decided, nothing set in stone.

'I'm sorry,' he said to both of them, his wife and sleeping son, and knew that it was inadequate.

Chapter Eighteen

It was late afternoon and Miranda was high up in the glen, her elbows propping her chin so she could read *A Wizard of Earthsea* from the beginning again, lying on her belly under the trees where a strong golden light still filtered down through the leaves like honey dripping from a comb, when she heard the raised voices and sat up to listen.

They were coming along the path a few hundred yards from where she lay hidden, loud male voices arguing with each other and occasional giggles from what were obviously girls. They had local accents, kicking loose stones into the undergrowth as they hurried past her hiding-place. Probably just some kids heading down for a swim before sundown, though there was a nagging familiarity about some of their voices.

She dismissed them as uninteresting and returned to her book, soon lost in the story again, following Ged as he served his long apprenticeship to the Mage of Re Albi, Ogion the Silent. Time passed, and the voices she had heard were forgotten. She became the story, in fact, and walked beside Ged through the long stretches of the night, no longer aware that the sun still shone for her. Ages later – she had no idea how long it had been since she first started reading – Miranda drew a sharp wondering breath, craning her neck to stare up into the flickering golden leaves.

She tried to remember when she had last spoken to anyone – except her shadow men, who didn't really count –

and whether she too would lose the power of speech if she stayed here long enough, cut off from the world. It seemed such a long way in the past, her other life: that cosy room in the attic where she kept her books and most precious possessions; her mother in the kitchen, snapping at her about something while elbow-deep in washing; Gil in his study, bent over the pages of some dusty book as usual. She imagined going back in years to come and finding them all still there, miraculously unchanged, while she had grown tall and strong and sun-tanned in these woods. Sometimes, in the long silences of this place, it was hard to be sure that any of them existed at all.

She rolled over onto her back and day-dreamed about the cold greasy sausage she had devoured for breakfast, simply unable to save any for lunch, its delicious fatty taste still lingering on her tongue. It was no longer a surprise to her that men stranded in desolate places could murder and eat each other without a second thought. If she could go back to that first cold dawn, waking to see a pretty little rabbit only a few inches from her face, she would have no compunction at all about snapping its neck, skinning it with her pocket knife and roasting it over an open fire.

But the rabbits seemed to have sensed her murderous intent, because they kept clear of her shelter during the day and the traps she had laid so carefully for them were always empty when she checked.

She had tried crouching in the shallows to catch fish with her bare hands, early in the morning when the fish were probably not expecting anyone to be about, but without any success. And she couldn't try again this morning, because the boy had slept on the beach overnight and didn't leave until well after the sun had risen. By then she had finished his last tasty sausage and was still grinning to herself about that well-planned theft when he packed up his sleeping bag and rucksack, and started on the long climb back up to the main road. But at least he had gone now and the beach was blissfully hers again.

It had ruined everything, waking up in the morning and knowing that he was down there, the intruder, walking on her pebbles and washing his face in her shallows. She determined not to let anyone sleep there in the future, if she could possibly stop them, and spat on her hand to seal the promise.

But when dusk began to fall and she finally wandered back through the cool darkening undergrowth, having discovered a secret way down to the beach that kept her clear of the main paths, she was infuriated to find the kids were still there. Most people stayed only an hour or two before hiking back up to the car park with their beach bags and little children, unaware of her watchful presence. These noisy pests were clearly planning to stay much longer than that, however, maybe the whole evening.

They had built a fire in the same place as before, piling the stones high to make a barbecue, and the boys were standing over the flames while the girls splashed about in the shallow water under the rock, screaming and ducking each other.

Miranda crouched out of sight and fumed. Her easiest route back to the den, straight down this path and across the open beach, had been cut off. To get home now, she would have to climb the cliff from behind, which meant retracing her steps and taking a damp little path she had found once which steepened almost impossibly above the glen and was so overgrown she would need a stick to beat down the nettles and gorse.

Thick smoke drifted across from their fire and stung her eyes. Like the idiots they were, they must have used damp wood to light it. For one crazy moment, Miranda was tempted to stamp down there and scream at them to go home. But of course she couldn't.

She was a ghost in this place. She was a shadow. She was not meant to be here at all.

She rubbed her eyes and stood up, squinting down at them furiously instead. It was only then that she realised he was there too. The boy who had tried to drown her and whose sausages she had stolen in revenge. He had not only come back to spoil another evening for her, but he had brought his friends as well. He was standing on a large boulder near the shallows, laughing at the girls in their bikini bottoms and wet tee-shirts, that unmistakable wedge of blonde hair falling over his forehead.

She stared, hating him more than ever before. There was a cluster of beach bags and rucksacks near the fire, and one of the lads had already started putting up a tent on the smooth grassy bank near the mouth of the stream. They were obviously all planning to spend the night there. Another boy played with a home-made bow, shooting stick arrows loosely over the rocks as though at invisible rabbits. The beach, once so calm and beautiful in the gathering dusk, now echoed to the sound of pegs being hammered violently into the ground and half-naked girls screeching like banshees as they were chased through the water.

It was clear she had been invaded, which meant this was war. They could expect nothing less from her now.

Grimly, she snapped off a thin whippy stick from amongst the branches of green-barked sallies and made her way up the overgrown path, slicing viciously at nettles until she emerged breathless but triumphant at the top.

The light had completely died by then and the sea was a whispering black void. Miranda considered what she might do to make them all sorry, terrible images of revenge flashing before her eyes: Vikings in long boats wading ashore and burning everything in sight – or whatever pillaging was, exactly; an angry cloud of wasps pursuing them across the beach; scorpions scuttling under the folds of their sleeping bags, curved tails poised to strike. But she couldn't think of anything concrete she could do on her own, except possibly repeat her crime from last night and steal some of their food, which would be next to impossible with so many of them keeping guard over the camp fire.

She crept warily across the rough grass of the cliff, and then peered down at the sheer black drop she had to navigate. She was starving again and the thought of more warm sausages was too much for her. Perhaps she could somehow cause a diversion, get them to move away from the fire long enough to snatch some of their barbecue and disappear again into the darkness. She liked the idea of that unseen entrance and exit. It would be as though an avenging angel had descended upon them and ascended again without any of them being aware of the enemy in their midst. She had a vague memory of Gil telling her how it used to be done in the theatre, the god dropping from the rafters at precisely the right moment. Yes, that would be perfect, so long as she could achieve a solid tactical diversion.

Miranda let herself gingerly down the rock face in the darkness, clinging on to the few tufts of grass that didn't come away immediately, her foot feeling around for an invisible ledge. She wasn't far from the safety of her den now, the gorse-covered sleeping bag billowing and rustling uneasily in the breeze as she dropped the last few feet into long grass.

Simply throwing a stone would not work this time, unfortunately.

It was less than half an hour later when she crawled fiercely back out of her low shelter again, ready to do battle. She had her box of matches in the pocket of her jeans, and her stick in her hand, yesterday's sausage grease still coating its tip like wax.

Her fingers stinging, she reached up and pulled some old dried gorse from the roof of her shelter, dragging it along behind her as she stumbled back towards the beach path in the dark. The thorns pricked at her skin but she ignored them. The wind had risen too, whipping at the grasses and her loose hair, and she wondered for a moment whether her plan would fail. If it was too windy, the gorse might not catch light properly.

From below, she could still hear occasional shouts and hysterical laughter from the girls, and tinny rock music hissing from someone's transistor radio. Their lack of respect set her teeth on edge.

She crawled down the path, almost on her belly to avoid being seen, no longer scared of those menacing black figures on either side, the innocent bushes and rocks of daylight. The bushes seemed like allies now, familiar and almost encouraging as she slipped past them, stick in hand, the dry bundle of gorse bumping at her heels. They knew the truth, that this was her place and it was worth fighting for.

The others were gathered around the fire in little groups, some of the lads smoking cigarettes on the rocks and passing round cans of what looked like beer, others squatting by the open fire to flip their burgers and sausages before they burnt. There was an ugly sizzling and a burst of acrid smoke as a burger fell accidentally out of the pan and into the flames. One of the boys burst out laughing and applauded, dodging as a stone was thrown at him through the darkness. Two girls in jeans and skimpy tops were kneeling next to the radio, play-fighting with each other, arms jangling with silver bracelets. One girl was apart from the rest, treading bare-foot through the shallows with her head lowered. Her red sarong flapped in the wind like a sail.

Hidden safely behind her boulder, Miranda searched for the boy of the night before and finally saw him lying on the grassy bank with a slim dark-haired girl, their bodies entwined as they kissed.

For some reason that made her angrier than ever. It was his fault her beach had been invaded, and now all he could do was lie there, ignoring the fact that his friends were wrecking her peaceful existence.

Miranda crept across the pebbles, keeping carefully out of the flickering circle of firelight, and arranged her bundle of dried gorse near the base of the vast sandy-looking rock which formed part of the cliff. Then, shielding the flame with her body and trying to stay low enough not to be seen by the older kids, she struck a match and held it against the gorse.

It was extinguished instantly by a gust of wind.

She stared, furious, then fumbled to strike another match, this time cupping her hands around the vulnerable flame. It leapt and jittered, scorching her skin, but did not go out.

When she touched the flame to the gorse, nothing much happened for a few seconds. Then the dry thorns seemed to singe before finally catching light. Before she could be seen, Miranda darted back into the shadows and waited for them to notice.

One of the girls saw the fire first, shouting something and pointing across the beach. Heads raised and somebody laughed, then several of the boys began to struggle across the pebbles to investigate.

Her chief enemy, the boy who had tried to drown her, finally stopped kissing his girlfriend and sat up to see what was happening.

In the smoky glow of the firelight, she saw his bewildered expression and couldn't help giggling, remembering how he had made exactly the same face the night before. Then he stood up and followed the others towards the burning gorse, holding his girlfriend by the hand. Miranda felt her mouth water at the thought of those sausages and burgers, waiting patiently for her in the frying pan. Nearly all of them had moved away from the camp fire now, and her only problem was the boy who'd been flipping the burgers, still standing a few feet away, his back turned. But this was her best chance. She had to act now or go back up to her den empty-handed.

She ran lightly over the stones, her feet swift and practised, and stuck the sharp point of her stick into the largest, juiciest burger in the pan. Then, without daring to risk taking a second one, she turned and fled back towards the cliff path as quickly as she could.

An angry shout went up behind her, and there was a terrible clatter as someone tripped over the stones. Miranda heard, rather than saw, the others turning away from the dying flames of the gorse but didn't stop to check whether of them were following her.

She raced back up the narrow cliff path with thorns snagging on her jeans and tearing at her bare arms with cruel fingers.

There was a yell from the beach, a girl's voice raised in anger. 'Stop, you bloody thief!'

Something struck Miranda violently in the thigh, pitching her forward onto the stony ground.

She lay there for a few seconds, winded and confused, her cheek pressed into the dirt, then managed to struggle to her knees and crawl the last few feet to the top, the pain in her right thigh intensifying all the time.

What had happened? What had they thrown at her?

She had no time to stop and investigate, she had to keep going, to get back to safety, to reach a proper hiding place. From behind, she could hear their voices coming nearer through the darkness.

She crawled a few more feet, dragging herself under some thorny bushes, then lay there dizzily.

After a while she twisted her neck and tried to look out through the spiky thorns, too faint to go any further. She saw the pale beam of a torch wavering along the overgrown path below as the hunters approached. Then it stopped abruptly.

'There's blood here.' It was a girl's voice, high and frightened. 'Shit, you actually hit him.'

The boys' voices raised angrily in argument for a moment, 'The stupid bastard shouldn't have taken our food,' 'He was asking for it,' and then another, muttering so low she could hardly hear him, 'Come on, let's get back to the car. Nobody knows anything, right?'

Their voices gradually died away and Miranda lay under the bushes for a long while, not really sure how long she had been there.

Later, she found some strength to drag herself out from under the spiky bushes, wincing as the thorns ripped her skin. That effort meant she had to rest again, face-down, listening to the uneven thud of her heart and the far-off drag of the tide up the beach.

She opened her eyes to see bright pinpoints of stars shining above her in the black sky. The sea was quieter now, whispering in the darkness below, and there were no voices from the beach. She was alone.

Miranda felt along her thigh to where a sharp piece of wood had pierced the skin and was still sticking out. It was too unbearably painful to remove so she left it in place, her fingers growing numb as she pressed down on the wound in a vain attempt to stop the bleeding.

Much later, the wind became bitterly cold and she forced herself back to her knees, fumbling across the rough blowing grass as though she was blind. But there was no moon tonight and it was too dark to find the entrance to her little shelter.

Her hands felt along the blank rock face in silence, her head spinning and a warm stickiness trickling down her jeans. There was a moment of dizziness and suddenly she was staring down into empty air. The sea was loud in her ears as she slipped on the crumbling edge of the cliff, and lost her balance, tumbling wildly through space.

Chapter Nineteen

He had been falling for ages, but now he had come to a stop. Lawrence opened his eyes to the rattle of a tea trolley. Stiffly, he shook off that strange dream and sat up in the uncomfortable bedside chair. Looking at his father's sleeping face first, he shifted his gaze to the bewildering bank of dials on the monitor. Everything seemed exactly as it had been when he fell asleep last night. Though there was light streaming through the thin flowery curtains, pulled round the bed for privacy, and someone had come invisibly into the room behind them.

The curtains moved slightly, metal rings rattling on the pole. Lawrence stifled a yawn, then turned to find a woman in her fifties, an immaculate white apron protecting her uniform, staring in at him. She nodded a greeting, then silently began clearing away last night's cups from the bedside cabinet.

'You look awful, love. Can I fetch you a fresh cup of tea?' she whispered.

'No thanks, I'm fine.' He stretched, glancing down at the creased tracksuit he had been wearing since yesterday. 'I'd better go home and change.'

'That your dad?' she asked, glancing at Gil in the bed.

He nodded. 'He's had a stroke.'

The cleaner made a sympathetic face. 'You stay here as long as you want, love. The doctors won't be round until about nine o'clock.'

Confused and aching, Lawrence studied his watch. The time made no sense until he realised it was nearly seven o'clock in the morning. He must have been asleep for hours, his head lying awkwardly on the edge of the bed. Once the cleaner had rattled back into the corridor with her trolley, he stood up and held his father's hand for another few minutes before leaving.

It was a cold drive back to the house through the quiet misty roads and he put the radio on for company, listening to the local station with its amusingly sober shipping forecast and brief recap of national news, the cheerful presenter reading out a list of birthday greetings before playing a Dolly Parton number. The mist finally cleared and the sun began to shine.

Port St Mary was still asleep as he drove through its empty streets, but the newsagents in the High Street was open. He pulled up and went inside to buy a paper. The shop was busier than he had expected and he had to wait, listening with quiet amusement to the two men ahead of him in the queue. They were both in their early twenties, and probably builders, judging by the dried plaster on their jeans and heavy brown boots. The older one was flicking through his copy of *The Sun* as they talked, shaking his head with casual disapproval.

'You ought to go to the police about that.'

The other said angrily, 'Yeah, and land my sister right in it. Not to mention her mates.'

'But he could be dead.'

'Shh.' The younger one glanced round at Lawrence and then cautiously lowered his voice to a hoarse whisper. 'You don't know that. Anyway, she said it was only some piddling home-made effort. Couldn't do that much damage even if it did hit him.'

'It wasn't one of them cross-bow jobs?'

'No.' The queue moved up and the younger lad fumbled in his pocket for some change. 'I told you. Like that bloke, lived in a forest.'

'Robin Hood?'

'That's him.'

'Ah, but you can do some real damage with a bow and arrow. Where was she again? Up at Dhoon Glen?' He shook his head pessimistically. 'Poor bastard could bleed to death there and nobody know anything about it for weeks. I wonder who it was.'

'It was too dark. They couldn't see him.'

'Bloody idiots.' The older one nodded at the man behind the counter and produced a ten-pound note. 'You all right? Twenty Marlboro on top of that, please, and a packet of mints.'

The two men were still arguing in low voices as they left the shop. Lawrence paid for his newspaper and followed them out into the early sunshine just in time to see them climb into a battered white van and roar up the road out of the village.

He strolled back to his dad's Land Rover, newspaper tucked under one arm. Below him, Chapel Beach arched round in a clean golden crescent of virgin sand, empty at this hour of the morning. He and Cathy had searched for Miranda down there in the dark, walking the long narrow path set on stilts between the bay and the rock pools, where she had admitted to him that the girl was his daughter.

It was still hard to remember that Miranda was actually his. After so many years trying in vain for a baby, he had grown accustomed to thinking of himself as a childless man; now it felt as though his world had subtly shifted since that night, throwing everything out of kilter.

Lawrence bent to open the car door and stopped dead, staring back in the direction that the builders' white van had taken. The hairs rose on the back of his neck and he shivered.

Dhoon Glen?

That was where they had gone on their first day here, him and Juliet and Miranda, the beautiful deep glen with the waterfall and that lonely path to the beach which he had taken without them. He recalled his wife's hysteria and how he had raced back up the slope, breathless and sweating in the brilliant sunshine, to find that stupid boy ducking Miranda under the water.

Had she gone back alone to Dhoon Glen after she ran away? It would make an ideal camping ground. The young builder had said someone had been wounded out there, maybe even left for dead.

But it couldn't possibly be Miranda. For a start, they had mentioned a man, not a girl. Though in the dark ...

He dismissed the thought, getting into his car and driving slowly back to the house. It sounded more like some stupid kids' prank that had gone badly wrong. He couldn't imagine Miranda getting tangled up in anything that dangerous.

Cathy was nowhere to be seen when he got back, but Juliet was sitting moodily in the kitchen, staring out of the window as she smoked a cigarette. He didn't bother to ask her to go outside and smoke it. It was hardly worth it now his father was in the hospital.

Lawrence made himself a mug of coffee and was about to retreat upstairs to change his clothes when she turned to look at him, her tone arctic.

'How is he, then?'

'Didn't Cathy give you my message? I rang last night to let you know what was happening.' When she shook her head, Lawrence put down the coffee and stuck his hands in his pockets. These days when they talked, he felt as though his wife were a stranger, finding himself oddly polite and distant. 'The doctor said it was a more serious stroke this time, but he's holding his own so far. I only came home to get changed, really. Then I'll be heading straight back to the hospital.'

'I've hardly seen you at all this week.'

He stared at her, speechless.

'I mean, I realise it's important, your dad having this stroke,' Juliet said, slowly stubbing out her cigarette. 'But it feels like I don't count anymore. Like our marriage is over.'

'I don't know what you want me to say.'

'That it's over.'

Bewildered, he asked, 'Is it?'

'How should I know? You said we'd talk about it, Lawrence, but you're never here. Now you're going to disappear again and I'll be left alone with that woman, and no idea what I'm even doing here.' She shook her head angrily. 'Wasting my time, by the look of it.'

He sipped his coffee, not sure how to reply. She was right, of course. He had indeed said they would sit down together and discuss the relationship, but nothing had gone to plan since then. She couldn't expect him to do it now though, with his father lying in hospital and Miranda's disappearance still unresolved.

Juliet's timing was impossible as ever.

The fridge hummed gently as Lawrence studied his wife's profile, turned away as she lit another cigarette before the remains of the last one had even stopped smoking in the ashtray, remembering how much he had loved her in the beginning and how lucky he had considered himself when she agreed to marry him. He wished he was able to reassure her, salvage this situation and move on, but he wasn't certain that he could. Too much had changed between them over the past week, though he knew the end had begun earlier than that, possibly even as far back as their first year of marriage.

'If only you had come over to the island with me for my mother's funeral.'

'You're not still pissed off about that?'

'Then I would never have slept with Cathy,' he continued, ignoring her furious hiss at the housekeeper's name. 'Miranda would never have been born and none of this mess would exist.'

'So you're blaming me for your act of adultery?'

'You weren't here when I needed you. Cathy was.'

With an exasperated sound, Juliet buried her blonde head in her hands. 'That's priceless. Only a man could come up with that excuse.'

'It's not an excuse, Juliet. I completely accept that what I did was wrong. I behaved like a dick. But if you hadn't put your job first that week – '

'My job?'

'You insisted on going off to that gardening exhibition or whatever it was, instead of coming with me to the funeral.'

'God, you're such a fool. I didn't go to a gardening exhibition.'

He stared. 'I don't understand.'

'I was with someone else.' Juliet shook her head at him. 'The timing of your mother's death was perfect. He'd asked me to go away with him, and I couldn't work out what I was going to tell you. Then your mother died.'

Lawrence couldn't hear anymore. He walked out of the kitchen, his whole body trembling.

'I'm sorry,' she cried suddenly, running after him and catching hold of his jacket. They stood in the corridor and looked at each other, her cheeks ashen with remorse. 'Look, I didn't mean to tell you like that. It was cruel and thoughtless of me. Please come back and sit down.'

He shrugged off her hand.

'Let me try and explain quickly then, before you run off again.' Juliet stood back from him and touched her forehead with shaky fingers, staring down at the red tiled floor. 'I wasn't ready for a baby, Lawrence. I kept telling you that but you wouldn't listen. Your bloody obsession with starting a family always came first. Never mind if I felt suffocated by the whole idea of being a mother, you needed a son and heir to carry on the line. Then I met Tony at work, and he was so laid-back. He wasn't interested in kids either. We used to sneak out to his flat at lunch times. I know you won't understand this, but it felt … innocent. We had such fun together, with no pressure to spend the rest of our lives together or make a bloody baby.'

He could hardly look at her. He felt like he was going to be sick. 'Innocent? Were you having sex with this guy?'

'Of course. And I loved it.' She watched his face change, and her tone became defiant. 'You were so bound up in your mother's illness, you never even noticed how happy I was. What does that tell you about our relationship, Lawrence?'

'That I should never have married you.' He swallowed, feeling like there was broken glass in his throat. 'So, are you still sleeping with this man? What was his name? Tony?'

'God, no. It was over years ago. Tony got married and moved away. But the damage was done. I never felt the same about you afterwards.' She kept going, seemingly intent on driving the knife in as deep as it would go. 'Whenever we made love, it was there in the bed between us, this huge lie, this black hole at the heart of our marriage. And you couldn't even see it.'

'But I could feel it.'

Juliet stared, her eyes wide. 'Could you?'

'I thought it was my fault.'

'Maybe it was.'

The phone began to ring, but neither of them moved for a moment. Then Lawrence shook his head as though waking from a dream, heading slowly towards his father's study. The telephone stood on the leather-topped desk near the window and he picked it up automatically.

'Is Miss Maddrell there?'

It was DS Quine, his voice excited. The detective talked for a few minutes while Lawrence listened silently, looking back over his shoulder at Juliet who remained motionless in the study doorway throughout the phone call. The policeman seemed oblivious to the tension at the other end of the telephone line. He was convinced they had a genuine lead at last. Apparently, there had been another sighting of Miranda, this time in the remote north of the island, and DS Quine was going up there himself to investigate.

'A girl matching her description was seen camping up near the Ayres lighthouse two days ago. I'll let you know immediately if it turns out to be Miranda.' The detective paused. 'Could you pass that information on to Miss Maddrell for me?'

'Of course.'

'I have a strong feeling about this lead, sir.'

'We'll wait for your call.'

Lawrence put down the phone and stood there without moving for a moment, staring out of the study window. The row of stunted-looking palm trees lined the lawn, astonishing in this British climate, spiky brown-tipped fronds fluttering in the breezy sunshine.

Watching the palms, Lawrence fumbled in his jacket pocket for his dad's car keys. They were still there, metal cold against his skin. Then he turned and walked past Juliet without speaking to her, leaving the house.

His wife followed him out onto the drive, arms folded across her chest. She seemed defensive now that her own confession was out in the open. 'Was that the police?'

'Yes,' he said shortly, unlocking his father's Land Rover.

He still could not bring himself to look her in the face. Not after what she had told him. Maybe it was hypocrisy, but he was still angry with her. His slip had been one night; hers had been a full-blown affair.

'Tell Cathy the police have got a new lead,' he told her. 'They're looking for her up at the Ayres lighthouse, though I doubt she's there. And ring the Steam Packet and cancel my ferry, would you? I don't know when I'll be able to leave the island now. You're free to go home whenever you like, of course.'

'But what's happened?' she demanded, looking bewildered. 'Where are you going?'

'To find my daughter.'

Chapter Twenty

The sharp stabbing pain in her shoulder came for a third time, and it was only then that Miranda opened her eyes reluctantly on the dawn light and turned her stiff neck towards the sea. There was a seagull, large-bodied but still quite young - she could tell that by the soft brown feathers across its wings - balanced crazily on the rocky ledge beside her, its angry beak wide as it squawked and then lunged forward to peck at her exposed shoulder again. This time she threw up an arm to defend herself and the bird fell backwards off the ledge, a comical look of dismay on its face.

From behind her raised hand, she watched the gull lift abruptly and soar high above the cliff as though on the end of a string that someone had jerked upwards. The bird landed on a high outcrop of rock and glared down at her balefully, still screeching in protest.

Presumably she was lying on its favourite ledge.

Lowering her arm and daring to glance down for a second, Miranda caught a brief glimpse of the sea, churning around the rocks a few hundred feet below her position, before gasping and dragging herself closer to the cliff wall for safety. The sudden movement was agonising, a terrible electric shock through her thigh as the embedded arrow shifted in the wound.

She must have fainted again, because the world dimmed for a while.

When Miranda opened her eyes again, her angry seagull had disappeared and the sun had come out. She tried to get up, but it was too painful and she slumped back. It was obvious that if she wanted to survive she must climb back up the cliff, which wasn't much further away than the height of a man, but she was in bad shape and it would probably take several attempts to reach the top. Her tee-shirt was torn from the fall, she was numb with cold, and her thigh was still oozing blood around the roughly-made arrow. Miranda was also afraid for the first time since she had arrived at Dhoon Glen.

She had to admit that, come clean about it, even though she hated herself for such weakness. But if she didn't climb back up to her den soon, she could possibly right die here from loss of blood. The ledge beneath her body was already sticky with the stuff and she had to keep jerking her thigh painfully to prevent tiny black flies from settling on the wound.

Once she had struggled through the agony of getting to her feet, Miranda managed to hoist herself up a few feet just using the muscles across her chest and shoulders. But she had to climb much further up than that. There were a few clumps of rough grass growing between the rocks which made useful little handles and footholds, but her first tentative step clear of the ledge still terrified her. The wind coming off the sea snatched repeatedly at her body as Miranda climbed, hand by hand, and with one foot trailing weakly behind in the loose dirt, gradually scaling her way up towards the top of the cliff without once looking down.

When she finally reached the top, she dragged herself over the edge and onto flat earth, collapsing there in silent relief while blood beat in her ears like the throbbing approach of a helicopter. She never wanted to do that again.

Her thigh was numb and tingling now; she could barely feel any pain from the slimy gash around the arrow. It was as if she had crossed some invisible threshold where her wound no longer hurt.

For a moment, Miranda wondered hazily whether she was actually dead, and this was some brain-dream going on after death. She had heard that could be possible. But if she was dead, at least she was no longer stranded on that narrow ledge above the sea where it might take weeks, or possibly months, for anyone to find her body.

Now that it was day, she had no problem finding the gorse-covered crevice in the rock that was her den. She crawled inside, dragging her leg like a spare part behind her, and allowed herself to collapse for a few minutes with her eyes blissfully closed. Eventually, she forced herself to sit up again and scrabble amongst her things for the Swiss Army knife which Lawrence had lent her. She had only used it the night before, and it wasn't long before she found it, lying hidden beneath one of her books.

Reaching up to the billowing sleeping-bag that formed the roof of her shelter, Miranda used the sharp blade to slice through the thin nylon of its outer lining, then yanked down several strips of material long enough to wrap around her thigh. It hurt far more than she had expected and she couldn't help crying a little as she tightened the nylon strips about the wound. But her make-shift bandages seemed to be working. The little bubbles of blood that had been seeping out around the arrow all night gradually slowed and then stopped altogether, leaving only a darkening stain on the nylon.

Miranda was desperate to pull the arrow out of her flesh completely, but some half-forgotten memory or instinct told her to leave it in place until she could get proper help. It was hampering her terribly, but if she removed it altogether, she might lose so much blood that she would be too weak even to drag herself along.

She needed a wee, and she also needed water. How ironic. Leaving her rucksack and her precious books behind in the den, Miranda slipped the knife into the back pocket of her jeans and began to haul herself over rough grass towards the beach path.

It seemed like hours before she stumbled those last few feet onto the cold white rocks of the beach, exhausted and stooped like an old woman. The sunlight burnt in front of her eyes and her mouth was so dry that her tongue felt as though it had stuck to the roof of her mouth. She badly needed to reach the mouth of the stream before she collapsed from thirst. But that short distance between the rocks and that sound of trickling water felt immense now, almost like some vast desert which had sprung up there overnight.

Miranda hobbled across acres of pebbles in agony, wincing at each jolt to her thigh. When the stream was within sight, she forced herself into a trot and pitched face-down into the sodden grass where the glen met the beach, scooping handfuls of its cool water into her mouth.

She felt better almost immediately. The long night on the ledge had left a strange bloom of salt along her lips and she licked it away, drinking greedily then until her stomach swilled and sloshed with water. Her body felt so revived afterwards that she forgot about her wound for a moment and stood up without thinking, her sudden yelp of pain echoing around the empty beach.

Dropping back onto the grass on her knees, Miranda realised it might take her the whole day to climb up through the steep glen to the main road, assuming she even managed to make it to the top.

It had to be done though, there was no other way. The beach was often deserted until lunch-time, and by then she could be half dead.

She broke off a branch from a tree hanging over the stream and used it as a sort of crutch, hopping up the path and letting out a little groan every now and then. She stopped for a wee in the bushes, which was very unpleasant and took ages because of the pain of pulling down her jeans and squatting. Afterwards, her forehead was covered in a clammy sweat. She had to keep stopping to wipe it, occasionally glancing ahead through the trees in the hope that somebody might be walking their dog in the glen today or out on a hiking trip.

Running away from home had been the right thing to do, but it would be nice to be rescued now. Hospital was starting to sound pretty good too.

She remembered Gil telling her stories about the two world wars, and how some soldiers had needed their legs amputated after stepping on mines or being blown up by grenades. If the surgeons hadn't operated fast, he had told her, then gangrene might have set in. Miranda had always imagined gangrene as some hideous creeping green fluid that moved slowly up your leg from foot to thigh. She didn't want her leg cut off, but then she didn't want it rotting from the inside either. If she could get to a hospital in time, they would have medicines to keep the wound clean.

'Don't worry, men,' she said, forcing herself breathlessly up the slope towards a wooden bridge crossing the stream above a miniature waterfall. 'It won't be long now.'

There was no one to hear her. The glen lay empty and oddly silent in the early sunshine. She paused on the bridge for a rest, leaning on the wooden barrier to stare down into the cool shaded water.

Her mouth horribly dry again, she wished she had not left her water bottle behind in the den. She could have filled it in the stream here and taken little sips on her way up.

'It won't be long now,' she repeated to herself, finding the words comforting.

Perhaps if she could wet her lips again ...

Lowering herself gingerly onto the wooden slats of the bridge, Miranda leant forward over the edge and stretched her arm down under the barrier, trying to catch some water in her hand. But it flowed tantalisingly through the tips of her fingers, just slightly out of reach. She had just given up and struggled back to her feet, when there was a faint clunk and Miranda saw something red and shiny drop through the slatted floor of the bridge into the stream below.

She cried, 'No!' and instantly threw aside her crutch, sinking to her knees with a sickening wrench and trying to peer through the slats.

Sure enough, it was the knife Lawrence had lent her, which she had tucked into the back pocket of her jeans before leaving the shelter – safely enough, she had thought – lying in the water now between two jagged white rocks. No, no, no, no. She couldn't abandon it. Even if she came back for it another day, the wonderful shiny blades would be all rusted and useless by then.

Miranda could have screamed with frustration. Now she would have to climb down there and get it back.

Further down from the bridge was a cluster of sprawling green ferns, pretty yellow and white flowers poking their heads out from under their fine spiky leaves, and an absolute mass of wild garlic. The smell was intense as she pushed clumsily through them to the stream bank, trying not to crush the delicate flowers underfoot, and lowered herself onto a crescent-shaped area of shingle lapped by the shallow water.

Her thigh had begun to throb fiercely under the nylon bandages and she winced, clamping her hand around the protruding arrow. When she looked down, her fingers were stained with what looked like bright red paint.

Exhausted, on the verge of giving into tears, Miranda wiped the blood onto her filthy tee-shirt and took a few dragging steps upstream. 'Come on, men. One last effort ... ,

The water was freezing in the shade of the huge ferns but only ankle-deep. She was soon weaving unsteadily back towards the two white rocks where she had last seen the knife.

She had to get it back, however much her leg hurt. It was the only thing she had left.

The water deepened into a pool as she reached the miniature waterfall, her jeans sodden and clinging to her thighs. Climbing onto the smaller rock, she bent to retrieve the knife, shining brilliantly under the water, and watched her blood ebb away in a slow drifting red mist.

So much blood. This was it, she was dying. Her resistance to the idea began to slip away. It won't be long now, she thought dreamily. Not long now. And perhaps it was better for everyone if she did die. Better for her mum, better for ...

There was a shout from the glen above her and the sound of hurrying feet.

'Miranda!' It was a man's voice, shockingly familiar, calling her name as he ran down the narrow path between the trees. 'Miranda! Miranda!'

Who ... ?

She straightened too quickly and something seemed to tear inside her leg, as if a muscle had wrenched against the embedded wood of the arrow, pain shooting through her like a thousand volts. The sun blackened to nothing and her whole body jerked, crumbling sideways into water.

Lawrence had not bothered to change his clothes. He had not even stayed long enough at the house to manage a proper drink or eat any breakfast. So it was that he found himself hurtling down through Dhoon Glen like a madman – famished, thirsty, and still in his creased tracksuit from the previous morning.

The winding path was near vertical at times, twisting and constantly turning back on itself like a corniche, and so hung about with creepers and indistinguishable greenery that it was impossible to see further than a few feet ahead in most cases. He hadn't intended such a precipitous descent, but the sheer slope had taken over after he tripped on a root near the top of the path and now it seemed impossible for him to slow down without colliding with the high earth banks on one side or the occasional wooden barrier on the other which protected walkers from the drop.

'Miranda?' he called out hoarsely. 'Miranda?'

No answer.

He crashed past the waterfall where Miranda had suffered her ducking at the hands of some stupid local lad, but the place was deserted this morning, the shady pool quiet and still as his feet thundered by.

After four or five minutes of that bone-jolting speed, the path flattened out as it emerged in the valley bottom and he was able to slow to a trot at last, glancing breathlessly from side to side through the sunlit undergrowth.

He cupped his hands round his mouth. 'Miranda?'

There was no sign of the girl.

Lawrence refused to give up though and tackle that appalling slope again until he had searched the place thoroughly, even if it took him all morning. He had a hunch that DS Quine's trip up to the north of the island would prove just as fruitless as the other sightings reported to the police. But that story he had overheard in the newsagents had stuck in his mind, as if his instincts were telling him to follow it up. It sounded like exactly the sort of crazy mess his daughter would get herself into.

His daughter. He couldn't quite get his head round that yet, but he was trying. Though she was more Gil's daughter than his, if he was honest about it, clearly worshipping her grandfather and hanging on his every word – which made it all the stranger that she had run away from home.

It was getting warmer now, gone half past nine in the morning. Lawrence picked his way along the stony banks of the stream towards the beach, his eyes constantly scanning the glen for the missing girl. He had felt the same way about his own grandfather, of course, listening to gory anecdotes about the war, scared but fascinated by the idea of death and danger.

Miranda was much closer to Gil than he had ever been to his own, rather stern grandfather. Once they found her and brought her safely home, how would she take the news that his father had been rushed back into hospital after another stroke?

'Miranda? Miranda?'

There was a little wooden bridge ahead, crossing the stream and sloping into the bushes. Beyond it were the faint blue waves of the sea, moving steadily around the rocks on their way to the beach. It was an idyllic scene, but a curiously empty one.

He began to doubt his own instincts, and came to a halt. Perhaps he should turn back and join the police search up at the Ayres lighthouse. But just as he made the decision to leave, Lawrence heard a kind of rustling up ahead and looked round, instantly alert.

'Miranda?'

He stood in the sunshine, listening hard. After a moment, he realised it was not rustling he could hear but whispering.

There were people whispering in the wild, tangled trees and shrubs that ran alongside the path. Whispering to each other, back and forth, like questions and answers, a conversation. He frowned, straining to hear what was being said. He could not make out any actual words, the voices were always just on the far edge of his hearing.

'Hello?'

The whispering stopped abruptly. Then started again, but more muted, as if the whisperers were afraid of discovery.

'I know you're there, so you might as well come out,' he said loudly, glancing from side to side as he kept walking, trying to work out where exactly the whispers were coming from. 'Who are you?'

The tall grasses on either side of the path shook, rustling in a warm breeze from the sea. The bushes shook too, as if people were hiding behind them. The whispering started again, but this time it sounded less like human voices.

Lawrence frowned, staring around himself. Were those voices whispering or just the breeze?

Far-off he caught a faint hint of music, and thought he must be going mad. Then the wind direction shifted, bringing a peal of bells with it. Lawrence checked his watch. Ten o'clock precisely. He grinned at his own idiocy. Nothing supernatural about church bells sounding the hour. Or leaves rustling in the wind.

He had come to the little wooden bridge now, and suddenly realised there was something in the stream below. Something gleaming pale in the dappled green shade of the ferns.

He ran forward, staring down over the wooden rail.

Miranda was lying on her side in a deep pool below a little waterfall, her head against a large white rock and her legs in the water. He stared, his heart pumping hard.

'Miranda?'

She did not stir. Her face was waxy.

Was she dead?

He could not face that possibility. To have discovered her existence only to lose her without ever having …

Lawrence swung underneath the barrier and dropped into the stream with a loud splash, his tracksuit soaked to the knee within seconds as he waded towards the girl.

She looked filthy and wild, as he might have expected after so many nights spent outdoors. God only knew how she had managed to survive out here on her own. She was wearing jeans, and her right thigh was strapped up with strips of some silky material, dark with what was obviously blood. When he turned her gingerly in his arms, he saw a thin piece of bark-covered wood protruding from the back of her jeans, a few inches above the knee. The wound was still bleeding slightly.

He remembered that conversation he had overheard in the newsagents, something about some kids up at Dhoon Glen and a bow and arrow, and his temper flared.

What stupid bastard could have done this to her?

'Miranda?' he said loudly, trying to rouse her, but there was no response. 'Can you hear me?'

He felt cautiously along the arrow towards the terrible gash in her thigh, then realised that it was stemming the flow of blood and shouldn't be moved. But it must have been steadily working its way loose, because as he touched it, part of the rough arrow came away in his hand.

The girl groaned, her eyes flying open.

'Gil?'

He was intensely relieved to hear her voice, but she needed to conserve her energy. 'Hush, lie still, it's okay.'

She stared up at him, her eyes glazed with pain. 'Lawrence?'

'I'm going to pick you up and carry you back to the car. Can you put your arms around my neck?'

Miranda managed a slight nod and he helped her, sliding her white arms up over his shoulders and gripping her waist. Her eyes remained fixed on his face the whole time. He felt for a stronger footing amongst the slippery pebbles of the knee-deep pool, then heaved upwards. The girl was freezing cold and wet from the stream, but he cradled her against his chest, trying to stabilise her temperature with his own warmth. She had started to shiver now that she was clear of the water.

Angrily, he wished he had brought a blanket or a coat that he could have wrapped around her. But at the back of his mind, even at his most confident this morning, he had known a terrible uncertainty about finding her alive. About ever finding her at all, in fact.

Lawrence staggered up the bank with her in his arms, slipping several times on the mud and shingle, his back aching terribly with the weight. She cried out in pain and then fell limply against his chest, her head lolling to one side.

He said, 'Miranda?' in a low voice, craning to see her face. But she didn't answer and her pale lids were closed.

He could hear the tide now, not far away. The sea winds swept through again and the tall grasses whispered around them, jostling together in the sunshine. From over the dark-green, tousle-headed trees came a fleeting music, which he presumed to be somebody's car stereo on the coast road. Not strange spirits blowing into reed pipes along the shore …

This time he didn't stop to listen.

Chapter Twenty-One

'Glad to see you're awake at last, Mr Cardrew. How are you feeling now? Not too bad?' The young nurse, probably in her early twenties, gave Gil a reassuring smile and dragged the flowery curtains closed around his bed. She stooped to pull back the bedclothes, then rolled down the waistband of his pyjamas with swift, unembarrassed hands.

'Time for your injection.'

Gil forced his lips apart. 'Australian?'

'You can tell, huh? I'm over from Sydney for a year, staying with some distant relations of mine.' She produced a long menacing-looking needle from her trolley and tapped it, pinching a fold of his skin before sliding the needle smoothly into him. 'Have you ever been to Australia, Mr Cardrew?'

'My great-grandfather, John Cardrew, was born there,' he managed to say, frowning at the pain.

'Really?' She smiled, rubbing his skin. 'That must have been a while back, I guess. Was his father a convict?'

'Wrongly convicted, but yes.' His voice sounded foreign to his ears, the words stumbling and slurred. 'John sailed back to England when he was twenty-eight.'

'Didn't he like Australia?'

'His father didn't want him to marry into convict blood.'

'Like me, you mean?' The young nurse laughed, making a face. 'I'm probably descended from someone like Jack the Ripper!'

Gil leant back against the pillows, exhausted but amused as he watched her bend to straighten his bedclothes again.

She continued briskly, 'It doesn't really matter though, does it? Who your ancestors were that far back. I mean, what's important is what you do with your life now, not what they did with theirs.'

'You think so?'

'God, yes. No point looking over your shoulder the whole time.' Clearly satisfied with her perception of history, the young nurse straightened up and beamed at him, a slight smear of lipstick on one of her perfectly white front teeth. Her eyes busily scanned his bedside cabinet as she pulled the medicine trolley backwards. 'I'd better get on. The doctor will be round later for a quick chat. Anything else you need, Mr Cardrew?'

Gil shook his head and she opened his curtains, rattling loudly out of the room with her trolley. He could still hear her whistling along the corridor as he turned his head on the pillows to stare out at the evening sunshine. His leg still hurt from that bloody injection, but at least he was able to speak again now, after a fashion.

He couldn't remember much from the night before; it was a disconcerting hotchpotch of real details and confused imaginings. Though one of the nurses had told him Lawrence spent some hours at his bedside before going home in the early hours. He certainly didn't remember any of that. But there was no one to keep him company now and it would be dark soon. Perhaps his son was still looking for Miranda.

The thought worried him. Why had the girl run away? Did she think he didn't love her anymore now that his 'real' family had come to stay? He and Cathy had been wrong to hide the truth from the child all these years. He understood that now.

Was it too late to make amends?

After a meagre lunch, he slept for a while again, his sleep disturbed by strange dreams of falling. Then there was some commotion in the corridor and Gil frowned, opening his eyes. For a moment, he was surprised to find himself in hospital. Then he remembered. What was the time? He could not see a clock but it had to be early evening, judging by the way the sun had dropped low in the sky, one whole side of the ward draped in shadow.

He turned his head stiffly as the door to the ward swung open, expecting to see the supper trolley. But it was Lawrence instead. He was pushing a wheelchair, and the young Australian nurse was by his side. Then he realised Miranda was in the wheelchair, wearing a hospital gown and with her right leg swathed in bandages. Her pale face trembled into a smile as she was wheeled across to his bed.

Gil struggled to sit up. The relief he felt at seeing her almost overwhelmed him, and when he opened his mouth to speak, his tongue was oddly heavy and he heard himself slurring again.

'Miranda! Are you hurt?'

'Shh,' the nurse said soothingly, coming to settle him back on his pillows. 'It's nothing to worry about, she'll be fine. But I don't want you getting tired out, Mr Cardrew. Five minutes, okay?'

Lawrence waited until the nurse had left the room, then wheeled Miranda closer to his bedside. He looked almost as exhausted as Gil, his tracksuit filthy and stained with blood. But he was smiling too, glancing down at his daughter with an affection Gil had never expected to see from him. 'I found her camping out at Dhoon Glen. She'd had a bit of a run-in with some local lads, but the doctor says it's not as bad as it looks. She'll probably be up and about again in a few weeks. I've got the police on it too, we'll soon find the lads who did this.'

'Miranda?'

She seemed embarrassed, taking the hand he held out to her but not quite meeting his eyes. 'I'm sorry, Gil.'

'What ever for?'

'If I hadn't run away, you wouldn't have got so ill again.'

Gil said angrily, 'Nonsense,' then felt her fingers tremble in his and realised the girl was more frightened than embarrassed. He remembered acutely how it felt to be in trouble at that age and smiled down at her, softening his tone. 'Too much butter, that's my problem.'

'You seem much better this evening,' Lawrence said, settling himself on the edge of the bed. There was a new light in his son's face that Gil had never seen before, a sort of restless energy in the way he held himself which didn't seem to fit with the filthy clothes and pale unshaven skin. Lawrence had always been so precise about his appearance. Gil looked from his son to his granddaughter and back again, but said nothing. He couldn't help wondering whether the girl knew now that Lawrence was her father.

'I see they've taken the monitor away.'

'Oh, I didn't need any of that paraphernalia.'

'You gave us a terrible shock.'

'I'll survive. You don't get rid of me that easily.'

'So I see.'

'But why did you run away from home, Miranda?' Gil was irritated to find he was still slurring his words. His mouth felt lopsided and alien, as if it was no longer under his control. 'Was it something I did, perhaps?'

'She overheard you and Cathy in the study.'

'Me and Cathy?'

'Discussing who her father was.'

Gil stared at Lawrence for a moment, then turned his eyes back towards his granddaughter. No wonder the child had run away from him. It must have seemed to her as though he had deliberately hidden the truth, and he could imagine the reasons for that which she might have come up with on her own, too young to understand how complicated the situation was. Now that he looked at the girl closely, he could see fading red scratch marks on her cheek and running up one arm under the loose hospital gown.

He could only guess at the seriousness of that wound on her bandaged leg but knew she must have faced some terrors out there at Dhoon Glen, alone and unprotected. It was anger then that filled him, a cold anger at himself for letting this dreadful thing happen to her, his own flesh-and-blood.

Could he not protect anyone?

Gil straightened up on the pillows and forced his heavy tongue to move. 'I'm so very sorry, Miranda. What a dreadful way to have found out.' His speech was slurred, he could hear it. But there was no escaping this duty. 'I wanted to tell you the truth, believe me. But it was never the right time.'

'It doesn't matter,' she said quietly.

'But it does matter,' he insisted. 'It matters a great deal.'

Her eyes were full of tears. 'You've just got to get well and come home again. That's all that matters, Gil.'

He couldn't speak for a while after that and gestured wearily to his son to close the curtains. 'Later,' he managed to say. Exhaustion had hit him like a wave and the evening sunlight was suddenly too much for his eyes. Gil sank back onto the pillows, meaning to rest for a few minutes.

When he looked up again, it was dark and the young Australian nurse was bending over the bed to straighten his covers. She looked up at him and smiled as he stirred.

'Had a good sleep?'

Gil frowned. 'Where's my son?' he tried to say, but his mouth wouldn't work properly.

'What is it? Do you need the doctor?'

He sighed and shook his head, turning on the rustling pillows to stare at the dark ward but Lawrence and Miranda had both disappeared.

He must have been more tired than he knew, falling asleep like that halfway through their conversation. There were only two other beds in the small side ward, and both had been empty and stripped down when he woke this morning, but now he could see an old man lying in the one nearest the door, snoring gently with his head back and his mouth open, neck thick and wrinkled like a turtle's.

Gil watched him for a while in quiet amusement, then suddenly realised that the 'old man' was probably about the same age as himself. He looked down at his pale hands, turning them over with an effort to examine the blue, knotted veins running from wrist to fingers and those light brown patches which had only begun to develop in recent years.

He managed to say, 'It's my birthday soon.'

'Your birthday?' the nurse repeated cheerfully.

'Next week.'

The Australian nurse raised her eyebrows and made an extravagant 'ooh' with her lipsticked mouth, smiling indulgently at him as she picked up his chart.

'That's nice. And how old will you be, Mr Cardrew?'

'Seventy-two.'

'Sorry?'

Irritably, he tried the words for a second time, and this time the nurse heard him.

'Seventy-two?' she repeated after him. 'Imagine that!'

The young woman bent to take his pulse, staring blankly at the hospital wall behind his head as she counted. She scribbled something on his chart, then popped a thermometer into his mouth and sat on the edge of his bed while she waited. An attractive girl, she was wearing fawn-coloured tights under the blue uniform, one hand rubbing absent-mindedly at her leg as if it was aching. A few strands of her blonde hair had come loose from under her white cap and lay coiled on her shoulder like tiny golden wires.

But when the young nurse leant forward to remove the thermometer, he saw with a shock that it was Dora's eyes below the blonde hair and the accent was no longer Australian, but reassuringly British.

'Are you tired, Gil?'

'Yes.'

Dora reached out to touch his hand and a faint electric shock seemed to jerk through his body.

'It won't be long now, darling. Not long now.'

Chapter Twenty-Two

Nothing out there in the world had changed, Miranda thought, staring through the grimy window of the old Land Rover. Which was odd, because inside she felt like everything had changed, like all the colours were suddenly brighter, and she would never see things again the way they had been before she ran away. Being alone in the glen had changed her. Or maybe it was the wound in her thigh, healing nicely now under a clean bandage, that had shown her the world as it truly was.

Whatever had made the difference, she felt as though every cell in her body had been polished until it glowed, and now she was shining.

But no one else could see the change in her. So what use was it?

Gansey was deserted as they drove along the circular sweep of the bay, the ruffled sea fading to a dull orange under the setting sun. It was the tail-end of the season now, and most of the visitors were heading home at last, the pub car park nearly empty, the pebble beach deserted except for an old man walking his dog. The ferries would be sailing back to the mainland across the flat, copper-coloured expanse of the Irish Sea, packed with weary sightseers, the island quietening down as the summer months shifted inexorably into September. Through the half-open car windows the air smelt of salt and freshening winds.

From the grey loom of the cloud-rack over the hills, she guessed there would be a touch of rain tomorrow. Maybe even tonight.

Miranda stared ahead as they approached Port St Mary, and felt a sudden dreading about returning to the house. She imagined her mother appearing in the doorway, perhaps in tears, more probably furious with her for running away, and herself standing there embarrassed, with no words left to describe where she had been, or why.

Lawrence had seemed to grasp her need to escape unquestioningly. But how could her mother ever understand those nights spent staring up at a sky which wheeled with strange stars, or days dragging on in the heat while she waited for the beach to empty so she could creep down and hunt for tiny fish in the shallows?

She searched for an easy explanation of why she had run away in the first place, but failed. Miranda knew her mother too well to offer her the truth. To mention the word 'lie' might seem too much like an accusation, and anything else would feel dishonest.

Silence was her best option, she decided. Silence and head-hanging. The sort of dumb show her mother would expect and not bother to pursue.

The Land Rover climbed the narrow high-banked lane towards the house, and Miranda felt a rush of fearful anticipation.

'What did you tell my mum?' she asked Lawrence suddenly.

'The truth.'

'And what's that?'

He glanced at her. 'That you were upset when you heard … When you realised I was your dad.' He hesitated, frowning. 'Should I have made something up?'

'No.'

'She isn't angry with you.'

Miranda snorted. 'Is that what she said?'

'You should have seen her face when we first realised you were missing. She was distraught, Miranda, and it wasn't an act. I think you underestimate how much your mother loves you.'

Love.

That was a convenient word, she thought, and simply couldn't imagine her mother feeling anything that powerful for her. Miranda couldn't imagine her mother in bed with Lawrence either, though she knew it must have happened at least once, and while he was married to Juliet too. The thought of that night filled her with instant revulsion and she knew it would be a long time before she could look her mother in the eye again.

'Why did you and my mum … ?'

'Make you?'

She nodded, too embarrassed to say any more.

Lawrence shook his head. 'It's too hard to explain. I know this won't help much, but when you're older, maybe you'll understand. I was lonely. She was … lonely too, I guess. It was only the one time. But you were the result.'

'And no one ever told you.'

'I had no idea you even existed until I arrived on the island last week.'

'I don't feel like I existed before then either.' She found herself shuddering as the car pulled slowly through the gates to Gil's house. 'And now I have to face my mum.'

Miranda felt angry. Angry that she could no longer enjoy the sight of those beautiful green window frames and white-washed walls. When she hadn't known who her father was, that secret act had seemed misty and lost in the past, something buried long ago that didn't need to be unearthed. But now it was right there, on the tip of everyone's tongue, and she was expected to listen without flinching.

There was something so ugly and careless about what they had done together, her mother and father. Like an accident. An afterthought. She had never been wanted by either of them; she had been created by mistake, then hidden away like a monster.

'She won't shout at you,' Lawrence said reassuringly.

But Miranda was less confident. Exactly as she had predicted, the front door opened before the car had ever stopped, and there was her mother, hair pulled into a tight ponytail, and wearing a dress for once. A knee-length white dress decorated with red cherries. Her mum never wore dresses, she thought, staring. Let alone pretty ones like that.

There was a moment of hesitation as Miranda hobbled out of the car, Lawrence helping to fit her crutches awkwardly under each arm. Then her mother ran forward, and squeezed her in a suffocating embrace.

Miranda stumbled, yelping at the sudden pain, and her mother let go instantly.

'I'm sorry,' she gasped, and Miranda wasn't sure whether she meant for hurting her leg or for lying to her. The mascara under her eyes was smudged black as if she had been crying. 'I'm so sorry.'

Lawrence asked, 'Should I carry her up to her room?'

'No, I've made up a bed on the sofa in your father's study. Do you think he'll mind?'

'Not at all. It sounds like the best place for her.'

Her mother met his eyes above Miranda's head. Her face was pale, and she was wearing lipstick the same shade as the cherries on her dress.

'How is your father, Lawrence?'

'Hard to tell, really.' He hesitated, cautiously glancing down at Miranda before adding, 'The doctor says he has to be very careful. That this may not be the end of it.'

It was the sort of conversation between adults she was not expected to understand. Code and semaphore. Her two parents stood above her like sentinels, guarding her from bad news about her grandfather, as if she was unable to grasp on her own that his stroke had been serious.

Miranda wished she was back in the glen, where at least she had been in charge of her own destiny. 'My things!' she exclaimed, suddenly remembering. 'I left my books behind in the glen. I left everything.'

Lawrence said smoothly, 'Don't worry. They're all up in your room. Yes, I found your den and brought everything back that looked worth saving. That was a pretty impressive shelter you built there, Miranda. It must have taken some time and effort.'

'But what about your knife? I'm really sorry, I dropped it in the stream.'

Lawrence reached into an inner pocket and held out his closed fist like a magician performing a trick, his eyes on her face.

'Did you find it?' she asked, astonished. 'Really?'

He unlocked his fingers to reveal the shiny little red pocket knife and smiled at her amazed expression.

'I got soaked retrieving this. So don't go dropping it off any more bridges, okay?'

She stared. 'You're giving it back to me? But it's yours.'

'I think you should keep it now, Miranda. Let's face it, I only ever used it to open letters, and a knife like this deserves a rather more adventurous owner. Don't you agree?'

'Thank you,' she said.

Lawrence stretched into the car to remove her hospital bag and she turned the knife over in her hand to examine it. The red enamel was slightly scratched from its fall between the rocks, but otherwise it was perfect.

He was right, though. The knife deserved to be used for a serious purpose, not just for slicing envelopes open or getting stones out of shoes. Miranda could remember sitting in her den, using this knife to sharpen her hunting stick to a fine point, or once, high up in the glen, stripping blackberries from a prickly bramble bush, bitter and unripe. She had felt herself to be a true survivor at that moment, like Robinson Crusoe or one of the early explorers, living off the wild land and eating whatever came to her hand. That was something even Lawrence would never properly understand, because it would be entirely hers forever, that private moment of triumph and revelation as she forced herself to swallow those tart greenish blackberries and gazed down over her jungle of trees and creepers.

Now, whenever she used this little pocket knife, she would be able to close her eyes and remember her secret kingdom.

Her mother helped her inside the house while Lawrence drove the Land Rover away to park it outside the garage. But the hand supporting her arm was no longer gentle. Just as she had suspected, that tearful welcome on the doorstep had been an act.

Miranda could tell by her voice that her mother was seething. She kept her eyes fixed on the red tiles of the passageway, listening to the echoing clunk-clunk as her crutches struck the hard surface.

'Do you have any idea what you've put me through this past week? Or Mr Cardrew?' her mother hissed. 'He's in hospital now, thanks to you. He might even die. I could lose my job over this.'

Miranda said nothing in reply – it was always better to stay silent – but her heart swelled with the sheer injustice of that accusation.

'Yes, I shouldn't have told you lies about your dad being dead. That was wrong of me. But I only did it because Mr Cardrew said he'd look after us if I kept quiet. You think about it from my side for a minute. I was pregnant, stuck in that pokey little place in the village, no one to look after me. What was I expected to do? Say no thank you and walk away from a blank cheque book? Oh yes, it's all very well for you to sit in judgement, but you'd better be hopeful you never have to make a hard choice like that.'

Her mother paused as they both heard Lawrence whistling in through the front door. The jab in her back was deliberately painful.

'You've got money behind you now, and I did that for you. You should be grateful and stop ruining our chances by running away.'

Miranda almost threw herself down onto the sofa in Gil's study, trembling with rage and a genuine desire to hurt her mother. Her crutches smashed noisily against the wall but she didn't care. She had known this would happen as soon as they were alone together.

It was so unfair to blame her for everything! It wasn't her fault, she was just caught in the middle as usual. That was why she had run away in the first place. Because she was always the last to know when something important was happening. She hadn't even been here when Gil collapsed.

Miranda could feel tears in her eyes and rubbed them furiously away, burying her face in the rough blankets so her mother wouldn't know she was crying.

She'd have been better off drowning in that stream. Why had Lawrence bothered to save her and bring her back to suffer this hell?

Her stomach hurt from holding back the tears, and she stifled a groan. Her mother must have heard it, but she closed the study door and walked away along the tiled passageway towards the kitchen.

Miranda shut her eyes tightly and tried to imagine the scene, the police standing over her pale lifeless body, grimly shaking their heads, and her mother crying real tears at last, realising how she had driven her own daughter to her death. But her mother wouldn't have cared if she had died out there in the glen. Her mother hated her for existing. And her father was too busy with his own dad to worry about a kid he had only just met.

She felt for the little knife in her pocket, closed her fingers around it. The cold metal gave her strength. *You'd better be hopeful you never have to make a hard choice like that.*

Yes, she did understand. It did not make her fury any less painful, but she had made hard choices in the solitude of the glen, and she did understand. Could she forgive though?

Lawrence paused outside the door to his father's study, his hand poised to turn the round brass door handle, then abruptly changed his mind. The poor girl had only just come home. She would need some breathing space to recover from her adventures, maybe a day or two at least, before he sat down with her and answered some of the unspoken questions he had read in her eyes. Though he couldn't put it off forever, of course, however much he dreaded the task.

He turned away and trod heavily upstairs to his bedroom instead, shrugging out of his jacket as he went.

It must have been a real shock for Miranda to discover the truth about her parentage, especially in such a brutal fashion. And his well-meaning homily on the way here, about Cathy and her 'good intentions', had probably not helped matters. Lawrence was not a good judge of character at the best of times, but even he could see Cathy was furious behind that conventional smile. He had been angry with the girl too, naturally enough. She had put them all to a great deal of trouble, running away like that. But her behaviour was understandable, given the circumstances. In her place, he would have been tempted to escape too. As he had escaped, in fact, after that stupid fling with Cathy, running home to his wife and keeping his mouth shut about the whole affair.

At the time, of course, he had thought he was merely escaping from an unfortunate mistake, not an unborn child. Would he have behaved any differently if he had known the consequences of his action? If he had known of Miranda's existence when she was still a baby?

He did not know the answer to that, of course. But he suspected himself of cowardice.

He opened the door to his bedroom and hesitated on the threshold, then tiptoed inside as quietly as possible.

Juliet was asleep on the bed in the half light, curled up with her back towards him and the curtains firmly closed. She stirred at the sound of the door and turned over lazily, her arms and shoulders pale in the strapless lemon top. Her hand fumbled for the bedside lamp and the gloomy room was illuminated.

Lawrence thought she looked like a child today, the slender body almost androgynous and her face turned towards him without any visible sign of passion, blinking at the light and vaguely owl-like, curious white circles around her eyes where she must have been sunbathing with her sunglasses on. She had unbuttoned the tight blue Levis and he could see the flat expanse of her belly, the tiny sunken 'O' of her navel flexing as she stretched.

For a moment Lawrence found himself embarrassed, glancing away as though his own wife were some half-naked stranger he had disturbed in his room, then was struck by how ridiculous he was being and forced himself to look back.

Juliet didn't seem to have noticed his reaction, lying back against the pillows with her arms curved above her head. She yawned delicately as a kitten, all her white teeth showing.

'I was just having a nap. Is she back?'

'Downstairs.'

'Mmm. I thought I heard voices. God, is that the time? I must have been really exhausted! I've been packing since lunch-time.'

'So I see,' he said, kicking one of the suitcases standing next to the bed. He felt a slight flush of irritation which he tried to hide. 'You're definitely leaving then? When's your ferry?'

'First thing in the morning.'

'Need a lift?'

'I've booked a taxi.'

Lawrence nodded and walked to the window. Pulling the curtains open slightly, he stared out at the darkening sky.

'So that's it?'

'That's it,' she agreed.

'What will you do?'

Her voice was so perfectly reasonable, they might have been discussing her weekend plans rather than the end of their relationship. 'Sort out what's mine and what's yours. Then put the house on the market, if you're still sure about that.'

'I'm still sure.'

Juliet moved and he glanced round at her. She had stood up from the bed and was buttoning her jeans. Her face gave nothing away. Lawrence watched her and wished he could drum up some sort of genuine emotion. Anger perhaps, or possibly even sadness; anything that might crystallise his feelings about her leaving. But there was nothing in his head but blankness.

He felt oddly uncomfortable about that. After so many years of marriage, he ought to feel something.

He asked simply, 'Where will you go?'

Juliet glanced at herself in the mirror, dabbing at what remained of her lipstick with an experimental finger, an unconscious gesture which told him she felt a little uncomfortable too. The knowledge made him feel better about himself and her reply seemed less brutal. 'Does it matter?'

'I suppose not.'

'Well then,' she shrugged.

Lawrence didn't know what else there was to say. Perhaps if they had managed to have kids together, the joy they had once felt would not have evaporated. But she had been so frighteningly dismissive of her decision to go on the pill. Oh, the inconvenience of a baby! He saw through her, as he had never done before, right to the heart of her selfishness. And maybe he had been selfish too, pushing her towards a motherhood she did not want. But now that he had found Miranda, he intended to put all that aside and be a proper father to the girl.

The decision surprised him.

Was that why Gil had summoned him to the island? Not merely to tell him about his illness, but to make him a father at last. To show him a better way.

She had left the mirror now and was lifting one of her suitcases onto the bed. Juliet rifled through her clothes before dragging out a crocheted cardigan which she slipped over her shoulders, shivering as if she were suddenly cold.

There was still a beauty to her, a pale childish beauty that Lawrence had once found mesmerising, but saw rather more distantly now, like someone glimpsed on the other side of a station platform.

He longed to feel strongly enough to kiss her and tell her not to go, that he would be lost without her. But it seemed like a faintly ludicrous thing to do under the circumstances, smacking of the worst kind of amateur dramatics, and untrue to boot, so he did nothing.

'What about you?' she asked.

'I'll stay on here for a bit. My father ought to have someone around when he comes out of hospital, and I'm not sure he'll want that to be Cathy.'

She nodded, unsurprised. 'I can pack up your darkroom equipment and have it shipped over, if you like. You'll need more clothes too, I expect.'

'That would be very helpful, thank you.'

She turned to the dressing-table again and looked at him in the mirror, reapplying her lipstick with a steady hand. 'What about everything else?'

'I want my books.'

'Furniture?'

Lawrence smiled thinly. 'Keep it or sell it.'

'I'll send you a cheque.'

He nodded and sat down on the edge of the bed, unlacing his shoes. His feet were aching.

It was maybe a little strange, at a moment like this, but all he could think about was lying down and grabbing some sleep. It was as if the events of the past ten days or so had finally caught up with him, his body reeling and his mind too exhausted to bother with any more details.

His separation could wait; they appeared to have sorted out the basics, anyway.

'Sorry,' he said thickly. 'I have to sleep.'

Lawrence stepped out of his clothes, leaving them on the carpet with uncharacteristic carelessness, then crawled under the covers without looking at her again.

Chapter Twenty-Three

The house had been waiting for him to return, Gil realised. The green-framed windows seemed like a woman in sunglasses, dazzling and blanked out by the morning sun. The front door stood slightly open as though it was a mouth, about to speak to him. The first time they had ever seen this place, Gil had come out of that porched entrance into brilliant sunlight, blinking and uncertain which direction his wife could have taken, for she had gone hurrying ahead in her anxiety to explore the gardens.

His memory leaping forward into the present, he could see Dora standing there on the path that looped round the back of the house to the top lawn. Her blonde head turned as the old Land Rover pulled up, tyres spitting gravel.

She waved at him cheerfully, then disappeared towards the sunlit terraced lawns at the back as though inviting him to follow.

It won't be long now, she had said to him in the hospital.

Gil watched his wife wander along the gravelled path, or what had appeared to be his wife a moment ago but was now a rich bed of Crocosmia Lucifer waving in the breeze off the nearby cliffs. It was becomingly increasingly difficult for him to think of Dora as being dead. She always seemed to be there, just around the corner or waiting silently inside whenever he opened the door of a darkened room.

Memory was a strange and fickle creature though. Gil never saw his wife anymore as she had been before she died, incoherent and stumbling, too gripped by her disease even to acknowledge his presence. Dora seemed younger each time she came to him, as though time had run backwards when she died and she had run with it, losing that grey hair and pale skin until she was whole and almost a child again.

His son opened the car door for him. 'Are you okay to walk on your own, Dad, or do you need some help?'

'Don't fuss, Lawrence.'

Lawrence shrugged and lifted his overnight bag from the back sear. His son's face seemed strained and Gil wondered if he too had been suffering from sleepless nights. Juliet had probably been giving him hell. Finding out that he had a child by another woman would not have been her idea of good news. But he had little sympathy for his daughter-in-law. Why Lawrence had chosen to marry such an iceberg was beyond him, unless it was simply that his son had wanted to irritate him. Though, to be fair, he seemed to remember Juliet being rather more animated in the early days.

Perhaps if he hadn't been quite so insistent that Lawrence get married and have children as soon as possible, his son might have waited and chosen more wisely. But Dora's health had been failing at the time and Gil hadn't felt able to concentrate on anything outside their little world.

'I'll put this up in your room,' his son said, hoisting the bag over his shoulder. 'So, are you tired or would you prefer to eat? I asked Cathy to knock up a quick salad for lunch, in case you were peckish.'

'I ate enough lettuce in that hospital to last me a lifetime. Isn't there anything else in the house?'

'The doctor said ... '

Gil interrupted him angrily, 'I don't give a damn what the doctor said! You seem to forget, this is my body, Lawrence, and it wants something more substantial than salad. Cathy knows the sort of thing I like. Just ask her to make me something hot and filling. Toad-in-the-hole would be nice, with plenty of gravy.'

He waved his son out of the way as he climbed out of the Land Rover, holding onto the metal door frame as his legs trembled beneath him. That unexpected hint of weakness made him even more impatient and Gil found himself growing peevish and irritable, like an old man.

Once inside the house, he made slowly for his study. The passageway was cool and dark and his slippers shuffled comfortably along the red tiles. It was such a relief to be back in his own home, amongst familiar surroundings, and no longer wired up to those stupid machines like an invalid. He could hear his son and Cathy in the kitchen, speaking in low voices behind the green louvre doors as if they thought he didn't know they were talking about him.

Why was it so difficult for them to grasp that he wasn't interested in hanging onto life at any cost? It didn't matter how many salads he consumed, he would still die in the end. Better to enjoy his life while it lasted than wither away in a corner like a turtle in its shell, too scared to poke his head out in case death leapt up and bit him.

Dora was already in his study, lying on the sofa under a red blanket, an open book in her hand. As Gil pushed the door further open, her head turned and she smiled up at him shyly.

'Hello, Gil. Are you feeling any better?'

'Dora?'

She hesitated. 'It's me, Miranda.'

Gil stood in the doorway and silently stared at her, too confused to speak, then gradually realised that the voice was not his wife's. He looked at her more closely and then came into the room, shaking his head at such a ridiculous mistake. The two did look a little alike, but all the same. Tick, tock. Time was moving on and leaving him behind.

The poor child must think he was going mad.

Miranda said, 'I hope you don't mind me being in your study. But I can't manage the stairs very well, so mum said I could sleep here until my leg's better. I could always move to the living room if you prefer. I don't want to get in your way.'

'Nonsense, you stay where you are.'

She looked relieved, throwing her book to the floor and pushing herself up on the cushions. Her voice was high and eager.

'If you like, Gil, we could go out into the garden later. There's an ants' nest below the stone lions that I wanted to show you. It's such a sunny day and I can almost walk without my crutches now.' Then the girl bit her lip and paused. 'Unless you're too tired, that is.'

'What sort of ants?'

'Tiny red ones.'

He nodded, 'We'll go after lunch.'

Miranda began to talk excitedly about her time in the glen, showing him her bandaged leg and describing the wound she had received. 'I had to give a statement to the police. Do you think they'll catch him?'

So the girl chattered on while Gil settled comfortably into his high-backed leather chair and watched that pale expressive face as she recounted her adventures, no longer surprised that he could have mistaken her for Dora. There was the same glint in her eyes, a determination not to be beaten, and the slender hands moved rapidly as she spoke, drawing little pictures for him in the air. He and Dora had sat in this room together many times in the first year after they moved in, while she was still able to think and speak clearly, listening to music in the quiet evenings or talking about the books they had been reading. But he had never noticed how much Miranda resembled his wife.

Dora had been gone well over a decade, yet he still missed her, still looked for her unconsciously whenever he entered a room. His wife's photograph on the wall mocked him with her strange smile. When would he see her again? And where would she take him?

It won't be long now.

Through the months that followed his return from hospital, Gil found himself slipping deeper and deeper into a sort of forgetfulness, a reverie which could only be interrupted for daily necessities such as meals and baths or a leisurely stroll into the gardens with his granddaughter. That was a strange word for both of them – granddaughter – and he used it hesitatingly at first, unsure of how she felt about his long deception. But the girl seemed to enjoy her new status, shy and red-faced at first, then beginning to call him 'Grandpa' quite happily.

He would sit outside in a deckchair and watch her, pretending to read his newspaper while she hobbled about on the lawn on her bad leg or knelt to weed the flowerbeds where he directed. He often wondered why on earth they had wasted so many painful years, himself and Cathy, trying to hide the truth from her?

Now that life had settled down into some sort of predictable rhythm again, it felt as though it had always been this way, grandfather and granddaughter, sitting out together on the darkening lawn as each day drew to a close. Juliet had gone back to England, of course, as he had suspected she must in the end, and Lawrence refused to speak to him on that subject. It was as if the boy had simply closed the door on his marriage and was now standing with his back against it.

Gil was not sure that his wife would ever come back to him. But perhaps that wasn't such a bad thing. He didn't think their relationship had ever got past that infidelity; even though Juliet hadn't known about it, he suspected that Lawrence had been unable to look at her in the same way after that. A lie of that magnitude was a terrible strain to put on any relationship, he thought. It had certainly threatened to taint his relationship with Miranda, though she seemed to have bounced back from it quite readily, as the young often do, unable to keep hating him forever. But there were still other ghosts to lay to rest.

Gil kept coming back to that, staring out at the fading evening light while Miranda read her book, curled up like a small animal at his feet. That appalling mistake. That one dreadful kiss. And his wife stumbling into the kitchen, confused and even seeming unsure who they actually were, asking for lunch in her plaintive voice. But there had been something in her eyes. Some suggestion of betrayal. The years in between had passed like a fraction of a second. Yes, there were still ghosts to lay to rest before he finished.

The weather turned and the leaves began to fall, vast acres of reddish brown lying in drifts against the bases of trees and cluttering the front porch with their strange dry rustling. Cathy swept them away each morning but by the time evening came, the dead leaves would be there again, relentless and indefatigable.

It was late October now, and there was still no talk of Lawrence returning to England. Instead, he had asked Juliet to send over his books and a suitcase of clothes, and installed himself in one of the attic bedrooms overlooking the sea, though he was too tall for its low sloping roof.

He had even turned one of the other rooms up there into a darkroom. 'I need to keep an eye on you at the moment, Dad,' he would say whenever Gil asked about his plans for the future. 'No more butter, remember. No more walking up mountains!'

His son spent his days out with his camera or fiddling about in his makeshift darkroom, and would only come down in the evenings to sit and play gin rummy with them or watch some television programme that Miranda liked. Apparently he was able to sell his photographs to magazines, and was even compiling a book of island-based photographs for publication. He had shown a few photographs to Gil; they seemed pretty good for an amateur, though the subjects were always landscapes or trees or flowers in close-up. Never people.

Now that school had started again, the girl had moved back into the converted boathouse to be with her mother at night, though Gil suspected that she was unhappy there and would prefer to sleep in the main house. But he didn't like to interfere, in case Cathy thought he was trying to take Miranda away from her and became difficult. The woman had been silent and withdrawn since the summer had ended, and he could see that her unhappiness was affecting Miranda too.

Gil wasn't sure what was troubling Cathy, but it worried him. Perhaps the woman had finally grown tired of her position as his housekeeper and was planning to escape.

There had been some talk of Spain recently, and going to visit her sister there. He couldn't blame her, of course – her situation here was an unenviable one, and Lawrence was not making life any easier by giving her the cold shoulder whenever they passed on the stairs. But he dreaded the day Cathy might come to him and give her notice. She was the child's mother and would naturally take her away if she left. Even to Spain, perhaps.

To be separated from Miranda was an unbearable thought. Gil could only hope it would never come to that.

On a glowering afternoon in early November, there was an abrupt storm after several days of sultry tension, autumn making its presence felt with fast-thundering rain and a fierce wind that shook the windows in their green-timbered frames. They sat inside the dark house like refugees, watching rain streaming down the glass panes and mourning the deckchairs which had been left outside and were now bowling across the top lawn towards the stone parapet that surrounded it, flapping there like seagulls stranded on their backs.

Once the storm had passed and the evening air was clear of rain, Gil wandered around the outside of the house, as he always did after strong winds, painstakingly checking the roof for loose or fallen slates.

It was a familiar ritual and one which he and Dora had often undertaken together. But tonight he was alone and she could not see her beloved flowerbeds destroyed, one muddy wasteland after another, their few remaining plants battered and stripped to bent stalks.

Dora had always hated this yearly annihilation, inevitable though it was here, so close to the cliffs and open sea that nothing could survive the salt gales for long. Debris from the rhododendrons had choked her square greenish pond with its stone heron and impoverished-looking reeds, and the vast sycamore which dominated the front lawn stood bare-armed and desolate now, like the survivor of some terrible slaughter, the grass beneath its sodden trunk littered with the last leaves of summer.

Gil stooped to pick up a broken slate here and there, leaning them against the white-washed walls to mark the spot where they had fallen. There was a cheerful little man in the village who would come up and replace them for the price of a few pints.

Then Gil suddenly remembered that the man had died about five years ago, and stood still for a moment, confused. So who had replaced them last year, or the year before that? Cathy must have arranged it for him. He seemed to recall a white van arriving and the job being done in a few hours. Yet the man's face was so clear in his mind, it seemed only yesterday that he had been here, grinning and clambering onto the roof while his son held the ladder steady. Where had the time gone?

He felt a hand on his shoulder and turned to see Dora there. She smiled at him, saying, 'It's like a kaleidoscope.'

'What is?'

'Time.'

'I forget things so easily these days.'

'But you remember others, Gil. Things that were lost.'

He blinked and picked up another blue-grey slate. It was cracked right across and could never be used again, but he laid it gently against the wall beside the others. Dora followed him slowly around to the front of the house as he finished his search. The sun was beginning to set. Her feet seemed to rustle drily on the gravel path behind him, like leaves blown by the wind, and he didn't look round again.

'Did I lose you, Dora?'

'I think you misplaced me. That's not the same thing.'

Gil went back into the house and wearily climbed the stairs to the first floor. The landing was dark but he didn't bother switching the light on.

He heard Lawrence call after him up the stairs and replied irritably that he would be down in a minute. Supper must be nearly ready, though he was not particularly hungry. There was mud on his cardigan and he intended to change it before supper. Gil found himself standing before the locked door to his wife's bedroom though, fingering the small ornate key in his pocket.

How had it got there? He must have picked it up earlier that day, perhaps in order to sort out some more of her clothes for the charity shops. Or maybe he had put the key in his pocket yesterday, he couldn't be sure anymore.

Well, the key was there now. So he unlocked her bedroom door and went inside, closing it after himself this time.

The curtains hung partially open in the evening gloom. Gil paused, then looked around at the shadows. He had been afraid of the dark as a boy, but there was nothing to be afraid of here. This was only a disused room that needed a good dusting and the windows opened wide. And he would do that. He would certainly do that, once he had found those pearls again. His wife would have wanted her granddaughter to have them now.

Gil watched himself in the mirror, an old man shuffling slowly across the room in the half-light. The pearls were still there in the small ivory box on the dressing-table, luminous and immaculate.

Gil clasped the pearls in his hand and lay down on his wife's old bed for a moment. The bedsprings creaked as he stretched out his legs and stared up at the ceiling with its pattern of mock white Tudor roses. It had been Dora's idea to have separate bedrooms when they moved to the island. She'd told him, 'I'm too much trouble, I'll only kick and keep you awake at night.' Gil hadn't bothered arguing with her. Being able to escape to his own bedroom at the end of each day had been a secret relief and his own insomnia had meant he could stay alert during the night in case she called for help.

His body felt oddly tired after that walk round the house, picking up slates – so many broken slates this year; it was a miracle the roof had not started to leak yet – and these pillows seemed to smell of lavender, one of Dora's favourite scents and a mild soporific.

Was it his imagination, that faint hint of perfume?

It didn't really matter. Dora was so close, he could almost touch her, if he shut his eyes and concentrated.

It must be nearly supper time, Gil could hear voices below and the clatter of plates as they began to lay the table. Miranda's voice floated cheerfully up from the stairwell. Her pearls felt heavy and smooth in his hand.

The girl would be so excited when he gave them to her. He would only lie here for a moment longer.

Chapter Twenty-Four

'Gil?' The voice was soft but insistent in his ear. 'Come on, sleepy-head. Please wake up, darling. It's time to go.'

Gil sat up slowly and stared at his wife, a misty face swimming next to him in the dimly-lit room. The heavy floor-length curtains had been drawn back slightly and there was a pale glow filtering in through the windows.

For a moment Gil was confused, unable to remember where he was or if it was the light of dawn or dusk that he could see in the sky, then he caught the smell of lavender again and recognised that large dark wood dressing-table over his wife's shoulder, silver-backed brushes and combs gleaming in the darkness below her tilting mirror.

'Where are we going?'

Dora slid off the bed and held out her hand. He took it without question and they left the room so silently he couldn't remember afterwards whether or not she had opened the door. They went down the stairs together, still hand in hand, and he glanced instinctively along the passageway towards the brightly-lit kitchen.

Something seemed to tug at his memory and he stopped for a moment and tried to go back.

The pearls! He had left them behind in Dora's bedroom. He ought to bring them down and give them to Miranda. They should belong to her now.

The house was so full of light and noise now the girl had been found and his son had chosen to stay. The old place had come alive at last, he could hear the walls breathing around him. And it was nearly supper time. Gil leant forward longingly, straining at the hand that held him so tight. He could smell something delicious cooking on the stove, and that was Lawrence now, talking to his daughter behind the closed green louvre doors, the girl's laughter high and infectious.

'Wait,' he told his wife urgently. 'I should let them know I'm going out. They won't understand.'

But it was dark and he was already outside. Dora had pulled him inexorably through the front door into the garden, her voice soothing.

'Let them go, Gil. They'll be fine.'

'How can you be sure?'

She smiled. 'There's something I want to show you.'

They walked together down the flight of stone steps at the back of the house, past the stone lions where Miranda had discovered her ants' nest, past the terraced lawns with their glossy rhododendrons and uneven clumps of moss ruining the grass, down through the small wooden gate at the bottom and onto the narrow path which led eventually to the sea.

He paused there and looked back up at the house, a white glimmering just visible above the shadowy tree tops, and wondered if any of them had missed him yet. Miranda would be so worried about him. But Gil knew he could not go back now, even if he wanted to. He had come this far and had to go on.

As if sensing that change in him, Dora dropped his hand and night fell around them as they walked in companionable silence towards the sound of waves breaking quietly against the rocks. There was only a faint moonlight on the ground but they seemed to find their way so easily, it could almost have been day.

After a while, Gil realised his body no longer felt tired and the chill November air was having no obvious effect on his arthritis. In fact, he felt so amazingly full of energy, he could have broken into a run if he needed to. Glancing down at his hands, he saw that the creases and the mottled skin over his knuckles had completely disappeared. They were the hands of a young man again.

He looked at Dora walking beside him. His wife seemed as youthful as when they had first met in Oxford, her face smooth and flawless, her blue eyes laughing as she caught his puzzled sideways glance.

She smiled, 'There's no such thing as a straight line, you know.'

'Am I dead?'

'Do you feel dead?'

He thought about it for a moment. 'No.'

'There's your answer then.'

'Are you real?'

Dora threw back her head and laughed. 'I'm as real as you are, Gil. See for yourself if you don't believe me.' She held out her hand, the slender fingers pale in the moonlight. 'Go on, touch me.'

She felt warm and alive, as perfect as she had always been, a pulse even beating strongly at her wrist.

'Dora.'

He leant in and kissed her, tentatively at first and then with passion, stroking his hands down her body as she pressed against him. Her waist and hips were as slim as he remembered, and the clean sweet scent as he buried his face in her blonde hair took him back to that first night under the sycamore, the breath catching in his throat. There was an urgent desire too, something he had not felt for many years, and he looked into her face, astonished.

'I love you!'

'I know.'

'But can it be like this forever?'

Dora hesitated, then extricated herself from his arms. Her expression was suddenly serious.

'Look down, darling.'

Gil looked and nearly fell, his hand flailing out to grip her shoulder as he fought for balance and suddenly realised why she had brought him here. They were standing right on the edge of a high cliff, so frighteningly close he could see the grim drop rushing away from him in the half light until it reached the white crests of the waves below. This must be where she had fallen, or jumped, whichever it had been in the end. He wanted to step back and save himself, but Dora was watching him intently as if this was some kind of test. He could not fail her this time.

Gil clenched his fists and forced himself to look down again. He tried to imagine the terrible sensation of flying, wind tearing at his lungs, but shrank back from the edge.

'I can't do it,' he said.

'You don't have to.'

'Then why ...?'

'Look again,' she whispered in his ear. 'Look there!'

He followed the line of her pointing finger and frowned. There was a small boat coming into shore, unsteady on the waves. He could see two figures on the deck, and as the boat rocked in the moonlight, approaching the base of the cliff with its narrow strip of shingle beach, he realised they were his son and Miranda.

The boat slipped precariously between the dangerous black rocks in the channel and ran aground with a grating sound, Lawrence leaping over the side into the shallow churning waters and dragging the boat up the last few feet towards the beach. Then his son held out his arms to Miranda and the girl jumped, laughing as he stumbled under her weight and they both crashed into the water, staggering hand in hand up the shingle afterwards with their clothes sodden and dripping.

They disappeared from view under the cliff and all that was left behind was the little boat, lying on its side in the shallows and shifting uneasily with each wave.

Gil said, 'I don't understand.'

'You have done everything you possibly could.' Dora took his hand, smoothing her thumb repeatedly across his palm, just as she had done with Lawrence when he was a child and upset, her voice deliberately reassuring. 'It's their turn now.'

'And that's it?'

'What else is there?'

He looked at her and she seemed to understand instinctively what he was trying to avoid saying.

'Oh, that.'

Her shrug was eloquent. Dora smiled and turned her head slightly, her eyes moving over the dark waters as though searching for something he was unable to see. The sea sounded much closer than before, its constant restless whispering louder and louder in his ears until he had to strain to hear her. He watched her lips move, her blonde hair silver again in the moonlight.

'That's not important. It never was.'

'I betrayed you.'

Dora turned to look at him again, gently touching his face. 'You're such a boy, Gil. How did you ever grow old?'

'Did you kill yourself or was it an accident?'

'I can't remember.'

'Try.'

'I can't, it's gone. Things like that just slip through your fingers. What you leave behind, that's what really matters.'

'And what will I leave behind?'

She was smiling, shaking her head. 'As if you need to ask that.'

There was a tight band about his forehead, he could feel it constrict and the sudden pain made him frown. The sea crashed against the rocks in great black waves below them. His foot slipped on the edge and he looked down to check that he had not fallen, no longer entirely certain where the land ended and the air began.

Desperate to be sure she forgave him, that his terrible mistake had passed away into that great darkness and left nothing but love in its place, Gil caught her hand and trapped it against his cheek, revelling in the comfortable human warmth of it.

'Do you forgive me?'

'Don't fuss, Gil.'

He repeated his question several times, absolutely insistent.

'Yes,' she agreed at last, her smile indulgent. 'Yes, I forgive you.'

He pulled Dora towards him again and kissed her mouth, his eyes closing without fear as he felt the ground slip away and them falling together, weightless as feathers on the dark air.

Shakespeare was right, he thought suddenly, and for the first time in his life fully understood the words to the song.

Full fathom five thy father lies;
Of his bones are coral made;

Those are pearls that were his eyes:
Nothing of him that doth fade,
But doth suffer a sea-change
Into something rich and strange.

She had forgiven him. Dora had forgiven him. The pain had gone too, and there was an abrupt and satisfying silence in his head. It was as though he had finally managed to shut out the hiss and drag of the sea.

Gil thought, well, that's it.

Chapter Twenty-Five

It was a little after seven by the time Lawrence finally excused himself from the kitchen and went hunting for his father. He had heard the old man come in and trudge upstairs at least half an hour ago, but there had been no sound since then.

He felt guilty. His father had asked him to go round the house and check for fallen slates after the storm, but he and Miranda had been watching an old black and white film on the television, *Passport to Pimlico*, and he had managed to wriggle out of the task. So Gil had gone on his own instead. The storm had passed now and the November skies were clear, though it was still quite chilly outside. Lawrence had already seen the Ealing comedy on many occasions, and his only excuse was that he had been enjoying Miranda's delighted bursts of laughter as she watched it for the first time.

He shouldn't have refused to inspect the roof with Dad. If nothing else, it would have provided them with a perfect opportunity to talk about the future without Miranda present. His father had been drawing into himself lately, spending long afternoons locked up in his study with a pile of musty-smelling books, supposedly researching their family history for a book on the subject. Lawrence suspected the old man did more daydreaming than actual research though, his answers always a little vague when asked how the book was coming along. And now Gil was late for supper, presumably still sulking in his room.

The study door was open and the chair behind the leather-topped desk was empty. Rather unusually, the radio was playing quietly away to itself in the corner, and he recognised the music as being from Mozart's *Don Giovanni*. There was a sudden clatter of dishes from the kitchen and he heard Cathy swear irritably. She had already sent Miranda upstairs to wash her hands, her face flushed from the oven, then complained to him that the salmon would be ruined if they didn't sit down to eat in the next five minutes.

Lawrence switched off the radio and headed upstairs to his father's bedroom, knocking softly at the door in case the old man had fallen asleep.

'Dad?' When there was no answer, he knocked again, a little louder this time. 'Are you there? Cathy says she needs to serve dinner.'

He tried the door handle and it opened, but his father's bedroom was empty and in darkness.

Frowning, he stood outside the room for a moment and looked along the landing. The bathroom door was closed but Lawrence could see a shadowy figure moving about behind the frosted glass. Miranda was still in the bathroom, singing to herself and running the taps noisily as she washed her hands. *'What shall we do with the drunken sailor? What shall we do with the drunken sailor? What shall we do with the drunken sailor, early in the morning! Hoorah, and up she rises ...'*

He smiled, remembering himself at that age, singing at bath time. Maybe not sea shanties though. She was an odd child.

The door to the spare room was standing open, but there were no lights on inside. Yet he had definitely heard his father going upstairs earlier and not coming down again.

Perhaps he had gone into his mother's old bedroom.

The heavy dark wood door at the far end of the landing was firmly shut, as though it didn't particularly welcome intruders, but there wasn't any other room his father could be in, unless he had carried on up to the attic floor. But that seemed unlikely. The stairs were fairly steep and it was only Lawrence's room up there which was occupied.

Downstairs, he could hear Cathy bringing the plates through into the dining area, her footsteps along the tiled passageway hurried and impatient. Supper was being served, whether there was anyone to eat it or not. Salmon waits for no man, he thought wryly.

He tried his mother's old bedroom, tapping briefly before pushing at the door which, to his surprise, was unlocked.

'Dad?'

He fumbled along the wall for the light switch, clicked it on, then looked around in the soft glow of the shaded bulb. For a second, he thought he saw someone standing opposite and started, backing away instinctively. Then he realised it was his own reflection he had seen, in a large oval mirror across from the door.

His heart jumping, Lawrence steadied himself in the doorway and gazed into his mother's old-fashioned bedroom. The dark oak dressing-table and floor-length velvet curtains spoke of her taste for the dramatic, a brass bell pull set into the wall beside the fireplace a throw-back to the servants of Edwardian days.

Lawrence had only been in this room on one other occasion, during the week of her funeral, but it seemed eerily unchanged since then. He remembered seeing the half-empty basket of logs by the hearth, and that pair of shoes abandoned in the middle of the carpet, one standing, the other still lying on its side. Like Miss Havisham's rooms in *Great Expectations*, a thick layer of dust had settled over everything, even her once-treasured hardbacks lined up along her mantelpiece and stacked in piles against the overcrowded bookcase.

It was like a private shrine at the heart of the house, keeping alive what had long been dead. Her silver-backed Art Deco hairbrushes were still ranged along the mirrored dressing-table, ready for use, and the wardrobe door stood wide open, his mother's dresses hanging in a row inside, exactly as they had been when she was alive.

Then he saw his father, stretched out peacefully on the bed as though he had fallen asleep there, his hand closed on something.

'Dad?' he said again, this time without much hope of an answer.

He had known at first glance that his father was dead. The lined face was ashen and there was an awful stillness about him that could mean nothing else. Lawrence went to the bed and bent over him. His father didn't move even when he spoke. He steeled himself to touch the white hand nearest to him. The skin was still warm.

Gently, though he knew it made no difference, Lawrence turned the limp wrist over and felt for a pulse. There was none.

He examined his father's face with surprisingly cool detachment. The relaxed features and slightly parted lips – a gasp of surprise or anticipation? – showed no obvious signs of pain. His father appeared to have merely stretched out for a quick nap on his wife's bed, and then forgotten to keep breathing.

Lawrence dropped his wrist and stood there in blank silence, staring down at the string of pearls clenched in the old man's hand. They had belonged to his mother; a wedding present, he seemed to recall, from his father. She had only worn them for special occasions, keeping them in a little box on the dressing table.

Lawrence bent and loosened the fingers around the pearls, gradually pulling them free. Weighing them in his palm, he was shocked by their strange residual warmth; it was as though the pearls themselves were alive.

He slipped them into his pocket and sat down on the edge of the bed, straightening the crooked collar of his father's shirt. He was not sure how many minutes had elapsed when he heard a voice calling his name from the landing.

'Hello? Anyone in there?' It was Miranda, finished in the bathroom at last. 'Mum says supper's on the table.'

He stood up at once, hoping to prevent the child from coming into his mother's bedroom. But it was too late.

Probably out of curiosity to see a room that had long been off-limits to her, Miranda had already pushed the heavy dark wood door a little further open and was standing on the threshold, staring past him at the motionless body of her grandfather.

It was clear she understood Gil was not merely asleep, her lip trembling as she took a few hesitant steps towards the bed.

He stopped her and shook his head. 'I'm sorry, Miranda. He's gone.'

For a moment she did not move, but continued to look at the man on the bed, a stricken expression on her face.

Then she peered up at him, her eyes full of tears. 'Are you sure?'

'I'm afraid so.'

It was a dry fact, and drily delivered. But he didn't think the girl would welcome an excess of sentiment at a time like this. There was another hesitation, then Miranda blinked and nodded her acceptance. She seemed neither afraid nor surprised by her grandfather's death, but the grief in her face was genuine.

'Please, I want to see him.'

There was an adult note in her voice, a new maturity.

Lawrence stepped aside without argument, aware that the ritual was important. He watched the girl approach the bed and stand there in silence with her back towards him. Her shoulders shook as though she was crying, or trying not to. Then she leant forward and touched her grandfather's face with an experimental finger.

Her hand jerked back at once and she shivered. 'I thought he'd be cold,' she whispered.

He could hear Cathy banging cupboard doors and shouting something angrily from the depths of the kitchen, so he slipped quietly out of the room to call her. She would need to come upstairs. There were telephone calls and official arrangements to be made, and he didn't want Miranda left alone for any length of time. The girl seemed to be coping at the moment but once the initial shock had worn off, she would need someone there to turn to for reassurance.

'What is it?' Cathy came thudding upstairs with a damp tea towel thrown over her shoulder, her face flushed and irritable. But as soon as she saw Gil's body, her anger fell away and she looked round at Lawrence with narrowed eyes.

'Is he dead?'

'Yes.'

She sucked in her breath. 'Another stroke?'

'Probably. I'm going downstairs now to ring his doctor.'

He kept his voice low so as not to upset the child any further. Miranda was sitting on the bed beside her grandfather, exactly as he had done earlier, her head bent as she whispered something in his ear, though her actual words were inaudible from where they stood.

'I expect there'll be a post-mortem and we'll know more then. But could you look after Miranda? She's had a bad shock.'

Cathy said simply, 'Are you all right?'

'I'm fine.'

'You don't look fine.'

He glanced at himself in the mirror. He'd woken late that morning, too lazy to bother with the irritation and mess of shaving, and his skin was pale under a growing shadow of stubble. There was nothing in his eyes, though, to indicate a shock.

'I'm fine,' he repeated.

Cathy was looking at the child, her expression distracted. He had the impression that she responded to family crises in what was almost a text-book manner – shocked or saddened as the situation dictated, but with no genuine emotion behind any of it. Her sympathy towards him had felt disturbingly automatic. Lawrence was seized by a sudden and irrational desire to save his daughter from this woman, but knew it to be impossible.

Cathy placed her hands on Miranda's shoulders, turning the girl to face her. 'Miranda, love,' she said, her voice gentle for once, 'why don't you come downstairs with me and have a bite to eat? Your grandad wouldn't have wanted you to starve.'

'I'm not hungry.'

'Of course you are.'

'I'm not.'

Cathy said coaxingly, 'But it's salmon in pastry tonight. One of your favourites. It's on the table and spoiling. Come and have a taste, at least.'

Lawrence could not bear to hear any more of the girl's dull-faced replies and discreetly made himself scarce.

Downstairs, in the magnificently panelled dining area which Juliet had so admired, the long dark wood table that was always kept polished to a high sheen had been laid with folded cloth napkins and cut-glass crystal as though tonight's meal had been for some special occasion. It was as if his father had anticipated his own death, ordering this splendid Last Supper to mark the occasion; a commemorative feast which, with almost deliberate irony, was destined never to be eaten.

Before each empty chair, a plate of salmon en croute and minted new potatoes stood cooling, that delicious smell following him along the passageway like an accusing ghost.

Heading instinctively for the haven of his father's study, Lawrence shut himself in and flicked through the phone book for the doctor's emergency number. His hands trembled over the pages and he wondered if he was really all right, as he had told Cathy. If he was honest with himself, he had no idea how he felt about his father's sudden death. It was too soon to tell, perhaps. And he was face-to-face with the situation, too close to see the pattern.

These things always took time to come clear of the shadow, he knew that.

He found the number at last and spoke to the doctor in a clipped matter-of-fact tone, keen to deal with the formalities as unemotionally as possible, noting down the details of which people he should ring next and gratefully accepting his recommendation of a local firm of funeral directors. But it struck him, after he had put the phone down, that his father must have gone through this rigmarole too after his mother committed suicide.

Lawrence had been too lost in his own grief and confusion to offer his father any help at the time though, and the wheels of bereavement had rolled inexorably on without him. Now it was his turn to shoulder the burden, and as he sat back in the leather swivel chair and looked up at his mother's photograph on the wall, he couldn't help feeling that he was somehow to blame for both their deaths.

There was an abrupt knock at the door and Cathy looked in. 'Would you like a cup of tea? I've just put the kettle on.'

'How's Miranda?'

'Hysterical. She started crying and refused to eat any supper. I've sent her to her room. You won't want her around when the doctor arrives.'

'Perhaps I should go and talk to her.'

Cathy frowned, her pale eyes sliding over the wall behind his head. Presumably she felt he was interfering with her methods of child rearing. Coming into the study without being invited and shutting the door behind her, she stood facing him. She had rolled her shirt sleeves up to her elbows. He noticed a small tattoo on her forearm, what looked like a rose intertwined with a snake, that he was sure had not been there when they slept together. He was shocked at first. But then he saw it for what it was. A rite of passage.

'Leave her for now,' she insisted. 'Miranda's upset, she needs to lie down. There's no point getting her stirred up again.'

He had forgotten how sinuously her hips moved, watching her pace restlessly to the window and back, her expression preoccupied. It was the first time they had been alone in a room together since Juliet had left the island. He had been deliberately avoiding the woman for weeks, aware that he still found her attractive in an irritating knee-jerk sort of way, but his father's death was obviously going to force them together now, whether he liked it or not.

The thought filled him with loathing.

Lawrence looked away, leaning his elbows on the massed books that had been left open on the desk. He tried to make sense of his father's notes, scribbled in pencil down the margins, but could only make out the odd word. Their own surname, Cardrew – next to a lopsided squiggle which might have been a question-mark – appeared several times on a list of convicts sent out to Australia in the early 1800s. Then Lawrence remembered that his father had been researching a book on their family history. He traced one finger lightly down the list of names and ships of the fleet.

Cathy stopped dead in front of the desk, bare arms folded tightly across her chest, and met his eyes with a defensiveness that alarmed him.

'So what happens now?'

Lawrence stared, unsure what she meant.

She waved her hand wildly towards him, leaning back in his father's chair behind the leather-topped desk.

'You look very comfortable there.' Her words felt like an accusation. 'Are you planning to stay on? Take over the house? He'll have left it to you, I'm sure. But what am I supposed to do now?'

'I have no idea,' he said, confused by this unexpected attack. 'It's a bit early for this discussion. What do you want to do?'

'I don't know.'

Cathy hesitated, still looking at him with that disconcerting intensity, then sat down suddenly on the edge of the sofa and burst into tears. She covered her face with hands that trembled, clearly more upset by his father's death than he had assumed, and drew her knees together in an oddly childlike gesture. He watched in mute astonishment. The grief seemed genuine enough, he thought, but it had always been difficult to see through that shifting facade to her true motives, and even now Lawrence couldn't find it in himself to comfort her.

He turned to gaze out of the window and let her cry for a few minutes, embarrassed and feeling a little vulnerable himself, then cleared his throat.

He said, 'I'm not going to kick you out, if that's what you're asking. Miranda's my daughter too.'

She lifted her head and looked up at him, wiping her face on her sleeve. Her voice was shaky but defiant.

'I might want to go away. To see my sister in Spain. Maybe even live there for a year or so. We've been planning it for ages.'

'Did Gil know about that?'

She shrugged angrily. 'He would never have let me go.'

'You're a free agent, Cathy. You can leave whenever you want.'

'And Miranda?'

Lawrence raised his eyebrows, certain that some form of blackmail must lie behind all this talk of going away. He tapped his fingers on the desk top. His father might have paid her to keep Miranda around, but he was not going to stoop to such desperate tactics himself.

'You're her mother. You will naturally have custody.'

She stood abruptly and crossed to the sash window, avoiding his gaze. There was no moon that night and it was dark outside. Wrestling with the stiff catch, she eventually managed to push the sash window up as far as it would go. The room was filled with the scent of late honeysuckle, growing invisibly below the window ledge.

Several minutes passed as Cathy stood motionless in front of the window, a slight wind lifting her hair and rustling the papers on his father's desk.

He shivered in the chill draught and tried not to think of the body cooling upstairs, the man whose death had set this conversation in motion. But it was impossible. Lawrence kept expecting his father to come shuffling in, clutching his usual armful of papers and demanding to know why his son should be sitting in his study, behind his desk.

Cathy was right though. He did feel comfortable here, surrounded by books which his father had pored over for months and which he himself might one day read, scribbling his own notes in the margin alongside that bold indecipherable scrawl. But there was guilt too, a creeping suspicion that he had not been there when his father needed him most and that he had now taken his place without right or permission.

In that uneasy silence, the doorbell rang, a short sharp burst. Lawrence stirred, pushing back his chair.

'I'd better go. That will be the doctor.'

Cathy did not seem to have registered the bell or its significance. Fists clenched by her sides, her spine rigid with some unfathomable emotion, she was still staring into the pitch-black as if she had seen something dreadful out there and could not drag her gaze from it.

The doorbell rang again, this time more insistently.

Lawrence knew he couldn't wait any longer, much as he dreaded the task ahead of him. He was about to leave the room when Cathy turned her head and asked, 'What if I don't want custody?'

Epilogue

Miranda stayed on her knees in the dirt several more minutes after having lit her candle. Kneeling was a sign of respect. To the spirits of the dead and the spirits of the place. The *genius loci*. She wasn't praying to anyone though, dead or divine. She was just remembering.

That was why she had come here, after all. To say goodbye to a dear friend.

Gil had told her about this secret place many times, the strange earth mound on top of a hill in Wiltshire and the bodies buried deep within it. He had been fascinated by ancient burial sites. Yet she had always imagined they would come here together some day, tramping up through the fields like two pilgrims, young and old. Never that she would be here without him.

Bereft.

It was a good word to describe this feeling. It had been over three years since his death, but she still felt his absence every day. Like a wound inside her that would never entirely heal.

She stared about herself in the glimmering darkness. Excavations about thirty years ago had shown that locals had buried their dead in this place for many generations, along with jewellery and axe-heads to be used in the afterlife, some skeletons even found in sitting positions as if still alive. It was obviously popular with pagans; she could smell dampness and incense mingling with the candle smoke. Beside her candle was an odd row of others left against the back wall like offerings. Most of them were cold and burnt down to the base now, but a few wicks still flickered in their puddles of wax.

She placed an experimental hand on the mud wall. It felt cool. Beyond it must lie dozens of unexcavated bodies, hidden by rubble and the shifting dust of centuries: fathers and sons, mothers and daughters, each one carried to the same resting place in the end.

They had come here to scatter his ashes. To add Gil to the chain. According to his will, it was what he had wanted. To be part of something bigger.

'I'm so sorry,' a strongly accented voice came from behind her. 'Am I intruding?'

Miranda wiped her eyes on her sleeve. She smiled at the woman who had slipped silently into the cavern and was crouching at her back.

'No,' she said. 'I only came inside to light this candle for my grandfather. We're going to scatter his ashes on top of the barrow.'

'That's lovely. What was your grandfather's name?'

'Gilchrist.'

The woman shuffled forward, then held a hand over the candle flame for a moment, her eyes closed as if praying. She took a deep breath and sighed it out. 'Rest in peace, Gilchrist.'

Despite the woman's odd appearance, her smile was reassuring. She had red hair and wore dungarees handpainted with colourful swirls and a bright blue jacket with little wooden pegs instead of buttons, like something a child might wear to nursery school.

In one of the dark side caverns, a strange booming noise suddenly began to swell and thump and fill the barrow with its deep echoes.

Miranda put her hands over her ears.

'What's that noise?'

The woman laughed, raising her voice to be heard. 'That's my partner, playing the didgeridoo. In Australia, it's a sort of call to our ancestors. Listen, isn't it wonderful? Like the sea inside a cave.'

They crouched there together in the semi-darkness as the music grew louder and more compelling, the candles around them dipping and bending as a gust of wind tore through the standing stones above the entrance. When the sound eventually died away, the woman slipped back into the shadows without another word.

Miranda felt the muscles in her calves begin to ache as she continued to crouch there in the silent cavern, waiting for ... what? She did not know.

Her father would probably be wondering why she was taking so much time down here. But she stayed where she was, listening to the echoes subside.

Gil had come to this place years ago as part of an archaeological dig. He had always been interested in history and anthropology, and had once described the West Kennett Long Barrow to her as a very special place, a place of beginnings. But was it so important to connect to the past, to come back to the beginning like this, especially when it felt like so many things were ending?

The ground beneath her feet seemed to vibrate through her heels and up the ladder of her spine to her scalp. It was almost as the barrow was some kind of machine, whirring constantly away behind these thick walls of soil. Like a human body, blood pumping unseen under the skin.

She looked into the candle flame, remembering her grandfather's face, and felt tears come to her eyes again.

Wohauy, whaoom, whaoom, whaoom.

Lawrence turned his head, listening. The strange booming note had to be the sound of a didgeridoo being played somewhere deep inside the earth barrow, though it sounded more like the chant of some long-dead priesthood, rising eerily over the green fields of Wiltshire.

The afternoon sky began to glower again.

It was getting late.

Lawrence hesitated on the lip of darkness, then reluctantly edged his way down out of the spitting rain into the sheltered mouth of the barrow. The excavations were not deep here, only about the height of a man at the entrance, but the air had cooled and dampened considerably.

He found himself shivering, and wished that Miranda would hurry up. She'd climbed up the hill beside him and vanished inside this barrow nearly half an hour ago. He was not sure it had been a good idea to bring the girl on this expedition. His father had made it plain in his will that he wanted his ashes scattered near the West Kennett Long Barrow, but there had been no mention of involving Miranda in the ceremony.

He should have come up here on his own, kept her away from this dank gloomy barrow. He was not even convinced they had permission from the landowner to be here. Though from the people he had seen descending the hill earlier, it seemed nobody cared very much about permission. But Miranda had been pestering him to make this trip to Wiltshire ever since her mother left for Spain, determined to be there in person when Gil's ashes were scattered and to say a few final words to her grandfather.

And he had waited three years in the end, letting time and his emotion settle before making this journey. His daughter was a teenager now, almost a young woman. It would have been impossible to ask her to wait in the car like a child.

The man with the didgeridoo appeared to have packed up. They passed in the entrance and the man nodded at Lawrence. 'Hello, how do you do?'

He had a goatee beard and a strong Australian accent, didgeridoo strapped to his back as if they went everywhere together.

'Fine, thanks.'

'Superb acoustics in there.'

Lawrence managed a smile. 'It sounded amazing.'

'Ah, it's these old places. The sheer weight of the earth up top. Like a miniature concert hall.'

'I'm afraid it's raining out here again.'

The Australian sighed and pulled up his hood, waiting for the woman behind to catch him up. He turned to help her fasten a bright blue woollen jacket over her clothes, his tone rueful. 'More English rain. We should have brought an umbrella. We're going to get wet again. Sort of goes with the place though, don't you think?'

Lawrence nodded and stood waiting until the smiling couple had clambered up through the damp rocks into the open air. The earth around the entrance was wet and muddied with many footprints like a watering-hole. Not wanting to venture inside, he hallooed into the cavern several times, his only answer a confused flurry of echoes.

'Miranda?'

There was still no reply from within.

Reluctantly Lawrence ducked his head and followed the narrow slope down.

Inside the earth barrow, there was a smell of decay and some exotic scent like patchouli oil. Somebody had left a handful of candles arranged along the dirt floor near the entrance to one of the side caverns. It must have been several hours ago though, because the candles were guttering and nearly out. The place was filthy with earth and dead beetles and rubbish left by other visitors. In the glimmering semi-darkness, he could hear rain pitting softly against the ground above as he moved further in, through a gap between two large stones.

Beyond the entrance stones, the height of the chamber rose to about that of a priest wearing a headdress. Lawrence had a sudden vision of antlers sewn onto a fur cap and some ancient tribal ritual danced by a shaman.

Would men have been allowed in here at all?

He glanced back at the two rocks on either side of the entrance, funnelling smoothly in towards each other before widening out into the main chamber itself, round and dark and womb-like.

'Miranda?'

Lawrence stood there uncertainly in the dirt, feeling like an intruder on sacred ground. Did ancient places like this have memories, he wondered? There seemed to be some sort of faint electric hum down here as though the sound of that didgeridoo still bounced off the walls.

'I'm over here,' came a muffled voice from behind the stones, and he saw his daughter at last.

She stepped out from the darkest cavern into the central passageway, her face pale and her shoulders hunched. He could see that she had been crying.

'You sure you're ready for this?' he asked gently.

Miranda nodded.

He squeezed her hand, hoping to reassure her. One by one, they stepped out between the narrow standing stones at the entrance, then climbed onto the earth mound above the barrow. It had stopped raining and the last rays of the sun were just touching the green hilltops in the distance. The afternoon felt refreshingly cool and bright after the grim interior of the barrow.

Somewhere below them, lambs were bleating. Lawrence shielded his eyes to search for them, and found himself staring across green fields towards the strange looming mound that was Silbury Hill.

Turning slowly to take in the whole vista, horizon to horizon, Miranda could see why Gil had chosen this particular spot for the scattering of his ashes.

It was perfect.

She felt a little silly for having burst into tears after lighting the candle. But it was only natural to be upset when somebody you love has died.

It had been so horrible, watching his coffin disappear behind the curtains at the crematorium. As though some awful mistake had been made and at any moment Gil would bang on the wooden lid, demanding to be let out.

But there had been no mistake. Gil was gone, and over the three years since his death she had grown used to the blank space left by his absence. But she had never managed to fill it with anything but memories. And even they were becoming blurred now.

Miranda shivered. There were lambs bleating in a hilly field to her right, racing each other across the grass on white stubby legs while their mothers grazed at the far end of the field, occasionally lifting their heads to call after them. She watched them for a moment, wondering if they were destined to be eaten as chops on somebody's plate.

Lawrence said, 'Perhaps we should say something first.'

'Okay.'

She scooped a handful of ashes from the box he held out to her, shocked by the unexpected softness in her palm, and threw them awkwardly into the wind. They blew sideways, rapidly separating into a thousand particles and vanishing over the hillside.

'Rest in peace, Grandpa.'

Miranda tried to focus on her memory of Gil's face as she cast another handful into the blustering air. But his face kept slipping away until all she could remember was his back, retreating up the stairs, and his laughter, lost now in the wind and the relentless bleating of lambs.

'What else?' she asked after a moment.

'Nothing, I suppose.'

Lawrence scattered his own handful of ashes across the mounded earth, unable to make any mental connection between the father he'd known and the grey flecks still caught between his fingers. But this is what we come to, he thought, brushing the stuff off his hands without sentiment. Lawrence glanced at his daughter's face and wondered what she was thinking at this moment. The pale face and even paler lips gave nothing away except that the child was cold and tired.

Muttering his father's name under his breath, he cast another handful of ashes across the hilltop. The earth just seemed to reach up and carry it away through the rough swaying grass.

It was getting late and the sun had almost disappeared when Miranda began to speak in a sing-song voice as though reciting poetry.

Although the language was unknown to him, Lawrence listened in appreciative silence as they cast the last of his father's ashes across the ancient barrow. Her strange guttural words seemed to fit their ceremony and the darkening skies exactly.

When she'd finished her recitation, Lawrence turned to her and smiled. 'What was that?'

'Old English poetry, the beginning of *Beowulf*.' Miranda stared over his shoulder as though at some invisible sea on the horizon. 'The mourners lay the dead warrior in his ship and send it out onto the open sea, saying they have no idea where his journey will finish.'

'Did Gil teach that to you?'

She nodded. '*Beowulf* was one of his favourites. He told me once that he wanted it read at his funeral. So I memorised the first few pages.'

Lawrence suddenly realised what he had forgotten to do. He pulled the small package out of his pocket and handed it to his daughter.

'I nearly forgot. This was a wedding present from my father to my mother. I have no use for it, and they both would have wanted you to have it, I'm sure.' He smiled. 'You were too young before but you ought to have it now.'

Miranda unwrapped the tissue paper with a puzzled expression and then gasped, lifting out a long string of pearls. She had never seen anything so beautiful and couldn't imagine them around her neck, they seemed too elegant and grown-up for her. But the pearls glistened irresistibly as she held them up in the gloomy light of dusk and Miranda knew she was not going to refuse his gift.

Instinctively she lifted her hair, and he bent to clasp them around her neck. 'There,' he said, and stepped back.

The pearls were strangely cold and heavy against her skin, as if they had been lying in a dark place for many years. Her grandmother's pearls. She found herself running her fingers along the necklace, tracing the shape of each individual pearl, and felt beyond any doubt that they belonged to her now. That her grandmother approved.

'Daddy?' she asked. 'How do I look?'

For a moment, Lawrence couldn't bring himself to reply. She looked beautiful - and strikingly like his mother, he realised. But it was also the first time his daughter had ever used that word to him. Daddy. He found himself surprised by a sudden rush of emotion.

He put down the empty box that had contained his father's ashes and held out his arms to his daughter.

'You look stunning.'

Miranda hugged her father tighter than she had ever hugged Gil. But he seemed to need it, his voice breaking slightly on the words. She muttered something in return, her face pressed tight against his shoulder, then lifted her head, amazed by the intensity of her feelings and barely able to get the words out. There was another strange tingle of electricity up her spine. She felt an urge to dance away across the mound and touch one of the ancient standing stones. To prove to herself that the place was real and not a dream.

'It's stupid,' she said simply, 'but it feels as though Gil's here with us.'

Lawrence watched as the sun dipped below the horizon and the sky to the west of Silbury Hill became diffused with red. He frowned, remembering something his father had said when his own grandfather died. The earth seemed to shift under his feet and he had to steady himself, tightening his grip on the child's hands.

'Well, maybe he is. After all, Gil is still a part of us. He made me and I made you. So he must be right here inside us both. In our blood and bones, like a name stamped through a stick of rock.'

'Until we die?'

'For as long as this family continues.'

'Forever then,' Miranda said confidently, looking out across the fields. 'Forever and ever.'

Printed in Great Britain
by Amazon